LAST SECRET KEYSTONE

A JOEY PERUGGIA ADVENTURE SERIES **BOOK 3**

PHIL
PHILIPS

A cataloguing-in-publication entry is available from the catalogue of National Library of Australia at www.nla.gov.au.

Requests to publish work from this book should be sent to:
admin@philphilips.com

Philips, Phil, 1978-

ISBN-13: 978-0-6482724-6-5
ISBN-10: 0-6482724-6-X

Typeset in 11pt Sabon

For more information visit
www.philphilips.com

Dedicated to my mom

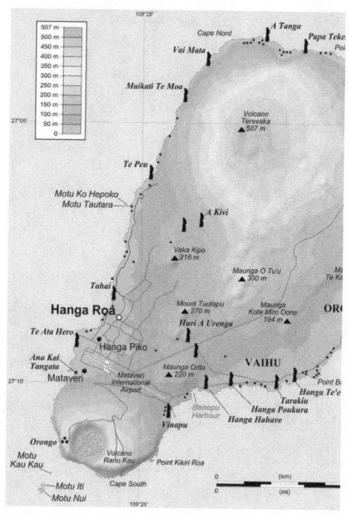

Map of Easter Island.

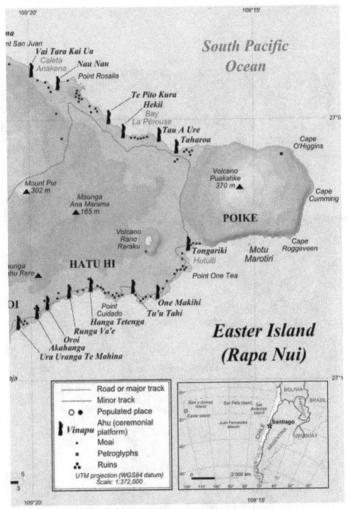

Home to 887 monolithic carvings called Moai statues.

Wernher von Braun and Peak Whiteness.

Fact: Operation Paperclip

After World War II, the United States gathered up Nazi scientists and brought them to America so the US could reach the moon before the Soviet Union. Wernher von Braun was a lead figure at NASA. A pioneer who had ties with Adolf Hitler himself.

Introduction

Translation of the 'Story of Our Ancestors'
Written in a book on Planet X

The true gods of this world visited our planet a long time ago, bringing with them their advanced technology. Needing a race to enslave, they found the primitive Homo erectus species and decided to improve on it, helping to evolve us into Homo sapiens – humans. We were engineered to be a primitive society with smaller brains and many defects, so we could be easily controlled.

Our population quickly grew and we spread out through the known world, worshipping the sun god, Atum. The men and women living in the promised land were charged with the work of the land, canals, and building structures. A portal enabling travel between worlds was erected deep within the Great Pyramid so the true gods could come and go as they pleased, taking with them hundreds of round-headed ones to help with the agricultural work on their own planet.

After thousands of years of coexistence with the true gods, the human race had spread to the far corners of Earth and new cultures had formed – and with them, we had developed our own theories on whom to worship. The king of the time sent his one and only son, Akhenaton, and his queen, Nefertiti, to govern in his name as Pharaoh to the people. During their reign, sadly, they bore only six daughters. Needing a male heir to rule, a round-headed secondary wife by the name of Kiya was chosen, and she gave birth to a boy they named Tutankhamun.

In the fifth year of his reign, Akhenaten was instructed by his all-powerful father, Amenhotep, to bring the people back to the one true creator, Atum. The people refused and incited an uprising, not wanting to worship the singular deity anymore. The king was troubled by the defiance and growing power evident in the primitive war-like humans his ancestors had nurtured. So, an army from his world was to be sent through the wormhole to exterminate them.

Fearing for her son's life, as he was half-human, Nefertiti declared religious freedom for all, and thereby gained the trust of the people. She blocked the Stargate on Earth so her son could rule over all mankind.

For this to be successful, the gateway on Nefertiti's home planet also needed to be disabled. The blue trigger keystone, Earth's gateway and identification marker, needed to be removed and destroyed. To save her beloved son, she entered the portal one last time, the task before her clear, and never returned.

Prologue

Easter Island
July 2019

In the shadow of the giant Moai statues of Rapa Nui, a team of archaeologists from UCLA had developed what they called the Easter Island Project to study and better preserve the artefacts found there. Through this work, the team had excavated several of the heads to reveal the underlying torso and body, suggesting that the inhabitants of this mysterious place were more advanced than was once thought.

The team's work was groundbreaking, but it didn't end there. A native boy in his teens told them he had seen a Moai deep inside a little-known cave, near Ana Te Pahu.

With this information at hand, a team of five experts including the director of the Easter Island Project herself, Joanne Turner, an adventurer at heart, went on a deep cave expedition to find this unknown wonder.

In a downward trek armed with a flashlight and a

Nikon DSLR strapped around her neck, Joanne and her team followed the guide into the darkness of the cavern.

And to her surprise, the boy was right.

A large grayish Moai buried from the waist down made from basalt rock, formed through the cooling and solidification of magma, loomed out of the ground with its massive eyebrow ridge, elongated ears, and oval nostrils. The face was, unusually, surrounded by dark soil, and a stairway of stone pillars, cut in the shape of tree trunks, led up to face the ancient monolith. When she first saw the Moai statue, Joanne felt a frisson of excitement and had an almost uncontrollable urge to climb the stone pillars.

She approached the enormous square opening that framed the grotto situated high up on the cliff top, flooding the cave with natural light. The fall from the lip of the cave dropped away some one hundred and twenty feet. It overlooked the Pacific Ocean and a U-shaped rock formation, giving the site a majestic and out-of-this-world ambience.

'Let's get to work, people,' Joanne said with a clap of her hands, then started to take photos with her digital camera.

Like a well-oiled machine, the team set about doing their jobs. Spotlights fluttered inside the already lit cavern. Buckets, trowels, brushes, and foldable shovels were extracted from backpacks.

'Dig around the black soil; let's see how far down it goes,' Joanne ordered, circling the face with wonderment. 'Why the hell is this thing here?' she murmured to herself.

Carefully, the two Polynesian men hired to do the heavy lifting began to remove the soil surrounding the square head.

A putrid odor suddenly engulfed the site.

'What is that?' queried Joanne, pinching her nose against the overpowering smell.

Ten minutes later they had all begun to feel ill, and were overcome with bouts of coughing. Then the coughing intensified, quickly turning into vomiting. The two Polynesian workmen stopped digging, kneeled before the structure and begged for mercy.

'We should not be here, boss,' one said to Joanne. 'I'm afraid we have interfered with the gods.'

Joanne was puzzled. She covered her nose and mouth with her dirty white T-shirt as sweat began to trickle down her cheeks. She coughed into her sleeve, rubbed her watery eyes, and decided, having come this far, that she would step up the tree-trunk stones.

The workmen begged for her to retreat, but she didn't listen.

'This statue is here for a reason,' she argued, carefully continuing up the stairway that encircled the face. She stopped at the square shaped elongated ear. 'What have we here,' she breathed, trying not to inhale too deeply to avoid the insidious smell, as she began to study the unusual shape before her.

'What is it?' asked her research assistant, wiping a shaky hand across his mouth.

Joanne frowned. 'It's a drawing,' she said, flabbergasted. 'One I've never seen before.'

On previous digs, she had found etched petroglyphs

on the backs of the colossal figures, commonly crescent-shaped to represent Polynesian canoes.

This was different.

It seemed more advanced than anything she'd ever seen before.

And it was deeply indented and here for a purpose, she was sure.

Joanne ran her finger along the grooves and snapped away with her DSLR. Then, seeing that the condition of her team was worsening, she decided to head back to her campsite so she could analyze her findings and return at a later time. She knew she had uncovered something incredible here; something that needed to be thoroughly researched and studied.

Two days later, all five team members, including Joanne, choked to death in the most brutal of ways. The cave was immediately quarantined and closed to the public, and warning signs erected until a detailed investigation could be conducted. Following careful analysis, the medical team established that the cause of all five deaths was toxicity due to inhalation of extremely high levels of arsenic found within the cave's disturbed soil. The local people dubbed it the curse of the ancestors.

Chapter 1

Major Dimitri Panos from the Direction Générale de la Sécurité Extérieure, otherwise known as the DGSE or the French CIA, watched on silently finishing his cigarette as the A300-600F Cargo Airbus prepared to depart into the cold winter night. The fuel truck vanished into the stormy darkness as heavy snow piled up on the plane's wings and fuselage. The loading ramp dropped from the rear of the aircraft's whale-like belly, and the freight doors steadily swung shut, protecting the artefact Dimitri had been sent to escort back to Egypt.

He boarded the plane unarmed in his casual attire, jeans, boots, and woolen sweater, taking in the grandness of the 1200-square-foot cargo bay. There were no seats. Instead, rows of floor-to-ceiling containers were locked in place like a giant 3D jigsaw puzzle.

Dimitri's brown eyes darted over to a knee-high timber crate covered in red tape with the words FRAGILE written all over its shiny surface, and an *Egyptian Antiquities* stamp visible, depicting the Great Sphinx.

Accompanying him were two armed soldiers also from the DGSE, each carrying nine-millimeter semiautomatic pistols in their holsters. Their mission was to chaperone the major and keep their eyes glued on the artefact at all times. The soldiers took their job immensely seriously, which explained the dour scowls that dominated their faces; their expressions said, *Fuck with us, and you die.*

Content that the crate was secure, Dimitri gave his men a friendly nod and entered the cockpit. He took the jump seat, situated on the left-hand side, right behind Captain Dean Butler. The captain was a clean-cut, gray-bearded man in his early sixties, his numerous years of experience apparent in his calm and professional nature. On his right was First Pilot Chris Little, a tall, slender man in his late forties about to clock his minimum 5000 hours of total flight time, to obtain his Cargo Captain's License. He was holding an iPad containing flight plans and charts, and busy working through a pre-flight checklist.

'Here we go, next stop Egypt,' Chris announced as the two engines roared to life.

'Buckle up,' warned Dean as he lined up the aircraft on the strip of asphalt which had been cleared of the worst of the snowfall. The halfway marker could almost be seen through the haze of white fluff. He pushed the throttle forward, and the bulbous nose of the plane was propelled into the blowing snow as the engines increased with power.

'One hundred knots,' informed Chris.

The captain confirmed.

The white runway lights blurred past the wings as Dimitri cautiously scrutinized the way the two pilots interacted. The captain scanned the instrument panel, making sure everything was in working order before liftoff.

'V one, rotate.'

When the control column was pulled back, the Airbus began its climb, the instruments reading 3000 feet per minute.

'Positive climb, gear up.'

'Flaps one, flaps zero.'

After a short incline, the plane broke through the clouds and leveled off at a comfortable cruising altitude, causing smiles of relief from all in the compact space.

'We should have a smooth ride from here on in,' said the captain, flicking the autopilot toggle on.

'These things seem to fly themselves,' said Dimitri. His eyes flashed to the altimeter watch on his wrist, which read thirty thousand feet, and was confirmed by the plane's odometer reading.

'That's an impressive skydiver's watch,' said Dean, who was wearing one of a similar design. 'Do you fly yourself?'

'Thanks,' replied Dimitri with a gracious smile. 'It was given to me as a gift. Yes, I'm a pilot, but these days I mostly operate choppers.'

'We must be transporting something of value back there,' said Chris, flicking a glance towards the back of the plane. 'We don't usually carry armed soldiers onboard. In fact, this is a first for us.'

'Yes,' said Dimitri, releasing his seatbelt and shoulder harness to stretch his stiff neck. 'The contents are significant. I even requested to be on this trip to make sure the item was delivered back safely.'

'Can we ask what it is,' asked the captain, 'or is it classified?'

'No, no – not classified, but it is a priceless artefact and therefore caution is always advised. It's an extremely rare vase,' said Dimitri.

'All this to protect a vase,' said Chris wonderingly. 'It must be old. What are we talking about here?'

'You're right, it's ancient. The carbon dating tests revealed it to be eight thousand years old, maybe even older.'

'Wow ...' said Dean, nodding slowly. 'Pre-dynastic.'

Dimitri flashed him a smile, impressed with Dean's historical knowledge.

'Where's it from?' asked Chris, turning a dial on his switchboard.

'We discovered it in Egypt on the Giza Plateau about a year ago.'

'So why were you here in New York?' asked Chris curiously.

Dimitri flexed his neck, uncomfortable with all this small talk, but he tried not to allow his unease to show on his face. 'In the basement laboratory of the Morgan Library and Museum here, they have the best X-ray scanner in the world. We wanted to know what was inside the vessel without damaging its core. They pumped these invisible beams at the structure and produced a 3D map of the inside, which has given us crucial information on what the people of the time used it for.'

Both pilots nodded their heads in interest as they continued to check and adjust the instruments on the console but, mercifully in Dimitri's view, they stopped asking questions.

Fifty minutes into the flight the clouds below them cleared and they saw Cape Cod Bay in Massachusetts, the last piece of landmass before they began to cross the North Atlantic Ocean.

'Is it okay if I stretch my legs?' asked Dimitri. 'I'm not a fan of sitting still for long periods.'

'Of course,' said the captain.

'I might grab some pillows for the troops,' said Dimitri, grasping them from near where he sat. 'Must be uncomfortable back there with no seats.' He made sure he closed the door behind him before he strolled over to his men. In his hands were two small blue pillows sealed in plastic bags for health and safety reasons.

His crew stood up in a flash to address their commanding officer. Dimitri noticed how noisy it was back there; a deep, loud humming sound consumed the bay, reverberating through the plane's naked steel frame.

'It's okay, stay seated,' Dimitri said with a warm hand gesture. 'It's a ten-hour flight. You can't be standing the entire trip. Here, I brought you both pillows.'

Dimitri threw them over, and the first officer caught his with a grateful smile.

'Thank you, Maj—'

The man's brains splattered all over the wall, brutally cutting off his sentence. Dimitri watched, unmoved, as the officer slumped to the floor. He had been killed instantly, the hat he'd been wearing now mashed into his shattered skull.

Nick, the second officer, removed the pillow he'd used to hide his silencer-topped gun and tossed it aside.

'Nick – move!' Dimitri commanded. 'As planned.'

Nick reacted swiftly, dragging the body out of sight, while Dimitri strode over to his crate. He kneeled and released the fragile red tape, then extracted his car keys from his pocket. There was a small, flat screwdriver amongst his keys, which unfolded like a Swiss Army knife. Using it, he loosened the four screws that held the lid closed, one at a time.

Once he'd removed the screws, he jabbed the timber lid with the palm of his hand until it came free. He placed it to one side, hitting one of the many metal rollers that filled the corridor and along which cargo was rolled to assist in loading them. Inside the crate, thick yellow foam and two skydiver backpacks were packed around the ancient vase.

Dimitri lifted the delicate pottery in his hands and used the dim glow of the line of LED lights on either side of the cargo bay to study the intricate pattern of square heads carved over the vessel's rough surface. His fingers caressed the grooves, and for a moment, he allowed himself to revel in the mastery of the workmanship.

The door to the cockpit swung open unexpectedly and curious, frowning blue eyes stared out at him.

'What are you doing?' Chris asked, stepping through the doorway. 'You can't open that in here.'

Dimitri stood with the jar in his hand and flicked back a cheeky grin, as though he'd been caught with his pants down.

'I think you should put the ancient artefact back in the box before you drop it or damage it. We could run into turbulence,' said Chris, his voice now cold.

'But that's exactly what I want to do,' said Dimitri smoothly.

The pilot's frown lines deepened.

Dimitri tossed the vase at Chris's feet, where it shattered, spilling its contents all over the pilot's pointy, shiny leather shoes.

Chris staggered backwards, his eyes bulging in surprise. 'What the hell did you do that for?' he gasped.

'That's why,' Dimitri replied, pointing to an object that lay amongst the pottery shards. 'That is a key, which was formed from a meteorite a long time ago. The key will open the door to a world you are not ready to know exists.'

Quad-Spiral Key

'I don't understand.' Chris's voice was shaking now.

'Believe me, my friend, you're not the only one.'

Chris picked up the intricate item at his feet and examined it, and then he looked to the rear of the cargo hold where Nick was standing. His eyes darted to and fro, and it was clear from his expression that the second soldier's absence concerned him.

Dimitri stepped towards him, which made Chris backtrack, the fear evident in his widening eyes.

'Stay there,' he said, his hands raised with trepidation. 'I will need to write a report on what happened here tonight.'

'Don't be stupid, that's not necessary.'

'Wait here until I discuss this with the captain. I will let him decide.'

Chris turned to re-enter the cockpit and Dimitri moved in a flash, crash-tackling the man to the ground. Dimitri grabbed hold of his neck and squeezed.

'Captain ...' Chris wheezed, his voice barely audible. He fought to free himself, kicking his legs and throwing his elbows, but there was no escaping his attacker's hands.

As Dimitri held the other man's airway closed, he thought about his time in the military and the countless men he had killed in the name of his country. He had promised himself when he had started a family that he would put all the killing behind him, and he had done so until tragedy had struck him to the core. Now, the emotion that had been building in him since that time seemed to have unleashed the monster within, and his hands gripped like an unbreakable vise. Like a lizard with its head chopped off, the pilot's limbs shook uncontrollably for a second or two, then fell dead still.

Dimitri shoved the limp body to one side, stood up and placed the three-inch key into his pants pocket. Nick approached, looking down expressionlessly at the dead pilot. As he did so, the sound of footsteps could be heard coming from the cockpit. Then the door opened.

It was Dean; his eyes came alive when he saw Chris spread-eagled on the metal floor.

Nick reacted before the older man could shut himself inside the cabin, extracting his weapon. He fired two bullets into the pilot's back, sending him flying backwards to collide with his captain's chair. Still alive, he managed to slide into his seat and reached for his headset.

Nick fired a perfectly aimed kill shot at the captain's head before he could alert the authorities. His frame slumped forward onto the computer console and pushed against the control column.

That's when everything turned upside down.

The plane nose-dived.

'Looks like we'll need to go with plan B,' shouted Nick.

'No, I might be able to land this thing,' Dimitri shot back.

'Remember, eighteen thousand feet,' warned Nick, smashing the red button above his head to open the exterior door and allow the sucking wind inside. 'If you can't, we jump.'

Dimitri sprinted into the cockpit. Pushing Dean's lifeless body aside, he gripped the control column and tried to pull the aircraft out of its dive. His arms shook with the force that was needed for the correction; sweat poured down his face, and he tried to ignore the alarms flashing red lights across the console.

After an intense struggle, he managed to bring up the airplane's nose and slow its descent, but it was too late. The damage to the ailerons caused controllability issues.

The aircraft was going down.

Martha's Vineyard Airport was in sight, but they needed to go with plan B.

Twenty thousand feet.

Nineteen thousand feet.

Eighteen thousand feet.

Dimitri darted out of the cabin and took the jumpsuit Nick had ready for him. An adrenaline junkie, danger had always been like an aphrodisiac to him: the more extreme, the better. He clipped himself in, and after a friendly fist bump, the two men leaped out into the darkness.

Ten thousand feet.

One thousand feet.

The plane hit the ocean with a loud splash. The front wheels snapped on entry like toothpicks. The nose collided and deformed the structure, creating large gashes through which water would find its way inside. Out of control, the belly of the 177-foot Airbus bounced on the water until the right wing snapped off in the opposite direction.

Sparks of flames ignited the sixty-eight thousand liters of fuel.

KABOOM!

A thunderous, billowing explosion erupted from the fuselage, causing an eerie crimson glow across the night sky as debris rained down over the water. Dimitri and Nick observed the destruction as they glided safely towards the inland.

The heavy Airbus slowly sank into the dark abyss.

Dimitri watched it all with a smile. He felt no remorse for the havoc he had wrought. He had obtained the spiral key, and that was all that mattered to him.

Chapter 2

DGSE Headquarters,
Paris, 5:00 am Local Time

A buzzing sound emanated from the bedside table. Boyce sat up, blinked several times, and turned his bleary eyes to a cell he only used for work purposes. For it to ring this early in the morning, something had to be up. Something important.

'Hello,' Boyce answered, his voice hoarse from sleep.

'Hi, Boyce, sorry for the wake-up call. The general wants you in his office ASAP. There's been an incident.'

'What incident?'

'Sorry, not at liberty to say.'

'Okay, on my way.'

Entering the DGSE building at the crack of dawn, Boyce strode down the empty tiled corridors that led to Julien Bonnet's office. It was the first time he'd been at work this early in the morning, and the abandoned hallways had an eerie feel about them.

There were no co-workers offering a handshake, no fist bumps, nothing but the quiet sound of his footsteps and his own thoughts. The anticipation of the news he was about to hear was a nervous kind of energy. Why of all the employees under the general's control had Boyce been the one chosen? Why had they not called in someone with a higher ranking?

Julien's door wide open and the light within his office bounced out into the corridor. Boyce stepped inside the spacious room to find the general staring intently at his computer screen, the bright-white light illuminating his aged face and snow-white hair.

'Hey, boss, what's up?' Boyce asked in a casual tone. Not many had the privilege of greeting the man in charge this way, but due to Boyce's youth and their unusual past association, the general let it slide. Boyce loved the general for that and had formed a firm bond with him over the years.

Julien turned to face Boyce, revealing the distinctive scar over his temple. An injury Boyce was told by his colleagues, to be the reason why Julien had invited Boyce to join his special unit team a couple of years ago, even though he was only fifteen years old.

The story went that the then thirty-year-old Julien had been on a diving expedition somewhere in the Red Sea, where he was said to have lost a young boy by the name of Ezra. A group that called themselves the 'Guardians of Egypt' had tossed explosive devices into the dive site, which had ended Julien's young friend's innocent life.

Julien had avenged the dead boy by killing those

men, but the incident had touched him on a personal level. It appeared that he had seen something within Boyce the moment they'd met that reminded him of Ezra, and he had felt compelled to protect him in a fatherly way. Boyce, an orphan, had welcomed the relationship with open arms.

'Good morning, Boyce,' Julien said, waving him in. 'I'm sorry to drag you out of bed so early, but I think we might have a huge problem.'

'What's going on?' Boyce asked, waiting patiently for the bad news. A hundred different possibilities flooded through his mind.

'Dimitri's cargo plane went down last night. It crashed in the Atlantic Ocean.'

'Our Dimitri?'

Julien confirmed with a nod.

'I'm so sorry,' Boyce said with sincerity. 'I know he was a close friend of yours and loved by our peers. No disrespect, sir, but why did you call me in regarding this? How can I be of any assistance?'

The general leaned back in his expensive leather chair and took in a deep breath. 'Boyce, I think this crash was deliberate.'

'Okay . . .'

Julien swung his monitor around to show a variety of 3D images on a rolling slideshow. 'Do you recognize this symbol?'

Boyce frowned and moved closer to examine the unusual-looking shape. He recognized it in an instant. His jaw tightened and his eyes flashed a warning as understanding dawned on him. 'The tri-spiral key,' he blurted. 'It's like the one Joey's uncle had locked up in his safe.'

'That's correct, the one that led you inside the Sphinx and to the Hall of Records.'

'Hang on,' said Boyce. 'This one is slightly different. It has four spirals on it, not three.'

Julien returned his gaze to the monitor and absorbed the information as if it were new to him. 'So it does . . . I missed that detail completely.'

'Where did you find this one?'

'The entire treasure trove you and your friends discovered last year was catalogued and moved to a secret warehouse in Egypt, all funded by the billionaire Elliott Magnus.'

'The space guy?' Boyce asked.

'That's him,' said Julien with a half-smile. 'Magnus has always had a fascination with Egypt and the alignment of the pyramids to the Orion constellation. This is just one of many pet projects he's involved in around the world, and he's dropped millions to secure the priceless artefacts. Millions we can ill afford ourselves.'

'I read an amazing article on him and the secret intelligence program they called Operation Paperclip,' Boyce said. 'After World War II, the United States gathered up scientists from Nazi Germany and brought them to America so they could fast-track the US to the moon before the Soviet Union. Elliott Magnus's parents were supposedly involved in that elite group.'

Julien gave him a soft smile. 'Yes, I know. Wernher von Braun was the man who ran NASA at the time, and the irony of it all is that he was good friends with Hitler. You'd be shocked to know how many Germans still reside at the Kennedy Space Center.'

Boyce nodded thoughtfully. The Americans had put this dark secret aside, knowing that offering safe harbor to German scientists, some of whom had shady pasts, was their best chance to get to the moon first.

'Here's an interesting fact you might like,' said Julien. 'Elliott Magnus was named after the man who pioneered rocket technology and space science. His full name is Wernher Magnus Maximilian Freiherr von Braun.'

Boyce chuckled. 'Wow, it appears Magnus's larger-than-life ego fits with his name. I'd be cautious having him snooping around.'

'Don't worry,' said Julien. 'Everything is under the watchful eye of the new director of the Ministry of Antiquities. You remember Hazim Saliba?'

'Hazim,' Boyce said with delight. 'I'm glad it's in safe hands, then.'

'We've gone off track a little, where was I?' said Julien, drumming his fingers on his desktop while searching the computer screen. 'Okay, so within the treasure trove was a vase, and we suspected it had something within it that we couldn't access. So, we organized a team headed by Dimitri to get it X-rayed in New York. The images you've just seen were sent back to us from the team at the Morgan Library and Museum. We recognized the key straight away.' Julien paused for a brief second. 'Dimitri was meant to bring the vase back to Egypt. However, I have a feeling that he could be behind the plane crash and now has that key in his possession.'

Boyce took a seat across from Julien and thought for a minute, confused. 'Why would Dimitri want it, and go to those lengths to get it? He's one of the good guys. He's your right hand. How did things come to this?'

Julien sighed and leaned over his luxurious computer desk, the tattoo of the winged lion on his wrist visible. It appeared there was more to Dimitri's story.

'Like yourself, Boyce, I gave the major a job in my unit and a reason to live not so long ago.'

'What do you mean, a reason to live?'

'Four years ago, his wife and thirteen-year-old daughter were killed in a terrorist attack.'

'Shit! That's terrible,' Boyce said, his eyebrows shooting up in surprise.

'It was at the Bataclan concert hall. One hundred and thirty people were massacred that night and more than four hundred injured.'

'Yes, I remember,' said Boyce, sitting back in his chair. 'What a tragedy to go through,' he said, shaking his head.

'Dimitri was a mess for a long time. The only thing that helped him through it was his faith, his Greek Orthodox Church. He finally found solace through religion and it helped him through the trauma, and he kept himself busy with work. He was doing fine, then last year we found the Stargate and the existence of another world out there in the universe. The question of whether we were alone in this universe or not was answered, and I believe this made Dimitri question his faith. If there is no God, no maker – or at least, not the one he believed in – and the Christian story is nothing but a myth, then where did his wife and child go? Which heaven did they ascend to? I think this rattled Dimitri to the core.'

Boyce took in the explanation and stared at a painting that was prominent in the room. It depicted the shape of the sun, which he knew to be the symbol used to symbolize Alexander the Great. The man whose bones they knew to reside in Saint Mark's Basilica in Venice. He snapped out of his reverie and asked, 'But, how would the major know about Planet X? He never saw us activate the Stargate.'

'Your detailed report on the entire experience has gone missing,' Julien said heavily, motioning with his eyes to his filing cabinet. 'Very few people have access to my office, but he was one of them.'

'So, he knows everything?'

'I hope I'm wrong, Boyce. But if I'm not, then he's on a quest to find answers. I think he's trying to find another keystone to initiate the Stargate once more.'

Boyce glanced upwards and pursed his lips in thought. 'But where is he going to find that?'

'Here.' Julien tapped his computer screen, which showed a line of square heads. 'Do you remember in your paper, how you explained that the reason the Great Pyramid of Giza was located at the exact center of Earth's landmass was to fulfill its one and only function, which is to activate the Stargate within?'

'Yes,' said Boyce, wondering where Julien was going with this.

Giza Pyramids · Center
of the Earth's Land Masses

'Did you know that many ancient sites like the pyramids of Giza are aligned on a single sweeping circle around our planet's surface? These monolithic human figures were depicted on the vase containing the key. Do you know where these figures are on Earth?'

Boyce shook his head.

Julien clicked his mouse a couple of times and opened up a Google Maps animation. The globe that was Earth spun slowly and stopped at a tiny landmass. Boyce craned forward to see the name printed next to it: *Easter Island*. 'If Dimitri is behind this, and I hope I'm wrong, I bet that's where he will go to find the keystone.'

'Are you planning to intercept him? Put men on the ground there?' Boyce got up from his chair.

'It's not that simple, my young friend. Think about it. If you had a key and needed to explore an ancient cave, don't you think you might want help in case of booby traps? Help from people who have been through a similar ordeal before?'

Boyce froze in mid-stride and stared out of the general's window into the distance. 'Joey and Marie?' he finally said, covering his mouth.

'Exactly. We'll need to warn them first in case he's heading their way.'

Boyce exhaled slowly. 'Here we go again.'

Chapter 3

Joey's Beach Club, Penthouse Suite, Santa Monica, LA, 9:00 pm Local Time

The night had rolled in over the beach, bringing with it the threat of a winter storm. The air was still and heavy, and thick clouds blotted out the stars. The view from the penthouse balcony never got old for Marie. She stood there soaking it in, breathing in the briny aroma, as the wind blew her long honey-brown hair across her face.

Her palms gripped the glass balustrade, and she shivered at the crisp December chill. Below, she spotted her man, who despite the cold was shirtless as he went about his late-night jog, and saw that he was heading back home. She smiled and rubbed her belly. A joyous feeling ran through her as she turned away from the beach and went inside.

She closed the door and lit a few candles she had arranged over the dining table to set the mood. Relaxed and comfortable in her activewear, she stirred the fragrant bolognese sauce she'd made, Joey's favorite, then dropped a handful of fresh pasta into the boiling water in another pot.

The door to their suite slammed and she smiled, knowing her husband was home.

Joey entered, smelling of sweat, but she didn't mind. He placed his phone on the granite benchtop and hugged her from behind, kissing her neck and sending a shiver running down her spine.

'That smells amazing,' he said, burying his face in her neck, causing her to quiver with laughter.

'Dinner will be ready soon,' she said, turning to face him.

'Okay, I'll quickly jump into the shower,' he said, playfully smacking her on the backside and leaving before she could react.

Soon, Marie heard the sound of the water and Joey's terrible singing as she drained the spaghetti into a strainer and turned off the heat on the bolognese sauce.

All of a sudden Marie felt a gust of wind against her neck. She spun towards the balcony and frowned. She could have sworn she had shut the door. Hurrying out of the kitchen, she saw that the door was ajar, and that the candles had blown out. She peered outside to the balcony but could see nothing but empty deckchairs in the blackness beyond.

She closed the door forcefully, making sure this time that it was locked. Then she turned back to her kitchen, and felt an eerie sensation in her gut. One she had felt before.

She was not alone.

Slowly, her heart skipping a beat, she twisted her head back to the balcony, and saw a man standing there. Her hazel eyes widened, and she startled in shock.

'Joey!' she screamed as her body trembled and her survival instincts took over.

Where had this man come from? Who was he? What did he want?

The man appeared to be in his mid-thirties and of Mediterranean background. He was attractive, lean, had a twelve o'clock shadow and wore his curly hair clipped. He was roughly six feet tall, and judging by the look on his face, he had enjoyed frightening her.

An awareness washed over her. She was behind the thick glass bi-fold doors, and they were locked. She was safe, but it was the way the man flashed her a smirk that caused her to fear his intentions. The stranger's sweater was branded with an Under Armour label. He was not a homeless person on the pier in search of money.

'What do you want?' she asked, regaining her composure.

The running water from Joey's shower had stopped, and she could hear him hurrying towards her. Her heart slowed down some more with the knowledge that help was on its way. Her husband had fought against incredible odds over the years against a variety of adversaries, one being an Atlantean soldier from another world, and he'd still come out on top. Marie knew that he would not take this threat to his home and loved one lying down.

A heavy hand came to rest on her right shoulder. She

turned with relief into her man's arms, only to come to the quick realization that this person was not Joey. He was considerably taller and broader, with dark, curly hair, and he reeked of cigarettes.

Panic set in.

Marie's heart raced and she started shaking uncontrollably. The man's other hand came across her mouth as she tried to scream for help, so nothing more than a strangled yelp escaped. Still, she screamed, hoping Joey would hear her.

'Shh!' His raw voice was like sandpaper against her ear.

Marie struggled against him. She wanted to cry as rage consumed her. She shot her right leg out, but her movements were far too slow. Hand moving from her shoulder, the stranger seized her arms, trapping them behind her.

'Relax, I'm not going to hurt you or your baby – unless you make a sound,' he said, slowly removing his hand from her mouth and reaching over to unlock the bi-fold door and let his partner enter.

Marie froze. How the hell did this man know she was pregnant, when she hadn't even revealed to her own husband that he was going to become a father? The only way he could know this was if he had seen her medical file. Which meant that his presence here was no coincidence. This was targeted.

Marie was, generally, utterly fearless and sure of herself. Her primal urge was telling her to strike, to go for her attacker's genitals. But with her pregnancy, her vulnerability, and the life of her baby, had introduced a new element of anxiety into her life. Her baby had to come first. She had to keep calm and think rationally. The days of being brave were behind her now; it was not worth risking a miscarriage.

She wrapped her arms around her belly and nodded her head in supplication.

She was at his mercy.

Chapter 4

On hearing his wife call his name, and recognizing the fear in her voice, Joey had flung himself out of the shower, grabbing a towel, and raced into the kitchen. His eyes narrowed, rigid, cold and hard, when he saw his wife being held captive by two strangers. His fists clenched tightly, causing his knuckles to turn white. In that frozen second between standoff and fighting, he saw the men's eyes flick towards him.

There were two towering men in his home. Their faces were unreadable and expressionless. The man standing away from Marie sneered at Joey then laughed, only adding fuel to Joey's wrath.

'Let her go!' Joey barked, ready to erupt.

The giant holding Marie did as Joey wished, and she darted over to her man and clasped him tightly.

'Are you all right?' murmured Joey, and when she nodded, he turned back to the intruders. 'Who are you?' he asked coldly.

'If you do as I ask, you will both be unharmed,' said the first man, who seemed to be in charge. He shared the same deep brown eyes as Joey's gangster father, who when alive had possessed a similar stare that could send shivers down one's spine. This man walked like a boxer and his skin was dark and deeply wrinkled. There was a seriousness about him that suggested he was a man of power who was raised to lead and who ruled with an iron fist. Joey knew the kind firsthand. He was a head taller than most people Joey would consider tall. There was bulk on him, too, muscles beneath the black sweater that clung tightly to his bulging biceps.

His curly-haired accomplice stood fast, like a well-trained soldier on guard, waiting for a command to act upon. He positioned himself so that Joey would know he was armed. His gun rested tucked in his waistband, showing off his black Italian leather belt. The smug expression on his face seemed to indicate that he felt entirely unthreatened by Joey's much shorter stature.

'Are you two military?' asked Joey, recognizing the type. 'Well, you're not Muslim – you're wearing a Christian cross – and your accent isn't French. I don't know of anyone else I have pissed off lately.'

'You are very observant,' said the leader. 'We are of Greek descent, but we live in Paris.'

'Paris,' Joey repeated. 'Did you know we're close friends with Julien Bonnet, the general of the DGSE?' Joey played the name card. 'If I were you, I would tread carefully.'

'I'm well aware of who you are, Joey and Marie Peruggia.'

Joey's back stiffened, and Marie's grip on his arm tightened.

The man glanced at his partner and flashed a mischievous half-smile. 'Being Greek, I especially loved reading about your discovery of Alexander the Great's remains. I can't believe his bones reside inside Saint Mark's Basilica. All this time the people of Venice have been praying to the general and not their patron Saint Marco ... That's genius.'

Joey tried to hide his surprise. How did they know all this?

The man in the shadows nodded his head in agreement.

'What do you want from us?' Marie asked from her protected position behind Joey. 'Presumably you're not here to talk about history.'

'You are absolutely correct. I want you both to help me find the last secret keystone, so I can activate the Stargate you both discovered not so long ago.'

Joey sighed, and Marie's expression instantly went hard.

'It's like a death wish that never seems to end for us,' Joey joked wearily. 'We'll never be able to escape our past, will we?'

Marie smiled at Joey briefly then stepped towards the two intruders. 'If you know all about the Stargate and our involvement in finding it,' she said, 'you would also know there is no red dolerite stone left on Earth. We destroyed the last remaining keystone, so you'll never be able to use the portal. You're looking for something that doesn't exist.'

'But you're wrong, my dear,' the man said, the corner of his mouth twitching into a cold grin on his rugged face. 'I wouldn't be here otherwise.'

The armed man circled towards Joey, and it made him feel uneasy.

'What do you mean?' asked Joey, keeping a close eye on the soldier's movement while preparing himself to defend his turf.

'We will find this precious gem on a tiny remote volcanic island on the eastern edge of the Polynesian triangle,' the man answered evenly. 'The South Pacific Ocean, if that helps.'

'Easter Island?' Marie guessed.

'Clever girl,' the man drawled condescendingly. 'Not that you'll care, but it lies on the same singular sweeping circle around our planet as Machu Picchu, the Nazca Lines, and of course, the Great Pyramid of Giza.'

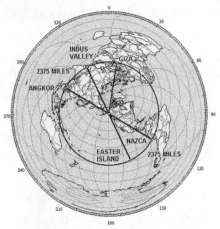

Joey was only half listening as he tried to take in his current circumstance – one he seemed to be continually re-living this past couple years. He discreetly scanned the room for possible weapons he could use in an attack. His firearms were locked away in his father's safe room, so they were out of the question. The only objects of relative usefulness were the pool-table cues and balls, and the hot pot of bolognese sauce bubbling on the stovetop, but those would be no match for a firearm, if the armed man chose to extract it.

Joey knew that if they were to have any chance of surviving this hostage situation, he would need to disarm the gunman first. The timing was crucial, so he waited for the opportune moment.

'I'm sorry, how rude of me,' the first man was saying urbanely. 'We've been chatting away all this time, and I haven't even introduced myself. My name is Dimitri, and this is my brother-in-law, Nick.'

Joey paused to think. He couldn't believe this idiot who had broken into their home was trying to play the friendship card. The same thing had happened last year, and in the end, the perpetrators had suffered Joey's wrath.

Dimitri reached into his black jeans and removed his cell. He entered his passcode and tossed it over to Joey to catch. After a near fumble in the air, Joey caught the phone and glanced at the five-inch display to see an image of the Moai statues located on Easter Island.

'What am I looking at?' Joey asked.

'Swipe through the photos until you see a symbol with noticeable swirls that was found on one of the enormous statues there.'

Joey swiped as ordered and Marie moved beside him to take a closer look.

Their mouths fell open once the image in question was in sight, and they glanced at each other for a moment.

'They can't be connected, surely?' said Marie with a shake of her head.

'It does resemble the keyhole that allowed us to into the Sphinx,' said Joey.

'Yes!' boomed Dimitri, focusing his attention on Joey. 'You are absolutely correct.'

'Okay, so even if you did find the entrance to a long-lost chamber that may or may not hold a keystone, you won't be able to enter it without the all-important tri-spiral key.' Joey took a quick breath and continued. 'What are you going to do, blow your way inside a cave? That would surely make it unstable and if it collapses, access may be blocked forever.'

Dimitri smirked. 'That won't be a problem, I have no intention of using explosives.' He extracted from within his dark sweater an object that had been resting on a delicate chain around his neck, underneath his holy cross. 'Help me find the red stone you speak of that will open the doorway to our makers, and I promise you on the memory of my wife and child that I will let you both go free. This is personal for me and my brother-in-law, so don't stand in our way.' He held up the object: it was a quad-spiral key very like the tri-spiral key Joey and Marie were familiar with.

'You say you're a family man, but what family man takes hostages?' said Joey, trying to buy time to work out what was happening.

'And what if we refuse?' Marie added, shooting a probing look over to Nick, who now stood closer to her.

Nick folded his arms across his chest, smirked and pointedly looked at Marie's athletic body up and down. Joey could feel his blood rush through him as rage built in him. He began to move towards Nick with an intent to end this once and for all.

Joey's eyes met Nick's and his fingers curled tightly into fists. He could see the man's neck snapping in his mind, and it felt good. He could feel his fist smashing into the man's nose, splattering red blood over the freshly painted white walls, but instead, he kept quiet as if his jaw were wired shut.

At that moment, feet away, Joey's cell, still lying on the kitchen benchtop, began to ring its harmonic default ringtone. Joey flicked his eyes towards it, and then noticed the caller ID.

'I have to pick it up,' said Joey, realizing the caller was Boyce. 'If I don't, he'll suspect something is wrong.'

'Don't test me,' warned Dimitri with a narrowed glare.

With hands held high, Joey slowly picked up his phone.

Nick reacted swiftly; he extracted his nine-millimeter pistol and aimed it at Marie's chest.

Marie gasped and then breathed deeply, trying to calm herself.

'Put it on speaker, and get rid of the caller,' said Dimitri from between gritted teeth.

'Hey, Boyce,' answered Joey, keeping it casual but thinking fast. 'How's it going?'

'Hi, Joey, sorry, this isn't a friendly catch-up call, I'm afraid. I just stepped outside of Julien's office to call you. He wants to warn you both of a dangerous man who could possibly be heading your way, but we don't know for sure.'

'What do you mean? Who is this man?' asked Joey, eyeing Dimitri who whispered to end the call.

'He's one of ours – or was. He's gone rogue. His name is Major Dimitri Panos, from the DGSE. Trust me, he's not someone you would want to go up against in a fight. The guy is a trained mercenary.'

'And why would he be coming my way? What did I do to him?'

'Julien thinks Dimitri could be behind a recent plane crash – involving a plane that had another spiral key on board, like the one your uncle had in his safe. If this is true, he might be trying to use it to find a keystone on Easter Island so he can activate the Stargate in Egypt. Unfortunately, it seems he stole my report on the events in Egypt. If so, he knows everything. And since you and Marie have been through this ordeal before, he might want to recruit you both to help him.'

'Why would he want to trigger the portal?' Joey asked, eyeballing Dimitri. 'What's wrong with Earth? On Planet X, humans are just ants in a much more savage food chain.'

'You don't need to convince me,' said Boyce. 'Try explaining that to a man who lost his wife and child in a terrorist shooting. It seems he's on a spiritual quest to find answers at any cost.'

Dimitri was signaling forcefully at Joey to end the call, but Joey pretended not to notice.

'Answers?' he repeated.

'Yeah, you know. Where we came from and where we go when we die. All that religious stuff.'

Joey and Marie's eyes met in resignation. Religious fanatics were not generally big on rationality, in their experience. It seemed the two of them would be part of Dimitri's plans whether they liked it or not.

'Hang up the phone,' hissed Dimitri so Boyce could not hear. He motioned his index finger in a downward direction. 'Right. Now.'

'Thanks again for the warning,' said Joey. 'I'll make sure to keep my eyes open.'

'As I said, it could all be a misunderstanding,' finished Boyce.

The whole time Joey held his phone, he had been picturing how this entire night would play out. He now had a weapon he could use. There were only two attackers. He was confident in his ability to strike. This was his domain. His subconscious spoke to the fighter within him; the warrior who had taken on larger-than-life opponents before. It was now or never to take these fools down.

He gripped the cell a little tighter in his fingers, placed his lip up against the speaker, and said one last sentence that would raise the stakes for everyone.

'It's been a pleasure chatting with you, bro, but now it's time for me to … *dance*!'

Chapter 5

There was a split second of stillness on both sides. Then Joey struck, tossing the smartphone at Dimitri's tanned and thinning hairline.

Dimitri reacted swiftly with a menacing grunt, deflecting it away with his forearm and sending it spinning over the Italian tiles towards the kitchen island bench. In that second, Joey saw the men's eyes flick upon him.

It was game on now.

'You will pay for that,' Dimitri hissed, taking a determined step in Marie's direction.

Marie shrieked and darted behind the pool table for cover. 'I can't believe this is happening,' she breathed.

Using the distraction, Joey leaped on Nick like a wildcat and reached for his nine-millimeter gun.

'Don't shoot him,' Dimitri warned Nick quickly. 'We need him alive.'

Joey and Nick collided against the island benchtop and fell in a tangle on the cold, hard floor. Nick's weapon was knocked out of his hand, and Joey used this brief moment of advantage to bring a fist up to Nick's face and smack his nose into a grotesquerie.

Blood pooled in Nick's mouth, but he recovered quickly and sank a punch into Joey's stomach, causing him to gasp. They stumbled apart for a moment to catch their breaths. Joey registered that Marie was screaming, but she'd armed herself with a pool cue and was still relatively safe behind the solid stone pool table. Reassured, he dove back at Nick, eyes narrowed in determination.

Joey dodged Nick's jab, his cerulean-blue eyes wide. He managed to tilt his head back, but incurred a glancing blow from the edge of Nick's flailing elbow.

Stars burst in Joey's vision, but he shook them off, throwing a sloppy leg.

'Is that all you've got?' Nick crowed.

Joey's blood thrummed in his veins as darkness began to spot his vision. He came in hard, teeth clenched, fists ready to rain blows. Dodging and weaving into his opponent's personal space, he found himself with an opening, and he took it. His favorite right hook caught Nick's cheekbone, snapping the other man's neck backwards like a willow whipping in the wind, and it sent him stumbling to the ground, out cold.

With his upper hand and fingers stained with Nick's blood, Joey sprang towards the nine-millimeter on the floor, but it wasn't going to be that easy.

Dimitri stood in his way, glaring at him with hatred in his dull eyes.

'You can do this, babe,' Marie encouraged, keeping her distance.

A confident smile curled the edge of Dimitri's mouth. 'Looks like you leave me with no choice,' he said quietly, then rolled his shoulders, ready to rumble. 'It's time to teach you an important lesson. The fact that you hurt my brother-in-law, my family, means a great deal of pain will be coming your way.'

'Yeah, yeah, grab a ticket and get in line,' Joey replied, putting up his hands in a boxing stance. 'You're not the first to want me dead.'

'You are but one man,' the major mocked, taking a step closer.

'That's what you think,' Marie barked back, hefting the cue in her hands. 'Surely you didn't think you could just waltz into our house without a struggle.'

Joey and Marie slowly began to circle the major.

Dimitri exhaled a long breath. It infuriated Joey that he was behaving as if they were a joke to him, a nuisance, like cockroaches that needed to be squashed.

Joey came in heavy with a thunderous right kick.

Straight after, Marie swung her cue like a batsman.

Dimitri instantaneously blocked Joey. He realigned his body and came in forcefully with a boot of his own that caught Joey's rib cage and sent him staggering back a couple of feet.

However Marie's maple-wood cue connected with a loud *bang!*

The monster took the hit in the shoulder and the cue snapped in half, leaving Marie with the jagged broken tip. Dimitri spun around, seemingly unfazed by the blow.

That was when Marie went in for a killer strike,

aiming the sharp piece at his chest. But once again, Dimitri was ready for her. He promptly deflected the blow, grabbed her by the neck and started to squeeze. Marie began to choke. She instantly dropped her weapon and used both hands to claw at the vise constricting her neck.

Fear was written all over her hazel eyes.

'Leave her alone,' Joey roared as he rushed at Dimitri.

Dimitri tossed Marie over to one side.

'I'm going to kill you.' Joey stormed the major with a flurry of punches and combinations.

Left … Right …

Right … Left …

Left … Left …

All were blocked without the major seeming to break a sweat.

Even though Dimitri was on the defensive, it seemed like he had the upper hand. Judging by the way he shielded himself, it became evident to Joey that this was not going to be a walk in the park. Boyce was right. Dimitri was a trained killer. He would not have earned his rank by being a boy scout.

'It's my turn now,' Dimitri chirped as Joey stumbled back to take stock. He stretched his neck and flexed his shoulders.

Then Dimitri grunted, moved forward, and threw his body weight behind a fist aimed squarely at Joey's face. It hit his jaw with force. Pain erupted in Joey's head from the point of impact as crimson leaked from both nostrils. Dimitri drew his hand back again, and this time it plowed into Joey's stomach. It felt like he'd hit a train head-on. Joey's guts mashed together, blood vessels bursting. On the floor, he was dimly aware that Marie was screaming. Dimitri continued the battering until Joey fell to the floor, completely trounced. His chest gently rose and sank with each shallow breath he took.

'Stop!' Marie shouted, crawling over to cover her beaten man.

Dimitri stepped back. 'Now you know what I'm capable of, so enough with this bullshit. I'm not going to ask you both again. Help me at Easter Island, or I will end you both in this stupid penthouse suite.'

'Okay, we'll help you,' Marie said, wiping blood from Joey's face with the edge of her shirt.

After a while, Joey managed to stand, his eyes already swelling shut and purpling with bruises. 'I can take him,' he said in a whisper, spitting blood out of his mouth.

'No, you can't,' Marie said shortly. 'We've lost this battle. Leave it alone, babe.'

Dimitri was addressing Nick in Greek.

Nick had come to and sat up, grasping his jaw. Slowly he found his footing. He turned to face Joey, a furious look on his face. His eyes narrowed, but Dimitri spoke to him again in Greek, and like a well-trained soldier, he walked away, shaking his head. Joey suspected he would have to watch his back with Nick around.

The major turned back to Joey and Marie and stared coldly at the couple. He was ruthless, to say the least: an experienced and skillful killing machine.

He stood with arms folded and feet apart, his chest muscles bulging and his biceps balls of strength. Tonight, he had made it clear who was running things. In the end the choice was easy: help him on this crazy quest or die.

Scanning the room, Dimitri spotted something out of the corner of his eye. It was Joey's phone, which was resting underneath one of three kitchen bar stools. He approached, picked up the device, and tapped the black screen to see it come alive.

The previous call had not yet ended.

Boyce had heard all the commotion.

Dimitri sighed and then began pacing back and forth, deep in thought.

'What's wrong?' Nick asked.

Dimitri flashed him a silencing gesture, before placing the cell over his ear to listen.

There was nothing but static on the other end.

After a minute of silence that felt like an eternity, he cleared his throat and spoke with what he hoped sounded like confidence, even though he now knew that the one man he feared most would be coming for him.

'If you want your friends to live, Boyce, it's simple. Be a good boy and tell Julien to stay out of my fuckin' way.'

And with that he terminated the call.

Chapter 6

DGSE Headquarters, Paris, 6:00 am Local Time

Boyce dropped his arms and his shoulders slumped as if suddenly weighted down by bricks. Dread crept over him like an icy chill, numbing his brain, and the shock was written all over his youthful face.

His friends were in danger.

Tucking his cell into his pocket, Boyce ran down the hallway to deliver the terrible message to his boss. He was young and fit, but the nerves building in his chest had set off a flurry of emotions that caused his heart to stutter.

Boyce dove into Julien's office. He was shaking and his breathing was erratic. He slumped into the chair opposite the general and rubbed his hands through his thick, curly hair. Raising his head to face his superior, he took a moment to compose himself. Eventually, he felt his breathing return to normal, although he still felt coiled tight with tension.

'By your body language alone, son, I gather the news is disheartening,' Julien said mildly.

'Yes, sir, it appears you were right. Dimitri was behind the plane crash, and he has now taken my friends hostage. We're too late.'

Julien bent his neck backwards in his own high-back leather chair as he considered this information. He wasn't one to show too much emotion. 'Boyce, it's not too late,' he said eventually. 'We know where he's taking them, and we can get there as quickly as humanly possible.'

'Do you think he would harm them?' Boyce asked, hoping that the man who had once worked for the DGSE might have some compassion still left deep inside his soul. He had played on the right side of the law at some stage in his life, after all.

'I can't be sure, but my guess is he won't harm them until he has what he wants,' Julien replied, staring into Boyce's concerned eyes. 'But he took down an aircraft. Only someone with deep psychological problems would do something like that. You never know what a man will do when it involves his family. This has become a spiritual quest for this man now, so all bets are off.'

'We need to stop him,' Boyce pleaded. 'Whatever it takes.'

Julien was silent as he watched the boy's red-rimmed eyes fill with tears, and passed him a tissue box. He then picked up the phone on his desk, dialed one and ordered for his jet to be fueled and ready to go. 'Time is critical,' he said with authority. 'The lives of my American friends depend on it.'

He then looked at Boyce with hard eyes. 'We'll stop him. Whatever it takes.'

Chapter 7

Joey and Marie exited the beach club. Down at the shoreline, mighty waves came crashing down on the sand, white foam roiling, while behind them the sea was an unrelenting black. Only a scatter of bright stars lit the heavens between voluminous gray clouds. Marie folded her arms tightly around herself to try to keep out the cold coastal breeze that blew right through the double-layered sweater, jacket, jeans, and hiking boots she'd been allowed to change into.

It had been an unbearable few hours for Joey as he had watched his two abductors shovel down his wife's pasta and mock her cooking skills.

'Aren't you concerned that Julien knows you're behind this?' Marie asked Dimitri as Nick licked his lips to wipe away the red mess on his face. Dimitri had administered first aid to Nick's broken nose and it was now all bandaged up and had stopped bleeding. 'He'll be coming for you.'

'Do I look concerned?' answered Dimitri, composed. 'Next time, in the sauce, throw in some fresh basil leaves, it'll help intensify the flavor.'

'I'll remember that,' said Marie flatly, rolling her eyes.

Soon after, Joey and Marie were ushered into the bedroom, where the two creeps perved on Marie while she and Joey dressed for what would inevitably be a dark, gloomy cave adventure.

'Come on, give us some privacy,' Joey had said.

'Yeah, right,' Nick had said smugly. 'So you can arm yourself? No way.'

'Yeah, that's exactly what I'm going to do in my wife's closet,' Joey had replied, shielding Marie as best he could while she had grabbed her clothes and scrambled into her jeans and sweater. 'I can use the rocket launcher,' he'd teased. 'To shove it up your ass.'

'Hurry up,' Nick had barked. 'We don't have all day. We've already stayed far too long.'

Outside the empty parking lot of the beach club, they were ushered into the back seat of a black BMW X series four-wheel drive and the doors were locked. Joey sat beside Marie and immediately comforted her with an arm around her shoulders, tucking her in tight, close to his warm chest.

Nick drove while Dimitri sat in the front passenger seat with an air of nonchalance.

'Are you okay?' Joey asked his wife, softly caressing her hair.

'I'm fine. But we have to do what they say.' Marie felt resigned now to their situation.

'What do you mean?' Joey whispered. 'If we get an opportunity, we need to act. We need to *dance*.'

'No, Joey!' Marie whispered with a vehemence that saw Joey's brows shooting up in surprise. 'There'll be none of that this time. It's not worth risking our lives.' Feeling a maternal instinct to protect her unborn child, she knew she needed to put her foot down. She stared into Joey's sweet perplexed blue eyes and wanted to tell him the fantastic news. She was carrying their baby, and he would become a father in about seven months. She had meant tonight to be a special occasion on which she would announce the pregnancy, and celebrate the first chapter in what would be a new life of many firsts: the first giggle, the first walk, kindergarten, dating, college, and all the glorious things in between.

But Marie knew that if her husband found out now, he would be overprotective and act emotionally. She needed him to stay sharp, which he could only do without the added burden of her news. She knew she would have to tell him before Dimitri did, though.

'Hey,' Marie called out to Dimitri. 'So, what's the plan?' She was taking a risk being so blatant, but she figured there wasn't much he could do to her while they were in the car.

Dimitri took his time before turning his pretentious head. 'I told you before,' he finally said sarcastically, 'we go to Easter Island and put this key into its keyhole.'

'Yes, I know that,' Marie replied slowly, as if speaking to a simpleton. She knew that would annoy him no end. 'When we get there, how will we know where to go?'

'Ah, yes. I have a guide who will escort us to the Moai statue with the markings.' Dimitri snapped back to face Joey, before glancing at Marie's flat stomach and smiling nastily. 'Try to relax, everything has been planned. We have a long trip ahead of us.'

After a fifteen-minute drive to Los Angeles International Airport, they pulled up into a vast private hangar. Inside the gray walls was a strong odor of petroleum and a Gulfstream IVSP aircraft with blue patterned stripes that ran across the fuselage. Nick extracted from the trunk of the car an olive duffel bag, typical of those used in military operations. The bag was heavy, it seemed, as the veins in Nick's forearms were protruding as he led the team up the retractable stairway and inside the aircraft.

Marie, Joey, and last of all Dimitri, boarded the plane and were ushered to their comfortable, earth-toned leather seats. Joey took his aisle seat, and Nick tapped him on the shoulder.

'We're taking no chances,' he said, handcuffing Joey's left wrist to his armrest. 'We can't have you planning an airstrike.' His tone was scathing. 'I've already jumped out of a plane this week and I don't want to do it again. I think I'm coming down with a cold.'

Marie watched as Nick clicked the handcuffs closed, trapping Joey to his seat, then without warning, Nick laid into him with a quick right hook that sent Joey in the opposite direction and into Marie's arms.

'Ahh!' Joey cried, grabbing his face with his free hand.

'You monster,' Marie hissed, placing a comforting hand on Joey's chest.

'Revenge is a bitch,' Nick said, sitting across from Dimitri, who smiled at Joey's discomfort.

Joey regained his composure and tried to stand, wobbly on his feet, wanting to fight back, but he was stopped short, pulled backwards by the cuffs.

'No,' Marie cautioned. 'Let it go, babe.'

'Sit down,' Dimitri commanded. 'Listen to your woman.'

Joey reluctantly accepted defeat and sat back into his seat with his right hand hovering over his left eye.

'Can we at least get some ice?' Marie asked. 'Injuring the help before you get what you want is a stupid move,' she added.

Dimitri nodded his head. 'I agree. I apologize for my brother-in-law's hot-headedness. I'll get the flight attendant to bring you some ice. Now get some rest.'

The jet taxied out of its hangar, and within minutes it roared into the night sky.

The plane's intercom chime played.

'Good evening, passengers, this is your captain speaking. We'll be flying 4247 miles and arriving at our destination of Easter Island in around nine hours. The local time there is three hours ahead of Los Angeles, so time at our destination on landing will be approximately eleven am. Thank you and have a pleasant flight.'

Staring out of the window with the flap shield raised, Marie gazed down on the whitish-gray clouds that seemed to amass just under the outstretched wings. Even with everything that had transpired tonight, the open sky always gave her a feeling of peace and comfort. She relaxed her sleepy eyes as she saw the outside lights blinking. Knowing that once they reached the island, it would be all systems go, her vision blurred and she fell fast asleep.

Five hours later, Marie woke feeling as though she had a terrible hangover. She was nauseous and felt she was likely to vomit at the slightest provocation. As she sat, the smallest up-and-down motion caused by the turbulence and the constant humming of engines amplified her queasiness.

'I need to go to the bathroom,' she gulped, holding a hand to her mouth and keeping the contents of her stomach down as best she could.

'What's wrong?' asked Joey, waking beside her, and worrying as he watched her leap out of her seat and hurry down the narrow corridor.

'Nick, you stay here!' warned Dimitri, pointing in Joey's direction. 'Watch him.'

'My pleasure,' retorted Nick.

Marie entered the compact bathroom and vomited into the stainless-steel toilet bowl. When the heaving stopped, she splashed water over her face and waited a moment to make sure there would be no further urge to vomit. She stared into the mirror at her pale complexion under the terrible aircraft lighting. Feeling confident that her insides were calmer, she slid open the entry door to find Dimitri standing there waiting with a bottle of water in his hand.

His leg was outstretched, blocking her path back to her seat. She was helpless against the enormous man. She accepted the water, took a sip to get the taste of vomit out of her mouth, and waited to hear what he had to say.

'How do you feel?' he asked evenly.

Marie quietly nodded to say better, afraid to open her mouth.

'I know you were the brains behind finding the secret chamber in Egypt. I'm counting on you to find this one, too.'

Marie nodded, her game face on.

'I once had a daughter,' he said abruptly, glancing away.

'What was her name?' Marie managed to ask.

'Bianca.'

'That's a beautiful name. How old was she when she passed away?'

'Thirteen.'

Marie could feel the pain in his voice. How deep the grief was inside. He was an empty void, and no find would ever be big enough to fill it.

'I'm so sorry for your loss,' Marie murmured. And she was.

Dimitri gave a hint of a smile. 'Joey doesn't know you're pregnant, does he?'

'Not yet,' said Marie. 'I was going to tell him last night.'

Dimitri stared into her hazel eyes, and it was as if he was reading her deepest thoughts. His gaze was powerful, like nothing she had ever felt before.

'You're sick because you're in the first trimester of pregnancy. It should pass at around the twelve-week mark.'

Marie once again nodded her head.

'I hate to repeat myself constantly, but I need to make myself one hundred percent clear before we land. Don't try to be brave. If you see your husband acting out, tell him to stop. If you don't want to lose your baby, I recommend that we work together, and everyone will be fine.'

'Promise me,' said Marie. 'Give me your word that once you get your trophy, you will let us go.'

'You have my word that I will let you go,' he said, 'but try to cross me and your family will perish.' His voice was hard, immovable.

Marie believed him, and she gave another nod of her head. Dimitri pulled back his leg so she could go back to her seat and dwell on their short but grave discussion.

He was cold and calculating and she feared his unpredictable nature. Marie knew without a doubt that there was nothing they could do against him.

Chapter 8

Easter Island,
11:00 am Local Time

Easter Island is located in the South Pacific more than 2000 miles off the Chilean coast. It is a place where 887 giant Moai statues carved from volcanic rock reside, turning one of the most isolated islands in the world into one of the most well-known – and most mysterious.

The jet landed smoothly at Mataveri International Airport, and the captain reported that the temperature outside was a warm seventy degrees Fahrenheit. Joey led his wife down the airstairs and onto the asphalt that was the runway. A short, friendly local Polynesian man was waiting, and he appeared to speak perfect English. He was dressed like a mini–Indiana Jones and even had a matching cowboy hat to go with his outfit. He greeted Dimitri with a smile and a handshake. His name was Anaru, which was another form of Andrew; at least, that was what he told everyone.

He pointed over to a sleek black Eurocopter, specially designed and configured for sightseeing. 'Our pilot is waiting if you will follow me,' he said, leading the group to a helmet-wearing figure with dark glasses who was hunched over the controls.

Nick, who was flanking Joey, nudged him forward. 'Move!' he said rudely.

'What's your problem,' Joey reciprocated, adjusting his sweater. 'I'm moving.'

Joey glanced at Dimitri, who didn't seem at all bothered by his brother-in-law's actions.

Marie was on his other side, and when she grabbed his hand Joey could feel his fingers being crushed: the warning sign Marie had used on numerous occasions. She was telling him that she was afraid. Heights had never been her strong suit.

'We'll be okay,' Joey promised, holding her hand tightly.

Anaru sat up front in the cockpit with the non-English-speaking aviator. Marie and Joey snuggled up together in the air-conditioned cabin, facing Nick, who was on constant lookout while keeping a tight grip on his duffel bag.

What's in the bag? Joey wondered.

Dimitri was the last to enter the helicopter. He leaned over to shut the door behind him. His long limbs took up most of the leg room in the limited space. The blades suddenly came alive above them, beating in the air. And before they knew it, they had vertically lifted, and Joey's fingers were firmly being squeezed the higher they rose.

Anaru coughed into his microphone to clear his voice as the forward-facing stadium seating gave them 180-degree views of the lush green landscape and an overall map of the land.

'Welcome to Easter Island,' he said in a cheerful tone, but no one smiled back. He continued anyway; he didn't seem to care. Joey assumed he would have been paid handsomely to take them to the cave. 'Our destination, Ana Te Pahu, is only a short flight away, so we'll do a quick fly-by around the volcano first. Don't forget to take with you a handheld torch and helmet located in the box before exiting the aircraft. It's extremely dark down there.' He paused for a second. 'If you look over the hilly sanctuary of volcanic origin, you will see that there are hardly any trees.'

He waited for a response … nothing.

Undeterred, he continued. 'The island received its current name, Easter Island, from the Dutch sea Captain Jacob Roggeveen, who was the first European to visit here, on Easter Sunday, the fifth of April, in 1722. We are now flying over the Moai, the massive iconic Polynesian figures.' He turned in his seat.

This too was met with absolute quiet.

Anaru whispered something to the pilot, who nodded his head. They were probably conferring over the tough crowd, Joey mused.

'Here are the famous stone statues at Ahu Tongariki, the largest *ahu* on Easter Island. Its Moai were toppled during the island's civil wars, and in the twentieth century, the *ahu* was swept inland by a tsunami. It has since been restored and has fifteen Moai, including an eighty-six-ton Moai, the heaviest ever erected here.'

The chopper banked left.

'I'm sure this next fly-by will get you excited.' Anaru smiled to himself. 'Framed by palm trees, white sand and turquoise-blue water is the exotic beach of Anakena. It is without a doubt the most beautiful on this island. Four hundred and ninety feet from the beach are the Ahu Nau Nau monuments.'

'Why are the monuments all facing inland?' Marie asked, breaking the silence and causing all eyes to turn to her. 'Why are they not fronting the ocean?'

The guide's grin grew. 'Yeah ... I have a reaction ... Well, that's a fantastic question and—'

'Can we just get to our destination,' Dimitri interrupted. 'Enough with the info, I'm starting to get a headache.'

Anaru turned back in his seat, visibly affronted by the rudeness.

'What's wrong, Dimitri, can't you store any more

information in that stupid brain of yours?' Joey riled, waiting for a response that didn't come.

Nick leaned forward only to be stopped by a single raised finger from Dimitri. Joey wanted to reply with a comment likening Nick to an obedient pet dog, but decided to hold it back this time.

Minutes later they hovered over a grassy hilltop. The view from here was spectacular.

As they descended, the blades beating above them had much the same effect as a mini tornado on the loose ground cover. Marie covered her ears, held her breath, and closed her eyes until they touched the ground and came to a stop.

'It's okay,' Joey said into her ear. As they landed Marie slowly released her grip, and his fingers began regaining their blood flow once more.

Everyone, including the pilot, stepped out of the chopper, taking with them their own flashlight and helmet from a box in the main bay.

'Where's the cave?' Nick asked the guide, who was stretching his legs a few feet away from the chopper.

'It's up this hill,' he replied, pointing. 'We can't land any closer, too dangerous. We'll need to hike the rest of the way up.'

'Let's go,' said Dimitri with a sharp gesture of his arm. 'Time is ticking.'

The navigator said something to Anaru in his native language, and Anaru stopped.

Dimitri and Nick turned to see what the problem was.

'The pilot just informed me that he will be staying with his helicopter. It is too valuable to leave unattended.

He said he will wait here for us to return.'

Judging by the expression on Dimitri's face, he wasn't delighted with this piece of news. His eyes had a deadness, a stillness to them. And the clench of his stubble-covered jaw wasn't a promising sign. He turned to Nick and said in a mild but clear tone, '*Skotóse ton malaka.*'

Nick extracted his gun and raised his armed hand at the unaware pilot, who looked back at him in confusion. Nick curled his finger around the trigger and smiled grimly.

Joey's eyes widened, and Marie clutched at him; they both knew what was to come.

The bullet entered the pilot's skull, the report echoing deafeningly and incongruously around them in the beauty of the vibrant green landscape. The pilot's head jolted backwards, his eyes rolling, and his entire body went rigid as a splatter of brain fragments hit the chopper's oversized windows. As a red hole blossomed in his head, his body dropped like a bag of cement.

Anaru screamed, falling to his knees and removing his cowboy hat to show his receding hairline. 'Who are you people?' he shouted, tears filling his eyes. 'Monsters!'

Joey felt for the man. His poor friend had just been brutally murdered right in front of him, for no apparent reason. Joey turned to the asshole he should have hit harder back in his penthouse suite, as smoke dispersed from the barrel. Nick's cold eyes, devoid of any emotion, bore directly into him. Joey knew that that bullet had been meant for him, indirectly.

It was a warning.

This was what Joey would face if he tried to be brave.

Chapter 9

Ana Te Pahu,
Cave of Bananas

The volcanic eruptions that gave rise to Easter Island thousands of years ago created lava channels that covered much of the subsoil. The most enormous caverns on the island are in the foothills of the Ma'unga Terevaka, and the best example of these are the large volcanic tubes that have been amazingly formed by the passing of magma.

The group walked the undulating slopes of the Ma'unga Terevaka. The site was covered with grass and sprinkled only with a few lonely trees and shrubs. Anaru had his head bowed and eyes to the ground the entire way and clearly felt threatened; he seemed to understand that he would be next if he didn't snap out of it and do what he was paid to do: guide the group.

After a one-mile hike along a muddy dirt road carrying their headgear and torches, the group of five reached the cave's open entrance. The top of a lava tube had worn away, and the bottom of the open-topped area was filled with banana trees.

'This is where it gets its name, Cave of Bananas,' said Anaru in a muffled tone, his eyes still reflecting the trauma of seeing his friend's vicious death.

'How deep do they go?' Joey asked gently, trying to distract the unfortunate guide while placing the yellow explorer's helmet with flashlight snugly over his head.

Marie and the rest of the team followed suit.

Before Anaru could reply, Dimitri asked, 'Will others be sharing the cave with us?'

Anaru said, 'There are several underground chambers that interconnect. The entire route exceeds four miles in length, but where we are going is off limits to the public.'

'Why is that?' asked Nick.

'The people on the island say this cave is cursed,' said Anaru. 'There have been some unexplained deaths of people who have visited the site in the past, including a team of archaeologists from UCLA who developed the Easter Island Project to study the giant statues of Rapa Nui.'

Joey sighed. That sounded like bad news.

'Let's go,' said Dimitri, nudging Joey forward.

The entrance to the cavern gave onto one of the sectors where the lava layer had collapsed. It wound deep underground, with high deteriorated stone steps showing the way. Joey held Marie's hand and helped guide her between the stones, avoiding slipping on the wetter areas where small reservoirs of water had pooled.

'Careful here,' Joey warned as he slid on moss, but managed to correct his fall.

Anaru took the lead, followed by Nick and his duffel bag. Marie and Joey were in the middle, and at the rear was Dimitri, strategically placed so no one would try to make a run for it.

After a short journey in the gloom, they reached an area filled with natural light thanks to a generous breach in the cave roof. The sun and rain that had entered through the opening had given life to a mass of greenery.

'Welcome to Jurassic Park,' Marie joked with hands aloft, trailing through the vegetation that draped from above.

Joey gave her a wink. 'Hope there are no T-rexes in here.'

'Here we go,' said Anaru. 'From here on, the cave narrows and darkens, so turn on your flashlights and watch your heads.'

Five helmets on and five torches lit, the flat roof above came into sharp relief.

'The smoothness of the rock was formed from the passage of magma and the pressure of gases,' said Anaru, touching the surface with one outstretched hand.

Joey stepped further in and watched his shadow dissolve into the surrounding darkness, his beam of light cutting through what was an uneven terrain.

'I can't believe I'm once again in another stupid cave,' Joey winced with a shake of his head as he searched for a safe footing.

'Yep,' Marie said with a shrug. 'Our life in a nutshell.'

'Stinks down here,' said Nick, holding the back of

one hand up against his face to lessen the impact of the smell.

'No, that's just you,' retorted Joey.

Marie let out a chuckle.

'Won't be so funny with a bullet in your head,' Nick spat.

'Yeah, I've heard that before, too,' said Joey.

'Shut up and keep moving,' Dimitri interjected.

After a thirty-minute trek that took them deeper into the cavern, the air became stale. The general shape of the cavern was ovoid, the walls above the rocky floor curving smoothly about fifteen feet upwards to where stalactites and bat roosts dotted the ceiling.

'Not so level in here now,' said Joey as the small loose stones and scree that littered the floor caused him to trip and graze his knee through his jeans.

'Watch your heads,' warned Anaru. 'The height shrinks from here on in.'

The wall barriers were now a muddy brown, jagged and uneven. In the darkness of the deep cavern, the beam from Joey's torch was lost in the blackness, and his helmet light seemed to die a few inches from his face. Joey stayed close to the others and ran one hand along the damp wall as he walked so as not to lose his bearings.

'It seems like we are heading in an upward direction,' said Nick, who was now dragging his bag as he walked behind Anaru.

'We are; watch your step,' answered Anaru. 'The last part of this trek has an incline to it. That's why this location has stayed protected and preserved for so long. No lava ever traveled up here.'

They came across frigid pools of stagnant water which had to be circumnavigated, and eventually had to focus all their attention on their footing as the precarious climb intensified.

'How much more of this?' said Dimitri eventually, sounding impatient.

'Not long now, just a little further and we'll squeeze through to an open void with plenty of natural light,' said Anaru. 'This is the hardest part, but it will be worth it, I promise.'

Ahead came the sound of water dripping into puddles. Joey could hear his breathing become labored. Water was beginning to seep into his boots from all the dampness underfoot.

'Just under here,' said Anaru, removing what seemed to be two long timber planks placed to stop wanderers from entering. 'This is it; we are here.'

With the boards removed, daylight shone through a small gap from the space beyond. On hands and knees, Joey and Marie followed Anaru and Nick through to the other side where they found themselves in an astoundingly unique place, one that caused chills to run down Joey's spine. Despite their dire circumstances, a grin splayed itself across his face and left him completely and utterly speechless.

Chapter 10

The Mysterious Cave

The large Moai statue buried from the waist down was silhouetted against a generous square opening that framed the bright sunlight of the outside world. The ocean waves appeared majestic on what was a cloudless and muggy day. To take a step into this hidden cave was like stepping back in time, or, more accurately, to a place where an incredible, intelligent ancient society once ruled the land.

Marie took in the wonder before her. She gazed up in awe at the giant monolith in all its glory. It stood eight feet high and was carved from incredibly hard basalt, which disappeared into the dark soil at its feet. It had a heavy eyebrow ridge, elongated ears, and oval nostrils. The clavicle was emphasized, and the nipples protruded. The arms were thin and set tightly against the body that disappeared into the dirt.

Long pole-shaped stones spiraled their way up around the structure, accompanied by six strategically positioned orange traffic cones and five wooden graveyard crosses. Marie thought they had probably been placed there to scare away locals and spread idea of the curse of the ancestors.

A sizable metal sign had been drilled into the rock nearby, with words on it in Spanish.

Peligro. El suelo es tóxico. No molestar.

Anaru read the warning out loud, signaling with his palms for the others to stop.

'This sign translates to *Danger. Soil is toxic. Don't disturb.*'

'Please,' Nick dismissed this, flapping his hand as he dumped the heavy duffel bag on the ground.

'No, this is no joke,' said Anaru solemnly. 'Previous explorers have died due to the toxicity in the soil. I think they said they found traces of arsenic.'

'Let's not be foolish, guys,' Joey warned. 'I think we should listen to our guide and keep our distance from the stuff.'

'I agree,' said Marie. 'But are we at any risk being so close to it?'

'As you can see, it's an open cave that brings in an abundance of natural air,' said Anaru. 'As long as we don't disturb the substance, we'll be fine.'

'It's probably one of the many booby traps in this place,' Joey said. He turned to Dimitri. 'Trust me, you don't know what you're getting yourself into.'

'I know exactly what I'm getting myself into,' answered Dimitri, scowling. 'This is bigger than you and me, Joey. Once you become a father, you will understand my reasoning.'

Joey frowned, puzzled by his comment, and Marie looked away. She walked over to study the lip of the cavern.

It dropped one hundred and twenty feet straight down to the sandy bedrock of crashing waves. 'You're right, Anaru, this explains why this Moai has survived the passage of time so well.' She stuck her head out over the cliff top. 'We're on an elevated platform here. Any lava from previous eruptions on this island would have flowed to the ocean using the channels under us.'

Anaru nodded.

Joey joined Marie at the cave mouth and shook his head, dumbfounded, when he saw jets of water blowing out of the many different-sized cave holes in the cliff below them, before flowing back in with the crashing tides.

'It's stunningly beautiful up here,' said Marie, admiring the U-shaped rock formation that curved into the sea. 'The rocks here remind me of a sad legend in Hawaii, at a place called Hanauma Bay,' she said. 'The story of the bay was based on a woman's love for two men. Keohinani, the daughter of the mighty chief and protector of Hanauma Bay, could not choose between them, so her father, a great magician, turned them both into lizards. She prayed to the gods of the land for mercy, and the gods heard her prayers and turned the two lizards into two enormous stone mountains, like these ones here. Now they guard Hanauma Bay and Keohinani forever and there they rest, but even now their tails remain locked together in the eternal battle for her love.'

'Wow,' replied Joey. 'How can you fit all that info inside your gorgeous head?'

Marie punched her husband playfully on the arm, and Joey pulled her in close for a hug.

'The marking we spoke about,' said Dimitri, obviously not interested in ancient tales, 'where is it?'

Anaru left the edge of the cliff and pointed to one of the Moai's elongated square ears. 'The symbol is up there. It can be reached if you walk up the stepping stones, but be careful not to fall into the dangerous substance.' After a pause, he asked curiously, 'Do you know what it means or what it symbolizes?'

Dimitri reached into his sweater and extracted the spiral artefact from his neckline.

'What is that?' asked Anaru in fascinated confusion.

Marie spun around quickly and faced the structure, deep in thought. A focused expression on her face, she approached it.

'What is it, babe?' asked Joey.

'This Moai faces the ocean,' she said softly.

'And?' asked Joey. 'What's the relevance?'

'Ah,' said Anaru admiringly. 'All eight hundred and eighty-seven Moai on this island face inland. I never even thought of that ... clever observation.'

'That's why I need you on my team, Marie,' said Dimitri, sounding genuinely appreciative. 'You think outside the box. As you know, I read Boyce's report on your previous adventures. I know everything that happened. He explained how you interpreted many of the clues that eventually led you to the Stargate. If you have anything to share, please don't hesitate. You have an open stage here.'

'Stargate?' said Anaru, frowning.

Marie stepped forward. 'The civilization that built the Moai believed that they were the only people in the whole world. All invaders, any criminals that would be coming, would have to come from within the island – not from the sea! So all Moai faced inwards to protect the community.'

'Except this one,' said Joey.

'Yes,' said Marie. 'Except this one,' she repeated, thinking hard. 'Why?'

'I bet we'll discover the real reason soon,' said Dimitri, passing the spiral key to her. 'Show us the way, Marie.'

'Can someone tell me what you are talking about?' said Anaru, as Marie grabbed hold of the object designed with four swirls that represented the big bang when the universe came into existence 13.8 billion years ago. Its core, she knew, was made from the same meteorite she had used not so long ago – the key that had guided them deep inside the Sphinx.

'Hang on, I'll do it,' said Joey, stepping closer to her.

'It's okay,' replied Marie, placing a palm gently against his chiseled chest. 'I have smaller feet. It'll be easier if I do it. Hold my flashlight.'

Marie handed the light to Joey and climbed onto the first sturdy pillar. She took a breath and a moment to compose herself, aware of the poisonous soil that loomed underneath.

Four beams of light now flashed across her path, illuminating the way, and giving the thick sandy soil below a wavy riverbed effect.

With caution, she climbed to the top of the winding

staircase, all her years of ballet classes as a child, learning the art of balance, paying off in spades. Her helmet light reflected the imperfect volcanic stone that was the grayish Moai head.

Reaching the height of the statue's ears, she found the grooved symbol there.

Grooved Symbol   Quad-Spiral Key

She knew what she needed to do.

'Here I go,' she breathed.

She pushed the key into the indented shape and it slid into position like a hand into a glove. It now lay flush with the stone's surface.

'I'm going to rotate it now,' she called out. Then she gave it a hard quarter-turn to the right.

A grim silence descended on the group.

The key locked in place with a loud crunch, then the walls inside the cave started to vibrate.

'Oh God,' Marie gasped. 'This can't be good.'

Chapter 11

The Entry

Dimitri, Nick, and Anaru reached for cover over to one side, as loose rocks from the cliff top began to plummet down to the shoreline.

Joey stood his ground rigidly, feet firmly planted. His initial thought was for Marie's safety. If she slipped, the dangerous soil below would be disturbed, possibly ending her life and killing everyone else in the cavern too. Not that he cared what happened to Dimitri or Nick – they deserved to die painful deaths.

'Hang on,' Joey warned, as Marie held on to the solid structure in front of her with outstretched arms.

'Ahh!' Marie screamed. 'I don't know how long I can hold on.' Her legs shook on the narrow foothold.

And then, as quickly as the trembling had begun, it abruptly stopped.

Marie didn't waste any time. She swung around and walked briskly down the stone pillar steps and into Joey's open arms. He squeezed her tight and gave her a passionate kiss. She was safe, and that was all that mattered to him. She was his soulmate, his rock, and if anything happened to her, well, all bets were off.

Moments later, they heard a deep crackling sound.

'What's that?' Joey asked while Marie leaned into his protective arm. 'It's coming from outside.'

Dimitri was the first to look out into the daylight, and when he turned back, he was laughing. 'At least this answers your previous question, Marie,' he said, pausing for dramatic effect. 'This is why this Moai faces out towards the ocean.'

Nick's face broke into a big smile. 'Of course,' he said. 'It's showing us the way.'

'It sure is,' said Anaru with a bemused expression, seemingly lost for words.

Joey approached the lip of the cavern and scanned his eyes over the cliffs that formed the U-shaped mass. Through the dust and debris caused by the movement of rock, they could all see that an empty void had opened up in the mountainous cliff face.

'We have a secret passage,' said Dimitri.

'Just above the waterline,' Nick added.

'Looks like we're going for a swim,' said Marie.

The two goons who had kidnapped them looked elated, but Joey knew this feeling was not going to last. There was no way it was going to be a walk in the park. He had been through an ordeal like this before, and it had almost killed him. Whatever was behind the new opening in the cliff had lain dormant for God knew how long, its booby traps most likely still operational and set to kill the unworthy who dared to enter into its innermost caverns.

'I think we're making a terrible mistake,' said Joey. 'I just want to put it out there.'

'Let's go!' ordered Dimitri in his hard, commanding voice, pointing the way down.

'I can't go down there,' said Anaru with a quivering voice. 'I brought you all here, that was the plan. I did my job. Please let me go. I will keep my mouth sealed; you have my word.'

'Well, if you're not joining us . . .' Nick shrugged, extracting his nine-millimeter, 'you're no use to us anymore.' He raised his armed hand at the local, who froze. 'Thank you for your services.'

It seemed Nick got off on taking out his weapon, Joey thought disgustedly. He had proven with the helicopter pilot that he felt no hesitation in using it.

'No!' Marie begged. 'Let him go.'

'He could help us,' Joey added quickly. 'Don't lose all your chips in one bet. Any information he has on Easter Island could be crucial to our survival down there.'

Dimitri signaled to Nick, his palm elevated like a stop sign.

Nick grimaced but did as he was told, concealing his gun back in its holster. 'You've been given a lifeline, Anaru. I suggest for your sake and that of your new friends that you climb down before I change my mind.'

Nick crouched and unzipped the duffel bag near his feet, while Anaru approached the edge with the knowledge that his life depended on it.

Joey glimpsed inside the bag. They had come prepared with all the tools needed for a cave expedition – a deep pile of light sticks, flares and ropes – but his eyes opened wide when he spotted six grenades secured safely amongst them all.

'What are they for?' asked Joey, not bothering to mask the concern in his tone.

'You, shut up and start your descent,' Nick ordered, standing and fixing his gaze down on Joey's much shorter stature, clearly trying to intimidate him.

'But you have ropes,' said Joey, staring at the cords now wrapped around Nick's arm.

'These aren't for you. Now go,' Nick barked.

'Don't be an ass, at least lower Marie down.'

'Don't worry, we're not monsters,' said Dimitri with an air of smugness. 'Marie will abseil down with Nick. Now go ahead and start your climb. We'll meet you at the bottom if you survive. Just don't slip and fall.'

'I'll be okay,' said Marie. 'Make sure to watch your step.'

Joey nodded, knowing he had no real choice. He managed to clasp onto the edge of the cliff with his fingertips and gently lower himself down to the first foothold.

The drop fell away beneath his feet as he clung to the side. He turned his head southward to Anaru and watched him struggle. Joey felt adrenaline spike in his bloodstream, and his muscles began to burn as he rested on a narrow ledge. The slope was steep, but lucky for him, there were many hand and footholds to grip onto. He found his footing and progressed down the cliff face with relative ease, eventually reaching Anaru's location.

'Are you okay?' Joey asked the native man, who looked scared out of his mind.

'My neck burns,' he replied, wincing.

'Don't give up, Anaru. You can do this.'

Moments later, a rope was tossed over the ledge feet away, hitting the rocky floor below.

Joey heard a yelp of fear from above. He whipped his head up to see his wife and Nick beginning to edge over the lip of the cliff. They were locked together, preparing to abseil in tandem. Nick was standing behind Marie, his duffel bag strapped over his shoulder. He moved his feet up against the wall. Marie was trapped in front of him in an uncompromising position.

She squirmed as Nick controlled their descent. His hands were all over her, his crotch tight up against her backside.

Joey turned away, trying to keep his rage in check. He was livid, the veins standing out on his neck.

Marie's voice was louder now, and Joey could hear the anger in it.

Nick bypassed Joey and Anaru's location. He locked eyes with Joey as he moved past, then ostentatiously sniffed Marie's lush brown hair, mocking him as he descended.

The jerk was enjoying this way too much.

'Son of a bitch,' Joey muttered, his blood now at boiling point. To distract himself, he kept moving, looking for the best way to tackle the next section of the descent.

Marie reached the ground where she was detached and pushed the creep away, but Nick held her close and continued to touch her inappropriately.

Seeing this, Joey gritted his teeth and closed his

eyes, his face burning with suppressed rage. But when he opened his eyes to see Nick set another finger on her shoulder, he snapped, and what he did next made Anaru's jaw drop.

Joey leaped to his left to grab Nick's rope, and like a firefighter going down his pole, he slid down fast, exceptionally fast, which ended with him knocking the taller man in his rib cage.

The unexpected blow sent Nick sprawling onto the rocky beach with his line still attached to his torso. The expression on his face was one of surprise and fear, rolled into one.

'I'm gonna kill you,' Joey roared.

His rage exploded like magma meeting seawater and it was just as destructive. Joey grabbed Nick's neck and forced his head into the sand as the waves came crashing in. Nick shut his mouth as the saltwater hit his face. Joey reached for the gun in its holster by Nick's side. He could end this now.

In that instant, an intense football kick collided with Joey's stomach, sending him into the fetal position away from Nick, struggling to breathe.

'Stop!' Marie yelled. 'Please stop!'

A second kick followed soon after, winding Joey some more.

'I'm in control here,' said Dimitri coldly, blocking the sun as he stepped over Joey. 'If you disrespect my brother-in-law, you insult me.'

Joey tried to crawl away from the giant standing above him.

Nick, spitting sand out of his mouth and getting to

his feet, extracted his gun and advanced towards Joey with clear intent.

This is where I'm going to die, thought Joey. Of all his ingenious ideas, this had perhaps been the worst.

Marie pleaded for his life.

Nick lifted his weapon.

'*Ton thélo zontanó*,' Dimitri said softly in his native Greek.

A dull thump struck Joey in the head.

Then there was blackness.

Chapter 12

The Talk

Cold water cascaded over Joey's face and he blinked as he came to in the painfully bright light. He rose unsteadily onto all fours, spitting out saltwater, and managed to avoid the next incoming wave. *Where am I?* He thought for a moment, trying to clear his head. He breathed in deeply, smelling the brine of the ocean and listening to the percussion of waves, and then felt an unpleasant burst of pain that was searing through his jawline. While still in a daze, his fingers searched for the source, and when he touched it, he felt a large lump. He opened his mouth in a yawn to diagnose how severe the injury was.

Then like a flash, it came to him.

Nick hadn't shot him; he'd knocked him out with the hilt of his weapon.

A shadow loomed over him. Joey looked around blearily, and saw an imposing figure standing there, quietly waiting, knee deep in water. In his hands were two pairs of goggles and two flashlights. He also had a cigarette in his mouth, and he tilted his head as he inhaled, as if enjoying the feeling of the nicotine entering his body.

It was Dimitri.

'I'm sorry Nick struck you in the face,' said Dimitri, flicking the half-finished butt into the water.

Joey shrugged despite the pain he was in, and felt for his helmet, which was still on his head.

'You are lucky he didn't blow your brains out.'

'Am I supposed to thank you?' Joey replied, struggling up to his feet to face his kidnapper. 'Where are Marie and Anaru? What have you done with them?'

'They have gone ahead and entered the cave,' the Greek man said, nodding his head in the direction of the opening in the distance. 'I wanted to have a little chat before we entered. Make sure we are on the same page.'

'And what page is that,' Joey asked before craning his neck, as Dimitri stepped closer. Nick was tall, but Dimitri was another level of tall.

'Listen to me carefully, I will only say this once. You will enter this cave and help me find the keystone that will activate the Stargate. You will not stand in my way – do you understand me?' He shoved a thick finger into Joey's chest, and even though it was just a single digit, it was enough to move Joey off his feet. 'I'm not playing around. If you cause me any problems, I will not hesitate to end you. You are expendable; your wife is all we need.'

'Your words don't scare me,' Joey lied, rubbing his jaw. 'I've dealt with people like you before.' He spat the words out of his mouth, words drummed into him by his late gangster father. *Never back down. Never show defeat, whatever the situation or adversary.*

'Yes, I've read all about your past dealings and hostage circumstances, once in Paris and last year in Egypt. You've become an expert on how to survive these difficult situations, and I commend you for it. You could write a book on the subject, but this time, my American friend, it's different. The odds are now *not* in your favor, not by a long shot.'

'What odds? What are you talking about?'

Dimitri flashed Joey a grin full of malevolent enjoyment. 'This time, you're a family man. This time, if you fuck up, you will endanger the fetus that is growing inside your wife's body.'

Joey froze in shock. No. Surely Dimitri was lying to him, trying to unsettle him. But suddenly Joey knew it was no lie. He recalled Marie's nausea on the plane and Dimitri's strange comment in the cave above; the way Marie had turned away. The way she'd cooked his favorite dinner the night they'd been abducted, and set the table with candles . . . *She was going to tell me.* Joey struggled to keep a bland expression on his face. He was in a nightmare he couldn't wake up from.

Joey had been surprised before, but this one topped them all. He was going to be a father. Dimitri was right – this time was different, and the odds were stacked against him now. If he didn't accept defeat and do as requested, his most prized possession on earth would also find its end.

'Are we clear about what needs to happen?' Dimitri confirmed.

Joey nodded, acknowledging that he would comply. 'Now that we've gotten that out of the way, ladies first.' Dimitri gestured towards the cave, passing over a pair of goggles and a flashlight. 'Let's not keep your family waiting.'

Chapter 13

The Cave Dive

Waist deep in water, Joey took a deep breath and plunged under the murky surface with his torch hand leading the way. He also switched on his headlight beam and directed it down and into the shallow water.

Ahead was a rectangular-shaped tunnel the size of a refrigerator that seemed to descend a long way into a secret underwater passage. A quad-spiral symbol was etched on a thick slab of rock that must previously have blocked the entrance. It was now positioned on its side on an embankment of different-sized stones.

The symbol was the secret marker showing the way, only known to a few fortunate people, and Joey knew he was one of them.

Joey grabbed hold of the edge of the cavity and pushed his way inside, allowing himself to glide through with ease. A light stick had been dropped in the sand ahead, which turned the walls an eerie green. After a short twenty-five-foot swim, Joey found himself at a shaft that ascended to what appeared to be an opening. He glanced upwards to the surface, and his heart leaped when he saw Marie. Or at least, a blurry image that he thought was Marie. Three spotlights shone down over him as he approached the final leg of the swim in a modified breaststroke and an underwater dolphin kick.

Bubbles slowly exited his mouth, and when he broke the water, he sucked in a much-needed breath of air.

'Joey!' Marie called out, moving towards a ledge that Joey saw was made up of stone steps.

She threw herself into his arms as soon as he was upright, and Joey hugged her tightly. When he pulled back and looked around, he saw that the enormous void around them was lit up like a Christmas tree. Multiple cracked light sticks and a single burning flare showed the way. Their reunion was interrupted by Dimitri, who sprayed water out of his mouth like a whale's blowhole as he broke the surface.

'Are you okay?' Joey asked Marie in a soft voice, gently rubbing her shoulders.

'I'm okay,' she said, touching his jaw. 'But you're hurt.'

'I'll live,' said Joey, then noticed Anaru sitting alone. The guide was staring blankly into the water. A sense of guilt washed over Joey for this local who had been propelled into his world. 'You alright, Anaru?' he asked sincerely.

Anaru didn't say a word but flashed him back a wan half-smile.

Dimitri swam to the ledge, and Nick, who'd been

standing behind them, was there to greet his brother-in-law. Joey saw that Nick was still carrying the duffel bag. The two men spoke quickly and quietly in Greek.

While the two men's attention was elsewhere, Joey pulled Marie back with both hands and looked into her hazel eyes, which appeared green under this lighting. 'Why didn't you tell me you were pregnant?' he said softly.

'I was going to, Joey. I had it all planned out, but then this shit happened,' said Marie, her eyes showing a gentle concern. 'I didn't want you to worry.'

'How many weeks are you?'

'Six, I think.'

'Well, that explains your upset tummy in the plane.'

Marie nodded and they hugged tightly.

Dimitri walked over to them. His size and shadow eclipsed them both. He was like Dwayne 'The Rock' Johnson on steroids, thought Joey. The close proximity made Marie hunch her shoulders into Joey's chest.

Joey's mind went back to his apartment, where he had felt Dimitri's wrath. He couldn't believe he'd been so naive as to go up against a man with his stature, but what was he to do, nothing?

'Nice to see a happy and healthy family,' Dimitri said sarcastically, with a smirk that splayed over his face. 'Let's keep it that way, eh.'

Nick approached his brother-in-law, and said something in Greek that sounded argumentative, but Joey knew it just looked that way. Joey's father's friends and gang members were all Italian and Greek. They were over-animated all the time, always the loudest people in a restaurant, but they'd be mostly joking and teasing each other.

Unless you crossed them.

'Looks like this is the way,' said Marie, pointing her flashlight beam at an upward spiral stairway that stopped at an arched doorway of utter blackness.

Anaru stood and moved closer to Marie and Joey, remaining silent all the while. Nick positioned himself side-on like the police were taught to do. Always equipped to act, he was constantly on the lookout for danger.

'Okay,' said Dimitri, clapping his hands together. The sound of his clap echoed within the space and everyone spun around to listen. 'Here's the plan. Marie, Joey, and Anaru will guide us through. Make sure we get a safe passage and no one is harmed by any booby traps, and we'll find what we came here for and you can go free. Okay, move.'

Marie and Joey held hands, and together, their wet clothes clinging to their bodies, they clambered up the first steps that curled around to the right. The stones were cold, even through Joey's wet winter boots. The sound of each squelchy step was emphasized as they cautiously ascended.

Anaru broke his silence. 'The stairs are made from basalt.'

'Like the Moai?' asked Nick.

'Yes and no,' said Anaru. 'Most Moai were made out of tuff, a soft volcanic rock native to Easter Island. It was used because it eroded easily and was easier to cut. Only fourteen Moai on this island were actually carved from the incredible hard basalt. The one within the cave was from the same material.'

At the top of the stone steps, they reached the arched opening. Joey shone his flashlight along the prominent curved coping that extruded an inch from the wall to see a triangular shape etched in the center.

'The link to the pyramids of Giza,' said Marie.

Joey nodded and moved his light source to shine through the mysterious entrance. 'The door here has been lifted.' He trained his beam on a heavy stone slab that appeared to be floating above them, but had presumably been drawn up into its own specially designed cavity, allowing passage through the doorway.

'Are they human skulls?' asked Anaru, sounding terrified pointing his beam of light over the floor where human remains lined their passageway.

'Looks like the Walk of Souls,' commented Marie.

'The what?' asked Anaru.

'Once we entered the Sphinx, we were led into an area called the Walk of Souls,' said Joey. 'Human bones like this were scattered everywhere on the floor and on the walls. It was the beginning of a set of tests that eventually led us to a Stargate.'

'What have I gotten myself into?' said Anaru thinly.

'You have no idea,' retorted Joey. 'Get ready to expand your mind.'

'On the positive side, hopefully the tests are the same,' said Marie. 'If so, we can avoid the dangers that we'll encounter.'

'That's precisely what I'm anticipating,' said Dimitri

with a satisfied smile. 'You two show the way. We are a team now, so let's get out of this place alive.'

Joey turned to face Marie, gave her a quick kiss on the lips, took one last anxious breath, and stepped into the gloom.

Chapter 14

The First Test

Marie gazed ahead with trepidation as she inhaled her first breath within the cave. According to legends, the very first breath in some of these ancient caves could be your last. Then again, having survived the trials she had in the past, she knew the air alone was the least likely thing to kill her. She was more concerned about what traps awaited within.

She tentatively examined the void engulfed in a chilling blackness. Joey took the lead with outstretched arms as if he was her own personal bodyguard. His flashlight cut through the dark of the tunnel, revealing the scattered bone fragments on the floor. He held her hand and she took a step, shivering. Even though she had gone through a similar ordeal before, not knowing what was before them was making her feel anxious.

Silence engulfed the group, which amplified the sound of bones cracking beneath their wet boots.

'So many dead people,' said Marie in a low voice. 'They wouldn't appreciate us walking over their corpses.'

'Don't worry, they won't bother us,' said Joey, breaking through a screen of cobwebs that was draped in his path. 'I'm more afraid of the hidden booby traps, giant spiders and snakes that could be lurking in this place. Keep your eyes open. Take every step with caution.'

After a few yards, the corridor expanded into a tall basalt box with a single arched opening up ahead.

'This looks familiar,' said Marie, sliding over to one side to accommodate the three men approaching from the rear. 'Wait!' Marie warned, pointing to a section in the floor covered in bones. 'The trigger stone,' she breathed, guessing based on previous circumstances.

'That's right,' said Joey, gazing upwards and keeping his distance from what was the doorway into the next room. He stepped carefully over to where Marie was pointing and vigilantly removed a handful of skulls to expose the contraption. 'Last time, in Egypt, this trap was activated and a boulder came crashing down and snapped off Hazim's leg.'

'*What?*' asked Anaru, the shock clear in his voice. 'And who is Hazim?'

'The last I heard,' said Joey, 'Hazim is now the head honcho of the Ministry of Antiquities, a government organization that serves to protect and preserve the heritage and ancient history of Egypt.'

'So, he survived?' Anaru asked anxiously.

'Yeah, he made it out, but with only one working leg,' said Joey.

Anaru swallowed hard.

Nick extracted two glow sticks from his duffel bag and tossed them at their feet. They immediately emitted an eerie yellow glow that revealed the hundreds of human skulls staring up at them.

Anaru squirmed under their penetrating stare. 'Holy shit.'

Nick also seemed to be startled by the sight.

As usual, Dimitri showed no emotion. There was no anger, no sadness, no joy or resentment. He had one clear objective, Joey realized, and nothing was going to stop him from obtaining his prize.

'This is a warning to all who decide to step further,' said Marie, looking at each of the men in the cave. 'This is just the beginning, guys. Are you sure you want to continue?'

'Yes,' said Dimitri. 'This place might have booby traps, but we have something that these dead people didn't possess.'

'What's that?' asked Anaru, regaining his composure.

'Two people who have lived through this before,' said Dimitri, nodding over to Marie and Joey and smiling unpleasantly. 'You've already informed us of the danger here. We can do this. All our lives are in your hands. Now let's go, keep moving.'

With only one way into the next cavern, they stepped carefully around the trap that would send the hefty boulder crashing down to block their path. They trudged into the narrow void that stretched away further into the darkness.

One hundred feet in, the hallway widened into

another larger area that resembled the apse of St Peter's Basilica.

'The devil's drop,' Joey warned with widespread arms, stopping everyone in their tracks.

Marie peered into the distance, her eyes following the thin stream of light from her flashlight down into a seventy-foot vertical drop, bridged only by twelve tree-trunk-like stone pillars separated by nothing but air. 'The jump stones,' she mouthed to herself, remembering the last time.

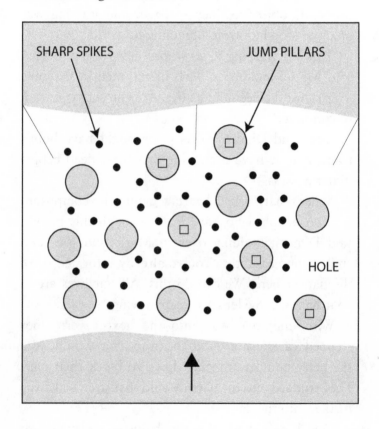

Once again, Nick dug into his never-ending supply of gadgets, lit a flare and held it aloft, illuminating the basalt walls that surrounded them. He pushed forward to see what was at stake. Then he tossed the incandescent light over to the other side of the drop, illuminating a thirteen-foot-wide ledge that gave onto an ominous opening that disappeared once again into the shadow – the chamber's only exit.

'How do we get across?' asked Dimitri, looking at Joey and Marie. 'Time to shine.'

'Are they booby-trapped?' asked Anaru. 'Looks like something you'd see in an *Indiana Jones* movie.'

'You sound like me,' said Joey, flashing the guide a warm smile to try to lighten the atmosphere.

Marie said, 'If this is anything like the chamber in Egypt, a triangular-shaped carving on the safe pillars will show us the way across.'

'Just a heads-up,' Joey added. 'If by any chance this does mimic the Egyptian chamber, and you step on the wrong pillar, the entire vertical shaft will retract downwards, and if you miraculously survive the fall, sharp arrows will be hurled at you to make sure you're killed.'

'Find the triangle shape,' ordered Nick, targeting his flashlight over to the long upright pillars. 'I don't see any.'

Uneasiness crept over Marie.

'Wait, there's a faint square image carved into five of the stone pillars,' said Joey. 'I remember in Egypt there were five shapes that guided us across. I wonder if the square symbols here represent the Moai statues on this island?'

'I think you might be right,' said Marie. 'It makes sense.'

'There is only one way to find out,' said Dimitri. 'Anaru, you're up.'

Marie glanced at the guide, who had gone chalk-white. She shook her head in disgust at Dimitri's insensitivity. 'Wait!' she said. 'Let's throw something on the supports and see if they move. That's what we did in Egypt.'

'No. Anaru will test them. Go!' Dimitri commanded in an ice-cold voice. 'Go, or you die.'

Nick reached for his holster. Any excuse to use it, thought Joey angrily.

Anaru composed himself and jumped across to the first of the square-marked pillars, tears of terror running down his face, making Marie sick to her stomach. A day ago, he was probably enjoying his uncomplicated life, taking tour groups around the island he loved. Now he stood petrified with outstretched hands as he found his balance. Nothing moved. Marie felt a wave of relief. Pointing out the next safe pillar, Anaru leaped onto that too, and then across the other three engraved with the simple quadrate symbol.

He had made it to the other side.

Now it was Marie's turn.

Chapter 15

The Second Test

Joey watched Marie jump across the obstacle, and for those brief moments his heart was in his mouth. He had never felt this kind of fear until now. It was his girl, his child, his everything. He watched anxiously as she made the leap and almost collapsed with the intensity of relief that racked his body when her feet landed on safe ground on the other side.

Now it was his turn.

Joey's mind traveled back to the last time he had jumped the stones, where he had pretended to slip, only to place a broken, razor-sharp skull fragment in an attempt to hinder Nader, a giant of a man with a size sixteen boot. The trap had worked, and Nader's leg had twisted up against the object, causing him to wobble and lose his balance. The sound of his horror had echoed for a couple of seconds before he'd fallen to his demise. Five sharp arrows had protruded out of his neck and chest, sealing his fate.

But this time was different.

Dimitri and Nick were brothers-in-law; they were family. If a planned attack killed one of them, the reaction from the other could be deadly, and could leave Joey with no family of his own. So, he ignored the two assholes behind him and jumped across to Marie and Anaru, who were waiting with trepidation written all over their faces.

Dimitri and Nick were over soon after, and Joey once again led the group onwards. Within seconds, his flashlight beam was enveloped and lost in the blackness of another narrow basalt tunnel. As they moved further along, it began to open out and grew exponentially in size.

A tall cavity loomed up ahead. It was an impressive sight to behold, similar to the grand gallery within the Great Pyramid. It rose up twenty-eight feet and stretched away about a hundred yards into the distance. The walls were hewn from the same basalt as the tunnels and were smooth to the touch.

Nick walked alongside Marie and took the lead. He cracked another light stick and held it aloft to help guide the way. Joey followed in third place, Anaru in fourth, and in the last position, as usual, was Dimitri.

Twenty feet inside the mammoth corridor, they saw a tombstone that rose up from the ground directly in the center of the void.

'I remember this,' said Joey, kneeling to examine the low structure. 'The Orion constellation.'

Marie nodded in affirmation.

Emblazoned on the stone's flat surface was an image

of three triangular pyramids from a top-view perspective.

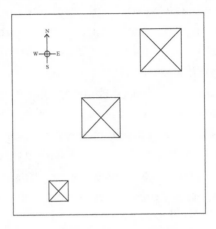

'What does this mean?' asked Anaru.

'The triangles represent the pyramids at Giza,' said Marie with a hint of a smile. 'They were strategically constructed to align in the same way as the stars of Orion's Belt: the most famous star system viewed from all around the world and mentioned by Homer, Virgil, and even the Bible.'

Joey sprang up from his knees and trained his beam of light over the stone wall and to the distant floor. 'Hand me your light stick,' he said, gesturing to Nick with an open hand.

'So you can use it as a weapon,' Nick answered grimly.

'No, you idiot, I want to show you the symbols that are marked all over the ground. This test is identical to the one in Egypt, and we need to tread on the Orion constellation to get through this alive.'

'What happens if we don't?' asked Anaru.

'The ceiling is resting on giant rollers spaced throughout this cavern,' explained Marie. 'Step in the wrong place, and the enormous slab from above will come crashing down and squash us like bugs.'

'Don't forget the sharp spikes that lance downwards,' Joey added. 'I almost became a shish kebab myself last time.'

Nick reluctantly handed him the light stick, and Joey tossed it further down the wide corridor. It bounced away, casting a green hue over square floor tiles that stretched away from them, each with its own unique pattern that repeated unevenly throughout the display.

'Which one is the Orion symbol?' asked Dimitri, towering in the back.

'That's the star constellation over there in its simplest formation,' pointed out Marie. 'The one with the three dots close together.'

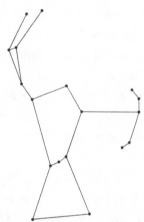

'Before we do this,' said Joey, taking charge, 'we must stay on this path and not deviate. The last time we did this, the group panicked and it almost killed us all. Please! No matter what happens, do not leave the Orion symbol.'

Dimitri flashed Joey a satisfied smile. 'Okay, Joey,' he said with an open-palmed gesture indicating that he should take the lead. 'We will follow your steps.'

Everyone moved into a single-file formation.

'Right, let's do this,' Joey breathed, starting the chain through the deadly labyrinth. He took the first hesitant step onto the Orion tile, careful not to overstep the lines. Broken debris of rocks was crushed underfoot by their boots. The gang mimicked his movements in a zigzag pattern at a snail's pace.

Twenty steps in and Joey reached the spot where it had all gone wrong in Egypt, and a jolt of panic ran through him, but he tried not to let it show. He didn't want to cause any unnecessary hysteria that might lead to what happened last time.

He stopped for a moment to compose himself.

'You're doing really well, babe,' Marie called out nervously. She had been there before and knew what he was thinking. She had seen the encroaching ceiling in Egypt, the lancing spikes, and Joey Superman-diving in the nick of time. 'You've got this,' she told him.

Joey shook off his negative thoughts, and after a treacherous walk that felt like the longest four minutes of his life, he reached the end of the corridor and the last person crossed the threshold onto the narrow ledge.

No casualties, no booby traps tripped, everything was as it should be.

Now to the next obstacle: one that involved descending a dark vertical passage.

Chapter 16

The Third Test

The hole before them in the adjoining chamber was circular, with high stepping stones that ran down alongside the wall in a spiral fashion. The hole had a thirty-foot-wide diameter so it was only just wide enough for a single-file formation to move downwards, and a sheer drop in the center if you were unfortunate enough to slip.

A marking was etched into the wall: the quad-spiral symbol.

Joey pointed it out.

Dimitri flashed his light on it then moved it to Joey's feet.

The walls encircling them were also of basalt, as were the stepping stones, and both appeared to be shrinking with every step as they moved further down the deep well-like passage. There was a musty smell, and the sound of dripping water intensified as they descended.

'I'm not looking forward to this swim,' said Marie, holding tight onto Joey's right hand as he guided everyone down.

'It'll be okay,' Joey said confidently. 'I'm just happy that so far everything has mirrored the way things were in Egypt. Makes it predictable.'

'What swim are you talking about?' asked Anaru timidly.

'At the end of this,' said Joey, gesturing ahead of them, 'we go for a swim. This will lead us further into the cave and to a sandy beach area. But it's not what you think. It's no Waikiki; the soil is quicksand. Once we're through, I'll instruct everyone on what to do to get us safely across.'

Nick lit up another glow stick and tossed it over the edge. It fell fast, and illuminated a pipe-like stone shaft that dropped a fair distance.

Splonk ...

It landed in the water, and the green light slowly disappeared as it sank.

Nick said, 'It appears to be deep.'

Joey didn't bother replying, and it seemed to displease the other man.

A few minutes later, they reached the base of the shaft: a gaping black well-like abyss. Its sides were sheer, plunging down out of sight. There was only a narrow rock ledge around a frigid pool of stagnant water.

'We'll need to leave our sweaters, boots, and helmets behind here,' said Joey. 'Might be an idea to leave the duffel bag here, too.' Joey hoped Dimitri would listen to him – after all, he'd been behaving thus far. And if

Nick and Dimitri happened not to remember that the grenades were in that duffel bag, all the better.

Dimitri faced his brother-in-law. 'Leave the bag here. Just take what we need.'

Nick agreed with a hesitant nod and slammed down the bag he was carrying. Joey flinched, thinking of the grenades inside.

'What are we facing, Joey?' asked Anaru as he discarded his shoes. 'How long is this swim?'

'If it's anything like Egypt it's nothing major,' Joey replied, removing his torch helmet. 'Maybe a minute or so.'

All helmets and sweaters were tossed to the ground.

Joey stripped down to his dark jeans, his chiseled, hair-free chest bare for all to see.

Marie stripped down to her blue denim and a midriff sports tank top, showing off her athletic body. Nick and Dimitri were in matching dark singlets and navy pants, and Anaru was in his khaki pants and white Easter Island shirt, where a Moai head stood prominent with modern text that read, *Rapa Nui*.

'Okay, Joey, when you're ready. We'll follow,' said Dimitri. 'Marie, you're next, followed by Anaru, Nick, then myself.'

Nick handed out goggles and made sure everyone had their waterproof flashlight. He then shoved half-a-dozen light sticks into his pants pockets, leaving the explosives bag behind.

Joey quietly breathed a sigh of relief.

All that was left to do was to get in and go for it.

Joey sat on the edge, fitting his goggles snuggly over

his face. 'Stay close,' he told his wife, then he took one last deep breath before plunging into the water.

The world went eerily silent.

A shiver ran along his spine when his entire body was submerged under the murky water. He swam downwards and slowly adjusted to the cold, and the shape of the underwater structure came into view in a pale shade of green. The light stick Nick had thrown in earlier helped to show the way.

The steps continued to spiral southward under the water's surface, tapering off at the bottom at a large distinctive man-made opening. Joey noticed that this one was not littered with giant stones blocking the entrance like it had been in Egypt. This site was untouched and preserved as it was thousands of years ago.

He approached the hole, which dwarfed him. He turned around to see that Marie had plummeted into the water above. Bubbles of air encircled her figure as she descended.

He waved for her to head his way.

More splashes followed.

Guided by his flashlight, Joey swam through the breach.

Just visible on the horizon were two blurry sets of colossal feet, which belonged, Joey assumed, to two enormous statues. A stairway led upwards from the center of the cave, inviting Joey towards it. His head broke the surface, and he sucked in his first desperate breath. It took a few moments for him to focus on what were two full-figured giant Moai statues on either side of the cave.

Joey frowned as he climbed the basalt steps to what was a towering cathedral.

'Holy shit,' he puffed, taking in another much-needed breath of air. A sudden fear rushed over him. He waited for Marie to join him and saw the mirror of his own thoughts in her expression.

Here was where the parallels between the two sites ended and the new threats began.

Chapter 17

The Cathedral

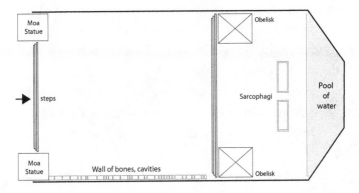

'Oh my God,' Marie gasped. She run her hands down her clothes, trying to squeeze out the water weighing her down.

She gazed over at the two complete, giant Moai statues on either side of the walkway, with their heavy eyebrow ridges, elongated ears, and oval nostrils.

They were the guardians of the underworld protecting this God-like place.

'This is different,' she acknowledged, taking in the vast space that stretched away from them like an airport hangar.

There was no quicksand, nor were there scary-looking granite sculptures of Anubis warriors, each with elevated scepters to climb over.

'Yes,' said Joey, trying to work through a million thoughts to figure out their next move. 'That's what scares me.'

Joey flashed his beam into the darkness and turned to the sound of Anaru, Nick, and Dimitri, who broke out of the water and advanced from behind.

Dimitri came up beside them and burst a flare over his head to reveal more of the site, which was at least a hundred yards deep, the distance of an American football field. 'Jesus,' he said. 'This is enormous. What do we do now?'

'From here on in,' said Joey, 'we're flying blind. This is different from what we experienced in Egypt.'

Dimitri's face fell and a flinty expression came into his eyes.

Nick extracted two more glow sticks and tossed them into the empty space, revealing carved drawings that had been etched all along the top end of the basalt walls.

'Look up there,' said Marie, pointing. 'Monkeys, hundreds of them, praying to their gods, the men with the elongated heads.'

'The Atlanteans,' Joey said. 'Christopher Walken.'

Marie understood the reference, smiled, and shook her head. 'Here lies the connection between Egypt and Easter Island.'

'What connection? Who's Christopher Walken, and what's with the primates?' asked Anaru, sounding fed up. 'Why are they carved on the wall?'

'These animals are domesticated,' said Nick, turning to face his brother-in-law. 'They have pickaxes in their hands.'

'We came across an Atlantean who wore his hair like the actor Christopher Walken, hence the name,' said Joey gestured to his wife. 'You can probably explain the rest better than I would.'

'Thanks for that,' Marie said with a raised eyebrow. She cleared her throat, and all eyes turned to her.

'Believe it or not, an advanced civilization visited Earth a long time ago. Needing a race to enslave to do their bidding, they found a species of archaic humans: Homo erectus. The term in itself means "upright man". They decided to improve on it, helping to evolve us into what we are today.'

Anaru's mouth dropped open.

'We were engineered to be rudimentary people with smaller brains than theirs, accompanied by many defects,' said Marie. 'This was so we could be easily controlled.'

'But that's science fiction crap,' said the native man, shaking his head.

'That's what I thought at first,' said Joey. 'But believe me, it's not. We've seen it, firsthand.'

Marie continued. 'Imagine a time millennia ago when a growing population of Homo sapiens were persuaded to believe in the sun god, Atum. Their society was charged with the work of the land and building these structural beacons found throughout the known world.'

Dimitri stood impassively, giving nothing away about what he knew of the story. Marie suspected, given his knowledge of the keystone, that he had somehow heard it before.

'After thousands of years of coexistence, the humans split off into different cultural groups and formed their own theories about whom to worship. This is when the king of the time sent his only son, Akhenaton, and his son's queen, Nefertiti, to govern in his name as Pharaoh to the people, and to restore the worship of the one and only true god. During their reign, Nefertiti bore six daughters – a tragedy in Akhenaton's mind. He needed a son to rule.'

'Yes, I've read this before,' Anaru said, looking as though things were falling into place for him.

Marie gave him a smile. 'Needing a male heir to rule, a round-headed secondary wife – that's what they called us humans, round-headed – by the name of Kiya was chosen, and she gave birth to a boy whom they named—'

'Tutankhamun,' finished Anaru. 'So, Akhenaten and Nefertiti, the Egyptian Pharaohs, didn't come from Earth?' questioned Anaru, wide-eyed. 'They were aliens?'

'Yes, sort of. Actually they were Atlanteans,' said Marie, 'the real first sentient beings of this planet. Some people also know them as the Anunnaki.'

'So, what happened here on Easter Island?' asked Nick, shining a saber-like beam of light through the darkness and onto the wall of kneeling anthropoids.

'I think once we get down this hallway, we might find out,' said Joey, pointing to a long stairway in the distance which was flanked by two obelisks and led up to a podium on which lay two sarcophagi.

Nick and Anaru took the lead and the others followed, their flashlight beams crossing over each other as they cautiously crept forward.

'Be careful, people,' Joey warned.

Nick tossed two light sticks which landed at the bottom of the stairs. In their green glow, Marie spotted a change in the side walls and gave Joey a concerned glance. The walls contained thousands of cavities of various sizes, far too many to count, and they littered the entire lower half of the rock face. Joey squeezed her hand reassuringly.

'Ape bones,' he said as evenly as he could. 'Looks like a gravesite.'

The wall to their right also featured a mural depicting monkeys. They were bent over and on their knees in what was a prayer position, worshiping the sun god, Atum.

'Something is wrong here,' Marie said softly. A chill ran down her spine as she took in the eerie graveyard consumed with cobwebs. Every step, every sound was amplified.

All of a sudden, a gust of wind passed her face, blowing her hair to one side.

Whip ... Whip ... Whip ...

From the sidewalls, brown flashes shot past her face, making a whistling sound. Marie covered her face with her hands and took in a shocked breath. Between her fingers, she exchanged a quick, petrified glance with Joey.

They were in mortal danger.

Dozens of primeval stone arrowheads were being propelled at them from the cavities in the side walls.

'Duck!' Joey screamed. 'Now!'

Nick dove to the ground as an arrow whizzed over his head, almost ending his life, but was grazed in the arm.

Dimitri dropped low for cover and escaped harm.

Joey yanked Marie to her knees just as an arrowhead whizzed through the air where her neck would have been, only to hear a howl of unbearable pain erupting from someone else in the team.

The sound of agony engulfed them.

Marie snapped her head around to see Anaru standing still, a dumbfounded expression on his face and an arrow-tip protruding from his neck. Blood gushed out of his mouth as he tried to gulp air.

'No!' she cried, watching as the life blood poured out of the dying man.

Anaru staggered forward, only to be hit by another arrow in his chest, right where the Moai monolithic figure was portrayed on his T-shirt, terminating his life in the most brutal of ways.

Chapter 18

The Sarcophagi

Marie and Joey needed no further encouragement. Both dashed forward, low to the ground, and spider-crawled the rest of the way to the flight of steps bordered by the two enormous obelisks. With their heads close to the ground, it was as if they were mimicking the mural, bowing to the sun god pictured on the wall.

'I should have known better,' Marie muttered under her breath once she was finally out of danger.

Joey rushed to her side and embraced her with a strong, warm hug. He could feel her rapidly beating heart through her wet clothes.

Dimitri and Nick followed, also keeping flat to the ground.

'That was way too close,' Dimitri snarled.

Nick's fear began to give way to anger. 'Why the hell didn't we know that was going to happen?' he spat, pushing Joey in the chest. 'You were supposed to be the experts.'

'This part is different from Egypt,' Joey told him calmly. 'I said that before.'

'Then what the hell do we need you for?' said Nick, reaching for his nine-millimeter.

'Yeah, that's smart,' said Joey snidely. 'Kill us before you have what you came here for.'

'Stop it!' Marie once again intervened. 'You two have been at each other's throats the entire time. It was a setback. We've already lost Anaru, so please, no more fighting.'

'Put it away,' said Dimitri in a quiet but authoritative voice. 'Marie is right. We are here for one thing, and maybe it's in one of those coffins.'

'Well, then,' retorted Nick, letting his arm drop but eyeballing Joey. 'Be a good boy and show us the way.' He gestured with a dismissive hand as though Joey was his servant to command.

Joey turned to face the sarcophagi and inspected them apprehensively before advancing up the stairs. His palms were sweaty, his nipples hard in the cool air, and goosebumps had broken out all over his naked torso, causing the hairs on his arms and neck to stand on end.

His mind started to race through the possibilities of who and what he might find inside those boxes.

He was now flanked by the two confronting colossal obelisks. The tall, four-sided, narrow monuments tapered to a point as they neared the ceiling. Carved into both pillars were images of the king and queen worshiping the sun god above them as the sun's rays descended over them, but the shaft on Joey's right bore the name of Akhenaten in hieroglyphics, and on the left, Nefertiti. He appreciated that the two rulers had shared equal power during the eighteenth dynasty. The columns stood proud. Joey knew it was a rarity to find two standing together unless you counted the obelisks deep inside the Last Secret Chamber. The only other known markers had been separated and given to France by the ruler of Ottoman Egypt in exchange for a French mechanical clock. One lived at the entrance to Luxor Temple in Egypt, the other stood at the center of the Place de la Concorde, Paris.

Marie began to follow her husband up the stairs, and after a few steps, so did the others.

'If you needed proof that Egypt and Easter Island are connected,' said Joey, standing at the top of the stairs with raised hands, 'here it is.'

'The queen and king of Egypt are mentioned all over this place,' Marie added, pointing to the obelisks and then to the two open six-foot-long sarcophagi that were cut from basalt and etched with hieroglyphs.

'The chamber seems to end here,' said Dimitri, looking at the dim rock walls beyond the boxes.

Nick ignited his last flare, and when he held it over his head, all eyes craned around and Marie gasped. There were murals above and behind the sarcophagi, spread over three walls like a Michelangelo masterpiece.

'What's this?' asked Nick, directing the dazzling light of the flare to the far side of the podium, a few feet beyond the sarcophagi, where there was a triangular-shaped pool of stagnant water. Lowering the light to illuminate the sarcophagi themselves, they all saw that the stone boxes were occupied by skeletal remains.

'Can you see the keystone among the bones?' asked Dimitri, turning everyone's attention back to the corpses.

Nick moved his flare close to the dark interiors of the sarcophagi to show the contents within.

Joey approached with caution. These last couple of years he felt he had become an expert on the dead. Sadly, he found himself almost comfortable around them.

'The remains are human,' he said with conviction. 'This one appears to be male, the other definitely female. She has a wider pelvis necessary for childbirth.'

Joey turned to Marie's hips and caught Marie's hazel eyes, and they shared a brief moment and a smile.

'What about the keystone,' Dimitri pressed. 'Is it in there?'

'Not in this one, sorry,' said Joey after a quick search.

'Nor this one,' said Nick, his search somewhat rougher. Marie pressed her lips together tightly at his disrespect.

'It has to be here somewhere,' said Dimitri.

'The murals,' Marie suggested, darting her beam of light onto them. The others followed.

On the north wall, above the triangular pool of water, were depicted rows of Moai heads. On a hunch, Marie began counting them. There were nine rows of about one hundred – but not quite.

'Eight hundred and eighty-seven,' murmured Marie, deep in thought. 'It's as if they were keeping a tally.'

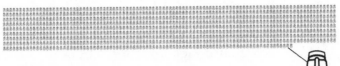

On the left, western wall, was an image similar to the chart of the Evolution of Man found in most modern-day museums: an ape on all fours, then a hunched caveman followed by several ever more upright versions of humanity, ending with what was known today as Homo sapiens.

To their right, on the eastern wall, was an image that resembled a modern-age DNA helix.

'I think we just stumbled across our species' origin,' said Marie.

'Holy shit,' Joey breathed, lost for words.

'I bet the eight hundred and eighty-seven Moai on this land and on that wall, represent all the failed attempts it took to evolve us,' said Marie. 'To construct a genetic DNA similar to their own, but adjusted to their specifications.'

'What has this got to do with the keystone?' Dimitri asked impatiently.

Marie continued, ignoring him. 'Anaru said it before: the Moai statues faced inland and not out to sea because there was no threat from the outside world. This is where life began for our kind ... This tiny stretch of land of Easter Island.' She then pointed to the western and eastern walls. 'Look, they're clearly showing us our evolution. This is the race that built these marvelous structures that are found all over the world.'

Nick seemed puzzled and stood unmoving.

Joey glanced back down at the sarcophagi in front of him and thought about everything Marie had divulged. An astonishing thought came to him. He shook his head and took a breath to calm his nerves, but he knew without a shadow of a doubt that he was right. 'Marie, Dimitri, Nick,' he said, his voice steady, 'I want to introduce you all to our first ancestors. Adam and Eve.'

Chapter 19

The Vase

Dimitri couldn't believe what he was hearing. He gazed down at the skeletons, who had until now lain undisturbed in their burial caskets for thousands of years. These were the two people, according to the creation myth of the Abrahamic religions, who had started it all. Adam and Eve, the Bible's first man and woman. He felt frozen, numb, as thoughts cascaded through his mind.

The Garden of Eden was Easter Island.

It had not been a Christian God who had created humankind in his image.

It was the Atlanteans who had evolved humans, and stories created by human cultures had rushed to fill the void they left when they departed Earth. Genesis 1 was one of these stories.

The loneliness grew until it dominated his emotions. Dimitri felt like a vise had gripped his heart, squeezing with just enough pressure to be a constant pain. His

Greek Orthodox religious beliefs had been crushed to smithereens. Ever since his wife and child had been taken from him, his inner light had been replaced with darkness, and now the only hope he'd clung to – that they had ascended to heaven – felt cold and dead and impossible.

One thought shone through the dimness of his frozen mind, and this was that he had nothing left to lose. He would roll the dice, open the Stargate, and hope to find the answers he desperately craved in the new world beyond. If the beings he found there had created humanity, then they might know what lay beyond the curtain of death.

'Hang on, I see something peculiar,' Joey pointed out, pointing down into Adam's thick stone coffin.

'What is it?' asked Marie, taking a step forward.

Joey pushed a triangular shape that was protruding from the base.

A sharp *bang* was heard, and Nick stepped back, startled.

'What did you do?' asked Marie.

Joey shrugged helplessly.

What followed was a whooshing sound that they soon recognized as sand pouring down within the sarcophagus, like a flowing waterfall.

'There's a small secret compartment,' Joey informed her with a relieved grin. 'It's opening up.'

It took a second or two for the new information to sink in, but Dimitri moved closer, excitement building in him. 'It's got to be the keystone,' he said.

Two bucketfuls of soft, white sand cascaded over the skeletal remains of Adam's left arm, covering it. In doing so, a rectangular stone moved up and backwards to reveal a laptop-sized compartment.

Marie quickly aimed her flashlight into the cavity, and Joey dug his hand inside and extracted an ancient blue vase.

Mixed emotions ran through Dimitri's mind. It was not the keystone as he had hoped. *Why another vase?* he wondered.

'It's like the first one, the one in the plane,' Nick said in a hushed tone.

'Give it to me,' demanded Dimitri, his expression serious. He scrutinized the pottery in minute detail, running his fingers along the grooves as he had done inside the cargo plane. 'The markings on this one are different,' he said eventually.

'What do you mean?' asked Marie. 'I don't understand.'

'The vase Nick is talking about was found in Egypt, and it brought us to Easter Island. The images on it depicted the Moai heads. This one is showing Angkor Wat.'

Angkor Wat,
Cambodia

They all stared at Dimitri.

'Are you talking about the temple complex in Cambodia?' said Marie.

'Yes,' said Dimitri. 'I am.'

'What do you think is there?' asked Joey, confused.

Dimitri slammed the pottery hard against the solid frame of the sarcophagus and it broke into small shards at his naked feet.

Marie was startled, visibly shaken. 'Why did you do that?' she cried in a horrified voice.

Dimitri kneeled to pick up a double-spiral key lying among the debris. He held it up. 'Now I know where to go next to find the keystone to activate the Stargate. Or perhaps there is another one there. It could be that the Atlanteans scattered them throughout our world.' His eyes scanned over Adam's corpse. 'It's fitting to have the father of all fathers show us the next location … Cambodia.'

double-spiral key

'Activating the Stargate will not give you the answers you seek,' Marie barked. 'It's not going to bring your wife or child back. It's just going to get you killed.'

'I didn't ask for your approval or your judgment.' Dimitri looked at her contemptuously. 'I need you to do what we brought you to do. If there is a keystone here, then you must find it.' He paused, thinking for a moment, then turned his head. 'The pool of water?'

Taking the still-lit flare from Nick and holding it above his head, Dimitri stopped short at the water's edge, while Nick kept a watchful eye.

'Why is there water here?' said Dimitri. 'What purpose does it serve?' Seconds later, he spotted distinctive markings on the floor inches away from the water line. 'There's something here,' he called out.

Marie approached, looking puzzled, and kneeled beside Dimitri. Together they saw four simple consecutive drawings laid out in a vertical column sequence.

Wavy lines.

A keystone.

A figure silhouetted by a circular shadow.

A line that ascended from the apex of a pyramid.

'This is it,' she said. 'It's similar to the granite pyramidion we found in Egypt. I think it's telling us that we need to enter the water to retrieve the keystone. There has to be an entrance down there to a secret room within the pool.'

Dimitri tossed the flare in his hand into the liquid, knowing the oxidizer chemical would provide the flash the oxygen needed to sustain combustion and continue to burn. It sank slowly to the bottom of the shallow pool to reveal a narrow tunnel that disappeared into the back wall.

'Joey, you're up,' ordered Dimitri, pointing to the American. 'Swim through and get my keystone.'

'No way,' replied Joey. 'Who knows what traps could be under there? It's a death wish. Why don't you send your dog to retrieve it?'

'What did you call me?' Nick said through clenched teeth, squeezing his fists and looming over Joey. 'Do as he says!'

'Why the hell are you doing this?' Joey asked Nick, trying a different tack. 'Your sister died, and that's always tragic. But all this isn't going to bring her back, or your niece. Is he paying you? Is that it? None of this is worth the risk to your life. You don't have to go along with it.'

'She was my blood, my family,' spat Nick as he nudged Joey roughly towards the water.

'Okay, okay, take it easy,' said Joey, holding his hands up in submission.

'Bianca was my niece, and she was my godchild,' said Nick under his breath. 'I never had kids of my own and treated her like my own daughter, and these terrorists took her away from me. How dare you judge me? You don't know anything about me.'

'*Afise ton,*' said Dimitri in Greek, trying to calm his brother-in-law down.

'*Tha ton skotóso!*' said Nick, extracting his pistol. 'I've had enough of his crap, Dimitri. We have his girl, we don't need him.'

'Don't be stupid, man,' Joey said quickly, taking a step back. Marie ran to his side and clung to him.

'Get on your knees,' said Nick in a bolder tone, holding his firearm out to his side in readiness.

Dimitri tried to reason with his brother-in-law, but he could see there wasn't much point. Nick seemed too far gone. His face was flushed and his eyes glittered with a sort of determination Dimitri had never seen there before. He looked to be at breaking point.

'Please,' Marie begged as Joey stood his ground before being forced to his knees.

Nick aimed his gun at Joey's scalp, executioner style, and pushed in hard, leaving a barrel imprint in his skin.

'Please don't,' Marie cried, turning to face Dimitri. 'Please stop him!'

Joey shut his eyes, at the mercy of Nick's gun.

'I'll go in,' said Marie, stepping into the water. 'But only if you don't shoot. Please.'

'*Mi ton scotosis*,' said Dimitri in a soft tone.

Nick's face contorted, blazing with fury, and without remorse he swung the hilt of his weapon into Joey's cranium, knocking him out cold for the second time.

Chapter 20

The Keystone

Marie screamed uncontrollably as Joey's body hit the ground hard. Rage coursed through her. Holding her flashlight aloft, she jumped out of the water and attacked Nick with a vengeance.

'You bastard,' she snarled through gritted teeth as she swung the implement at the hateful man's head, only to be blocked with ease.

Nick exploded into maniacal laughter. 'Get over yourself,' he practically spat, still smiling. 'You have no chance against me.'

Before she'd even had a second to contemplate her next move, Marie came in quick with her opposite hand and slapped him in the face. The smile fell from Nick's face. The slap was loud and it clearly stung. Nick grabbed hold of his rosy cheek, his face a mask of irritation and fury. Marie stepped back in fright as he charged her small frame, sending her tumbling backwards into the pool of water.

She landed unceremoniously with a loud *splash!*

Holding on to her waterproof flashlight, she broke the surface to see two figures standing there with folded arms.

'I'm pregnant, you asshole,' she spat at him.

Nick gave her a smug smile. 'Think I care?'

Marie looked away from him in disgust, and her gaze fell on Joey. He was still unconscious. Sadness and worry overwhelmed her.

'It seems like you are going for a swim,' said Dimitri lightly. 'Don't blame us for your husband's choice of words. He should think twice before calling the man with the gun a dog.'

'It's true, isn't it?' Marie taunted.

'Shut up and go retrieve the keystone,' said Nick contemptuously. 'Before I shoot you in the head and go get it myself.'

She really had no choice, she thought, and yet she hesitated, looking at Joey's inert form.

'Get my key, Marie, and I will let you and your sleepy husband go,' Dimitri said evenly. 'That's my promise to you.'

'Swear it?' Marie asked vehemently, staring back into the murderer's eyes.

'You have my word.'

Marie made a deal with the devil and took a moment to compose herself. The dazzling incandescent flare that had been tossed in the water continued to glow, showing the way.

It was now or never.

She took a deep breath and plunged once more into the cold, murky liquid.

Instantly, her body temperature dropped, and the world went eerily silent.

She tried not to think about what might be lurking in this darkness. She swam down to the tunnel the flare had illuminated, and saw that it was a square seven-foot entrance hole constructed from the same gray basalt as everything else. She pushed herself inside, flashlight first, and used her hands to feel her way along the narrow tunnel. Her yellow beam of light wasn't enough to see much further into the distance than a few feet at a time. She kept it trained on the tunnel floor beneath her as she flailed her arms and legs.

The swim felt like forever, even though it had only been a few seconds. Marie's heartbeat intensified as her need for oxygen grew. Where was the end? Her legs and arms were working overtime as she clawed through the water. Her throat burned, and she came to a point where, if she proceeded, there would be no turning back.

She pushed on. She needed to survive this, and to save Joey. Turning back would mean death for them both.

Thankfully, her worry was short-lived, and relief washed over her as she noticed the channel widening into a vast space.

She broke the surface of the water and gasped for air. A set of stairs led up into a grotto, and she swam over to them. But there was something much bigger in this space that dominated her attention. 'Wow,' she breathed, scanning the structure above, which resembled a pyramid. The base was wide and square, and the top tapered to a single point.

As she returned her gaze to the base, she said aloud, 'Holy shit,' and a thrill of excitement flushed through her in spite of her present circumstances. There, on the apex, just as in Egypt, sat a massive transparent crystal, held in place by giant claws. Marie smiled, understanding the stone's purpose, having seen a similar design on a much grander scale back in Egypt.

Once her feet found dry land, she shone her flashlight upon the translucent jewel and a stream of light bounced around the room. It rebounded on strategically placed mirrors or high polished discs, giving off an abundance of light, as though somehow powered by electricity.

Understanding that if she moved her light away, she would be plunged into darkness once again, Marie positioned her torch securely among some heavy stones and aimed it at the jewel. The yellow beam continued to collide with the reflective surfaces and voilà, she was free to roam as she pleased.

Marie's eyes drifted to a raised basalt platform that was hewn from the rock of the northern wall; the only other feature in the room. She approached with caution and the suddenly saw what the light had revealed: breathtaking murals that could have been thousands of years old.

The western wall depicted Angkor Wat in Cambodia and its iconic temple complex.

The eastern wall showed the Moai statues of Rapa Nui on Easter Island.

The northern wall above the podium showed the Great Pyramid of Egypt in superb detail, and included a large cross.

'X marks the spot,' breathed Marie, committing it to memory.

As she ascended to the podium, Marie noticed a stone basketball sized globe at its center, which had marked on it the continents of Earth, and markers at the three sites depicted in the murals around her. The positions were linked by a single line that formed a triangular shape; the symbol for the pyramid and the location of the Stargate residing in Cairo, Egypt.

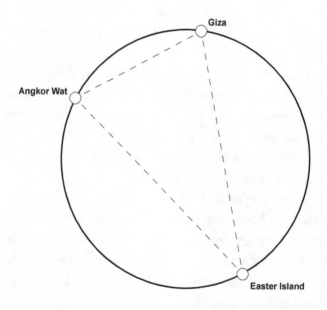

Marie studied the information intently, and then realized that there was more on the podium than she'd thought: beyond the globe was a sort of stage on which was displayed a fan of gray keystones. The display was stunning, the keystones laid out like a floral arrangement.

Four grayish-colored basalt stones, each in the shape of a triangular prism, surrounded the outer edge in what she surmised was just for ornamental purposes, and one lone red dolerite stone was at its core. The all-powerful red rose. A rock not from this world that had the power to activate the portal.

Marie came to a decision. Dimitri would kill them both if she did not deliver him a keystone, so she really had no choice in the matter. She carefully removed one of the keystones and held it in her hands, admiring it. Then she regained her composure, took another deep breath, and dove back through the dark tunnel, leaving behind her flashlight knowing the dazzling flare on the other side would guide her back safely.

This time she was not coming back empty-handed.

This time she held the prize that promised to set her family free.

It was a long shot, but it was her only hope.

Chapter 21

The Handover

Marie's head broke the water as two beams of light shone down over her, and then found the item she was clutching in her hand. She inhaled and her eyes found Joey on the ledge, his feet touching the water.

Joey was pinching the bridge of his nose, struggling to stem the flow of blood that was seeping out like a lazy river.

'Joey, oh my God, are you okay?' Marie asked, seeing the awful pain in his every movement. She moved towards him and watched him place a shaky hand up against his bloody, sun-bleached hair.

'I'll live,' he said, clenching his jaw, always one to try to hide his pain. 'Just a massive headache and my ear keeps ringing.'

'The keystone,' said Dimitri, stepping forward, the excitement written all over his unshaven face. 'Finally, the key to unlocking the answers I seek.'

'Hand it over,' ordered Nick, his gleaming, ruthless eyes on her.

'You don't understand what you're dealing with,' Marie said, handing over the dark stone. 'Your emotions have blinded you both to the danger you'll bring to yourself and possibly our planet.'

Nick took the stone and passed it to Dimitri, who exhaled a long, satisfied breath.

He held the solid triangular shape in his hand and examined it carefully, as though he were holding a precious newborn baby.

Joey rubbed his bruised eyes, squinting at the stone. 'Hey, the keystone—'

Marie squeezed his forearm painfully, and he broke off. He gave her a discreet, questioning look, but she refused to meet his gaze and instead gave him another light squeeze.

'You have what you want,' Marie said firmly, pointing to the gift in Dimitri's hands. 'Now please be a man of your word and let us go as you promised.'

Nick extracted his nine-millimeter, and Marie moved defensively back into Joey's embrace. 'Surely you're not that naïve,' Nick snarled. 'It's been a pleasure, but it's time for you both to die.'

'I'll be a father soon,' Joey pleaded, holding Marie tight to his chest. 'Please, let us go,' he asked. 'We're a family now.'

Dimitri flashed Nick a stop sign with his hand, and Nick sighed heavily. 'Ah, come on,' he breathed.

Marie could only hope Joey's words had touched Dimitri in some profound, meaningful way.

'Yes, family, it's the most important possession you'll ever have in your life,' said Dimitri in a flat, emotionless tone, but his gaze was menacing. 'Until it's taken away from you.'

'We're not the terrorists who killed your family,' interjected Marie gently. 'Those idiots deserve to die. Please don't lower yourself to their level by behaving the same way they did. Let our family live. We kept our end of the bargain. Surely you are still a man of honor?'

A long silence followed. It was as if the sentiment played in Dimitri's mind.

'Put your weapon away, Nick.'

Nick craned his head in displeasure and kicked angrily at the loose debris near his feet.

'I will do you this one favor,' Dimitri said to Marie and Joey with a hesitant nod. 'You are free to go, but if you interfere with my objective in Egypt, I won't be as magnanimous.'

Marie nodded her head. 'Of course.'

'From father to father, and for what it's worth, thank you,' Joey said.

'Do not tell Julien anything,' said Dimitri. 'If he tracks you down and asks, we found nothing on Easter Island. If Julien and his men are heading my way, I'll make sure that child in your belly never sees the light of day. Do I make myself clear?'

'Crystal,' Joey said, turning to face Marie, but she was still looking straight ahead. Joey followed her line of vision and tensed once more.

Nick approached them as though they were the scum of the earth, visibly irritated by Dimitri's decision. 'You're lucky,' he said, spitting at their feet. 'If it were up to me, you'd both be dead.'

Dimitri moved his brother-in-law away and stopped to deliver his final words. 'You two wait here for about thirty minutes before you follow us out.'

'We will.' Marie nodded. 'I would like to say it's been a pleasure, but I think you'll understand we hope never to see your ugly faces again.'

Surprise lit Dimitri's eyes and he gave her a hint of a smile, as if liking her spunky attitude.

'You better pray you don't see us again,' said Nick, and they both turned and backtracked down the corridor, ducking low to avoid the killer arrows.

At the end of the hall, Marie could see Nick sticking his finger up at them, and then, just like that, Dimitri and Nick disappeared into the water and, Marie fervently hoped, out of their lives.

When they'd gone, Marie didn't waste any time lovingly embracing her wounded husband, squeezing him tight. She cried into his shoulder as he wrapped his arms around her. His touch made her wet skin warm, and she pressed him close, not wanting the moment to end. The emotional roller-coaster ride had taken its toll on them both, but somehow, like the many other tumultuous adventures they had shared, they once again had survived.

'You're too smart for your own good,' Joey murmured into her ear.

Marie suddenly stopped crying and pulled herself away with a trembling smile. 'You're not too bad yourself,' she said, turning to face the pool of water. 'Although you almost let the cat out of the bag.'

'I've said it before, but I just love how your brain

works,' he said as she stood and walked over to the stagnant water a few feet away. 'What was in the last chamber, anyway?'

'I'll tell you when I get back. Don't go anywhere.'

'Where would I go, without you?'

Marie blew him a kiss and dove in, intending to retrieve the one and only stone that could trigger the Stargate; the dolerite that can only be found on Planet X and the three secret locations on Earth.

The key soon to be in Marie's possession.

The red keystone.

Chapter 22

The Trap

Air bubbles made their way to the surface with every exhaled breath. Dimitri exited the shaft behind his brother-in-law, who was already rummaging through the scattered sweaters and shoes they'd left behind.

Dimitri's shoeless feet found solid ground, and his eyes darted over to a burning flare that continued to illuminate the space. It lay there undisturbed on the cold floor, bathing the entire cavern in an orange glow.

Climbing out of the water he approached Nick with a bounce in his step, knowing he was close to fulfilling his destiny. 'Here, put the keystone in the duffel bag,' he said, passing it over.

'We shouldn't have let them go,' said Nick, who was using Joey's sweater to dry in between his toes. Nick placed the gray stone into the bag, and then shoved his leather boots back on. 'They take you for a fool. He only played the family card because he recognized it would be your weakness.'

'Who said I'm letting them go?' answered Dimitri with a sly grin, reaching for his own steel-capped shoes.

'What do you mean?' Nick stared at his brother-in-law as he swung the bag over his right shoulder.

Dimitri pointed at the duffel bag. 'Remember what's in there? We'll let God decide their fate and toss all our grenades into the water.'

Nick's smile stretched from ear to ear. 'That's more like it … With pleasure!'

'Hang on, safety first,' said Dimitri, craning his neck backwards. 'From the high ground.'

'This place will crumble.'

'That's what I'm counting on.'

After a short trip up the high spiral stepping stones, Nick laid down the bag and extracted the six grenades, lining them up ready to activate. He removed two grenade pins and held in the safety lever, then shut his eyes for a brief second as if he was savoring the moment and all the havoc he would wreak.

Dimitri glanced at the other man's ecstatic, exultant expression and a sliver of worry arrowed through him.

'You still taking your meds?' Dimitri asked, aware of Nick's bipolar disorder and his erratic psychopathic traits.

Nick half-opened his eyes. 'I stopped taking them when Bianca and Katherine were murdered.'

'That was four years ago,' Dimitri said, aghast, realizing just how compromised Nick's wellbeing had been all these years. 'Are you sleeping okay?'

'A couple of hours here and there,' said Nick, shrugging one shoulder like it was nothing. 'I seem to fall asleep fast but wake up soon after.'

'Nick! Why didn't you tell me? That's terrible, and you might have another psychotic episode.'

'You promised me answers,' Nick said, turning to face Dimitri with cold eyes, the two live projectiles still in his hands. 'You said that once we enter inside the Stargate, we will learn truths about where we came from, and maybe where Katherine and Bianca have gone. I've had wild dreams of this event, where I've seen my sister and niece.'

'And I will deliver that promise,' said Dimitri carefully, playing on the other man's insecurities. 'Now, how about we have a little fun and blow this place to kingdom come.'

Nick needed no further prompting. He released the hand grenades, which dropped into the void and splashed into the water far below. The other four followed right after, and they all sank to the bottom of the shaft, quietly waiting to detonate.

'Move!' warned Dimitri. 'There's no time to spare.' He turned to enter the mammoth corridor of tiles depicting the simplified star constellations. 'Remember, stay on the Orion constellation!'

In swift, cautious movements, they leaped across, careful not to detour from the designated Orion symbol, and that was when the bombs exploded, in sequence, one after the other like dominoes.

Boom! Boom! Boom! Boom! Boom! Boom!

The walls around them shook wildly, as if a volcano had erupted.

'Go! ... Go! ... Go! ... The whole place is going to come down!' Dimitri shouted, sprinting away from the chaos that would, he hoped, see the entire cavern cave in on itself.

'Ah, shit!' Nick grunted. 'I think what's coming is coming our way.'

A deep rumbling sound was getting louder no matter how fast they ran, as if chasing them from behind and building in intensity.

Then in an instant, water exploded into the chamber like a tidal wave, knocking both Dimitri and Nick off their feet and washing away their flashlights. In a rolling struggle, their limbs flailing amid a cloud of bubbles, they were pushed into the darkness.

The power of the water took hold of them, carrying them through the chamber at speed just as the ceiling collapsed and crumbled all around them.

Dimitri gulped in several breaths of air when his head rose above the water's surface, and he tried to keep from colliding with the stone walls on either side of the passage. Remembering his whereabouts, a rushed, petrified thought crossed his mind.

'The jump stones,' he yelled, hoping Nick would hear. Dimitri caught sight of his brother-in-law a few yards away. He, too, was fighting to stay afloat, and seemed to be losing the battle.

The traitorous devil's drop was fast approaching.

It was now or never, or die by being sucked down into the void around the stepping stones and impaled on killer spears – if they didn't drown first.

Dimitri noticed a stone ledge running along one wall, and he reached out and grabbed hold of it, utilizing the rock's indentations to cling on to.

'I'm gonna die,' Nick shouted hopelessly.

'No, you're not,' Dimitri spat out, managing to grab Nick's arm with his other hand, saving him from disappearing with the pounding water continuing to funnel through the passage. 'Pull yourself my way,' he yelled.

Dimitri stretched himself away from the wall, and his arms started to feel the burn as he held on to his brother-in-law's 180-pound frame.

'The force is too strong,' Nick cried. Dimitri saw that the heavy duffel bag was dragging the other man downstream. 'Let me go.'

Dimitri stared at the lip of the void ahead and shook his head with dread and regret. He should have crossed the stepping stones and then thrown the grenades into that void instead; that might have given them a better chance of escape. Now he faced his own mortality. Watching the rushing torrent of water, he understood that he would not be able to leap onto the correct rectangular-marked pillar that would lead him safely across.

At that moment, something collided with Dimitri's shoulder, and he saw that it was the low tombstone from the previous chamber, the one depicting the pyramids of Giza from a top-view perspective. He winced and gulped for air, as he let go of the wall and Nick.

They were now at the mercy of the seventy-foot drop about to consume them both. Water was pouring down into the void like a waterfall. There was no escaping the plunge to their deaths.

Panic rushed right through Dimitri in the darkness.

Then Nick screamed, disappearing into the churning water head first, still holding on to the bag. His voice was swallowed up in an instant.

Then Dimitri was sucked into the vortex. He gave up, his only thought that he was prepared to meet his family in the afterlife. He shut his eyes for a moment as the water took hold of him. But as he reached the peak of the waterfall, he realized he wasn't plunging downwards as he'd expected.

Splash!

The fall was only a few feet and then, incongruously, Dimitri felt himself being lifted up. Opening his eyes, he realized what had happened. The void had filled with water, and the overflow was now carrying him across the void, over the top of the stepping-stone pillars towards the ridge on the other side. He saw Nick sprawled on the ridge ahead, the duffel bag still hanging from his shoulder.

'Nick!' he bellowed, and the other man looked groggily around.

The surge of water continued, the water level rising with each second that passed.

'Quick, this place isn't stable,' warned Dimitri, wading through what was the beginning of the Walk of Souls. 'Nick, don't let go of that bag.'

Nick didn't reply but he renewed his grip on the bag, clinging to it as if his life depended on it. The two men staggered onwards through the water, pushing aside skulls which were washing out from the walls along the Walk of Souls, until finally they reached the spiral staircase and final pool that led to the outside world.

Dimitri and Nick swam out onto the beach and lay on the sand, exhausted, breathing in the briny aroma once more. Eventually Dimitri sat up and looked towards the breaking waves. Relief washed over him as he took a moment on the soft, golden sand and felt the heat of the afternoon sun shine warmly on his face.

With the stone still protected in the bag, Dimitri and Nick trekked back to the abandoned chopper, where spattered brain fragments still covered the side glass panel. Wasting no time, Dimitri climbed into the pilot's seat and started the rotor blades, which came alive as Nick buckled himself into the passenger seat.

That was when an unexpected visitor swooped in, his aircraft displaying a familiar symbol emblazoned on its tail. It was the emblem of the DGSE.

Dimitri's hands began to tremble. He tightened his grip on the steering column, and hot sweat started to trickle down his neck.

'Who is that?' asked Nick as the helicopter lifted off the ground.

Dimitri didn't answer, knowing he needed to get the hell out of this place in a hurry. But he knew perfectly well who it was.

This was a man who commanded respect.

A man who was once his boss.

A man you never wanted to cross.

It was the one and only Julien Bonnet.

Chapter 23

The Red Keystone

A smug smile spread over Marie's face as she thought of how she had outsmarted Dimitri and Nick. She entered the secret cave where the red keystone was still sitting on its altar on the stone podium. The beam from the flashlight she had cunningly left in position still bounced off the crystal and lit the room. Marie swam over and began to climb the steps that would take her to the altar, only to stop dead in her tracks halfway up when she heard a deafening roar.

What was that? she thought, and fear spiked through her. Then the cavern began to shake uncontrollably around her exposed position. Looking down, Marie saw a flurry of spider-web cracks blooming all over the stone stairs. Several more deafening booms followed, and Marie could hear water churning around her, as though she were in a washing machine.

'What the hell,' she gasped, trying to keep herself

balanced. She could feel adrenaline coursing through her veins and her heartbeat thumping wildly in her chest.

Then a tennis-ball-sized mass smashed into the steps right beside her.

Afraid of being hit, she dove back into the water and swam for cover over to the eastern wall. With her hand up against the solid rock, she could feel the vibration coming from the other side. It was as if she was caught in an earthquake, she thought. She tried to calm her pounding heart by taking a few breaths, but it hammered itself almost out of her chest when a book-sized chunk of the ceiling came crashing down only inches away, causing water to splash up and over her face. Terrified now, she screamed and began swimming back in the direction of the main platform, though she struggled through the choppy swell of the water, whipped into waves by the tremors.

The chamber was not safe and was coming down fast.

She thought of her chances of retrieving the keystone only feet away. She knew she couldn't just leave it here, knowing Dimitri would not hesitate to come back for it, once he discovered he was tricked.

I can dart over and snatch it. I can be quick.

Another solid chunk of stone dropped into the water, then another and another.

Splonk! Splonk! Splonk!

The side walls were cracking and crumbling around her and the ceiling was raining rubble. As Marie watched, a shower of rock pieces plummeted down onto the altar, crushing it and sending the flower arrangement of keystones skidding apart.

She covered her eyes for a brief second, trying to decide what to do, and when she opened them, she spotted a red coin-sized piece fly into the water. Before it sank out of sight, she snatched it in her hands. A remnant of the red keystone was before her. She pocketed it and realized her decision was made.

To stay here was suicide and if the keystone was broken, it's likely her problem was solved – and it can't be used.

Then everything went black. Marie realized that debris must have fallen on her flashlight and knocked the beam away from the crystal. Probably the flashlight had been crushed, too.

She acted swiftly, taking a quick breath and dived below the surface to escape through the dark tunnel. She said a silent prayer, hoping the tunnel hadn't been blocked by the event that had shaken the caves. She powered through while a burst of bubbles chased her from behind. Loud, muffled sounds continued, and Marie quickly realized she'd been just in time as the roof of the tunnel behind her completely collapsed and blocked the way through to the keystone's final resting place.

Just as her lungs seemed likely to give out, Marie spotted the incandescent glow of the flare ahead and swam desperately towards it, emerging into the triangular-shaped pool.

She struggled out of the water, hoping to find Joey waiting, but came to a shocked standstill when she saw the cave around her – or what was left of it. It was as if a missile had struck it from above, violently belching fiery smoke and dust out of an enormous gaping hole in the cave ceiling that had breathed in the afternoon sunlight and exhaled the vapors. She could see the sky. Despite everything, Marie felt enormous relief.

Then something else grabbed her attention: the sound of an engine. Marie scanned the gaping void above, much too high up to climb out of, and saw a helicopter swoosh overhead. It was the same chopper they'd flown in on; Marie spotted the grisly streaks of blood and brain on the window. Not wanting to be seen, she stepped back into the shadows as the loud rotor blades beat from above. The helicopter was hovering over the hole.

Moments later, the chopper banked left and disappeared from sight.

Marie turned her attention back to the cave, and Joey. *Where is he?* she thought desperately. After a quick search of the chamber, Marie saw her man lying face down a few yards along the uneven tunnel leading back the way they'd come. He appeared to be unconscious and in a precarious position, with loose rocks falling over his bleeding body.

'Joey!' she screamed. 'Hang on, I'm coming!'

Her vision was almost nil through the maelstrom of sand, dust, and soot billowing in the air and matting her hair and wet clothes. She plunged into the triangular pool once more and extracted the incandescent flare that was still burning at the bottom. She tore off a wet strip from her sports tank top and tied it around her nose and mouth as a face mask. Holding the flare over her head, she set out.

She hurried towards Joey, guided by the burning beacon, the light allowing her to make better headway in the opaque air. But her sigh of relief was short-lived as a dozen killer arrows were released.

'Shit!' she breathed, instinctively ducking as two of the arrows zinged dangerously low, just over her head. She stumbled and fell onto all fours, then weaved and zigzagged through the unstable terrain towards Joey, scraping her shoulder against the rough debris. She winced, feeling the gash on her skin, then picked herself up and dove onto a safe platform as rocks and rubble rained over her last location.

'I'm coming,' she told Joey again, then gasped as the unstable floor began to shake wildly again, creating unwalkable rolling hills of basalt.

After a treacherous climb, she finally reached Joey. Looking beyond him in case of further danger, she suddenly noticed that the water that had separated the super cavern from the caves beyond had disappeared. For some reason, it had been sucked out, leaving this place dry.

Marie turned quickly to Joey.

'Wake up,' she said, slapping Joey in the face and praying for a response.

But there was none.

She felt for a pulse in his neck; it was weak, but he was alive. She felt tears of relief trickle down her cheeks. But they weren't out of this yet.

The ground beneath them continued to tremble, choking the air with dust and sand.

'We need to get out of here,' Marie told the

unconscious Joey, tossing her flare onto the ground. She reached down to grab Joey's battered and bleeding upper torso. It was impossible to lift his dead weight over her shoulders, so she grabbed his hands and with an excruciating effort managed to drag him back to the cavern with the now open ceiling. When she finally reached it, she almost collapsed. She knew they were still far from safe, but at least Joey would be able to breathe the fresh outside air.

Facing the sky, she yelled and waved, hoping someone on the island would see the dust clouds and come rescue them. Surely someone would come to investigate the earthquake, or whatever it was, she reasoned. Luck had worked for her in the past, and for the sake of her family, she hoped someone up there was listening.

Chapter 24

The Reunion

'Look over there!' said Boyce, staring out his window to see a billowing cloud of dust escape from a gaping hole in the ground. 'I didn't know Easter Island was still active?'

'It's not,' said Julien, his cold stare suddenly focused on a chopper hovering over the crater.

'What's wrong, sir?' Boyce asked, feeling the general's anxiousness.

'Not entirely sure,' answered Julien as he rushed into the cockpit. 'The scenic helicopter over there,' he asked the captain, pointing. 'Can you make contact?'

'I can try different frequencies and hope they are listening.'

'Yes, do it.'

The captain spoke into his headset, asking the occupants of the chopper to identify themselves and then changing stations and repeating the process.

There was nothing but static.

'Is everything okay?' Boyce asked, stepping into the cockpit.

Julien lifted a pair of binoculars to his eyes and his jaw dropped as if he had seen a ghost.

'What's wrong?' asked Boyce.

'It's Dimitri, and he's flying the chopper. I see another man in the passenger seat. No sign of Joey or Marie.'

'Oh no! Are we too late?' murmured Boyce.

Julien shrugged and ordered the pilot to land the jet as close as possible to the hole. 'If it's Dimitri, he blew this entire section for a reason. Marie and Joey might be in danger. We need to act quickly.'

The pilot aligned the plane to descend on a flat piece of grassland. As he did so, the helicopter banked left and flew in the opposite direction. It was as if the bad guys knew they needed to flee, knowing the general would kill first and ask questions later. Even though the general was in his seventies, Boyce had witnessed firsthand what Julien was capable of doing to men half his age. And judging by the general's suddenly bitter face, staying as far away as possible was the best move for the men in the helicopter.

Boyce peered out of the cockpit window to see an incredible sight. Long sections of earth were literally sinking before his eyes. Huge basalt stones were emerging through the earth as the soil above subsided into what were previously hollow underground chambers and tunnel systems, Boyce assumed. The site was like a *Lord of the Rings* movie, complete with dust and sand.

The jet flew past the jagged-edged hole in the ground

and landed a hundred yards away before taxiing to a complete stop. Boyce, Julien, and two of his men from the DGSE disembarked the plane and approached the site with haste. All four men were dressed in military greens, all armed, carrying flashlights and backpacks of supplies. After a short hike over the rocky terrain, they reached the gaping hole in the earth and withdrew their Mk47s, in case a trap was set.

'Joey!' Boyce called out, keeping his distance from the edge while dust clouds continued to pour out of the gaping crater. 'Marie!'

Boyce thought he could hear someone coughing below.

'Joey! Can you hear me?' he shouted with renewed urgency.

'Boyce, is that you?' Marie called out in a choked voice. 'We need help!'

'Yes, it's me. You okay?'

'I'm alright. But hurry, Joey's been hurt, and the whole cave system is unstable; I don't think we have much time.' Marie began coughing again.

'Let's get them out of there,' directed Julien. 'Time is not on our side.'

Gun anchors with crank pulley systems attached were fired into a nearby rock formation. Without hesitation, Julien clipped himself in and dropped into the cave, commando-style. This was a controlled fall but at pace, and Julien made it look like child's play. Boyce was always amazed that at his age, the general was still willing and able to base-jump into a dangerous situation. His men were more than capable of doing the physical work, but that was not Julien's style. This was the reason he was such a highly respected leader, Boyce knew. He was the first on the front line in battle, always putting the safety of his people before his own, and his soldiers knew it.

Julien landed safely near Marie's position. 'I'm down,' he confirmed for his crew. After a few minutes, he called up to them again. 'Joey will be coming up first. He's secured, pull him up. Go! Go!'

Using the crank pulley system, Joey was lifted carefully out, secured by a rope that ran through the belt loops in his pants. His was conscious and holding on weakly, but Boyce was shocked at his friend's condition. His naked torso was bruised and bleeding, and when his feet found solid ground, he fell back down to his knees, then onto his side.

Boyce ran over to him and embraced him. Then he quickly unclipped the rope from Joey's belt and tossed it back down to Julien, who was waiting to strap Marie in.

'Shit, the floor is going!' Julien yelled up suddenly.

Boyce left Joey in the care of one of the commandos and hurried as close to the hole's edge as he dared. Clods of earth and stones were breaking free of the lip of the hole and raining down into the cavern below.

'Get ready for extraction,' Julien called in his deep, commanding voice.

Boyce and the other commando prepared themselves.

'Now!' Julien ordered, and the two mean cranked the rope as hard as they could. Moments later, Boyce could make out the two figures rising through the billowing dust. The general and Marie were swinging slowly in midair as they were winched out of the cave, inch by inch. Finally, they were lowered back onto solid ground, and Boyce and the commando struggled over to them, breathing hard.

'I'm so glad to see you,' Marie said when she was freed from the rope, wrapping Boyce in a fierce hug. She coughed and held him tight for a moment. Behind them, Joey, sitting up now, tried to smile but then winced, still holding the back of his head where a nasty, bloody gash was visible.

'I can't believe it,' said Boyce. 'It's the first time I've seen Joey speechless.'

Joey's lips twitched in a smile-grimace, and then he once again tightened his jaw in agony.

'Poor guy was tossed around like a ragdoll down there,' said Marie. 'Don't worry, you know Joey – when he gets better you won't be able to shut him up.'

'We need to get Joey to the plane,' said one of the commandos. 'We have medical supplies to treat him there.'

'Steve is a medic,' Julien told them. 'He'll take care of you.'

'Looks like a concussion,' Steve said solemnly. 'Lots of minor injuries too. You'll need to rest so you can recover.'

Marie nodded. 'Let's get out of this place; we can catch up in the air. We have heaps to tell you both.'

The two commandos helped Joey to his feet as the light of day drained away. Holding the injured man between them, they carried him away from the site that had just swallowed forever the all-important keystone.

Chapter 25

Santiago International Airport, Chile, 10:00 pm Local Time

The last vestiges of the setting sun disappeared over the horizon as Dimitri flew the Eurocopter in an easterly direction over the South Pacific Ocean. After five hours flying on fumes, he landed his renegade chopper in Chile, near a clearing in the Santiago International Airport.

'Hey, sleepyhead, time to wake up,' said Dimitri, who had let his brother-in-law sleep, hoping it would settle him down.

The singlet-wearing pair stepped out into the warm twilight air and headed for a hangar that was within walking distance.

'What time is it?' asked Nick, yawning, still holding the very battered duffel bag. 'And what's the plan?'

'You should buy yourself a watch,' said Dimitri as he glanced down at Nick's naked arm. 'I have another jet waiting here.'

'You sure have connections everywhere.' Nick smiled, staring at Dimitri's eccentric wristwatch. 'Can I have yours?' he asked, motioning his eyes towards it.

'No.'

'Why not?'

'It was a gift from a friend.'

The hangar was vast, like an endless desert of concrete.

'There it is,' said Dimitri, pointing to the aircraft that would take them to Cairo, Egypt, a fourteen-hour trip. *The place where I'll activate the Stargate and find my closure*, he added mentally.

'Those men aren't going to be a problem, are they?' Nick asked, reaching for a gun he no longer possessed. 'They're carrying M16s.' From behind the plane had appeared a group of men, all carrying machine guns and none looking especially friendly.

'Don't react,' Dimitri said, approaching the group at a steady pace. He had concocted a deal through an acquaintance, but this was Chile, and his contact was as ruthless as they came.

'For the record, this is your doing,' hissed Nick as the firepower turned in their direction. Even if they wanted to run, they wouldn't be able to escape the automatic trigger of the thirty-round magazines pointing their way.

The mysterious man in the middle wore a *chupalla*, or traditional Chilean horseman's hat made of straw. For some reason, it seemed like wherever he moved, he was always in the shadow. He was a short and stubby figure who appeared to command the respect of the rest of the group.

'*Buenas tardes*,' said Dimitri in his best Spanish. 'You must be Carlos. I have paid for a safe passage to Egypt and some supplies.'

Carlos stepped out of the shadow to reveal a deeply scarred face. He took a moment and looked closely into Dimitri's eyes. He appeared to be analyzing him as he scrutinized his face, but his stare intensified when they all became aware of the sound of sirens wailing in the distance.

'Are you setting me up?' the man asked.

'No, sir, I would never betray a contact,' said Dimitri firmly.

In that instant, two police cars rounded the corner of the hangar and came to an abrupt stop feet away, their flashing red-and-blue lights reflecting off the runway. Within seconds the group was surrounded, and four armed policemen approached.

'I can't do jail, brother,' Nick said darkly, gripping the duffel bag tightly. 'Maybe we can try to outrun them all.'

'No!' Dimitri warned. A confident smile curled the edges of his mouth when he suddenly noticed how comfortable the hat-wearing man seemed to be around the authorities.

'*Policía, pon tus manos en el aire*,' said the policeman.

'They want you to put your hands in the air,' translated the Chilean man with the hat. His eyes almost sparkled, even in the darkness.

'I'm sorry to bother you, Carlos,' said the officer, stepping forward to greet him. 'Are they with you? They landed an unauthorized chopper into our airspace.'

Nick was gripping his duffel bag so hard now his knuckles were white, and his eyes were darting left and right in fright. To see him this way was reassuring to Dimitri. Most of the time, his brother-in-law was cold and ruthless. Among these men, truly dangerous men, Dimitri guessed, he was as quiet as a mouse – a very sensible reaction, under the circumstances.

Carlos spoke to the commanding officer in Spanish. The policemen relaxed when he assured them that the two newcomers were with him. His pulling power over the authorities was apparent as the police turned around and drove away without even a word to Dimitri and Nick.

'Who is this guy?' Nick whispered to Dimitri.

Dimitri kept silent, not wanting to share that Carlos was from the Madariaga family, a multi-billion-dollar drug-trafficking cartel that controlled this side of the airport.

Carlos reached out and shook Dimitri's hand, thanking him for the generous donation, and gestured towards the airplane that had the look of a billionaire's private jet.

'As requested, I have surveillance equipment and guns waiting for you in first class.'

Dimitri thanked him.

'Santiago, the pilot will take you to your destination. He's waiting for you inside the plane,' he replied. 'Safe travels, and if you ever want to do business again, please don't hesitate,' he said, and then gestured to his armed soldiers and left.

Dimitri and Nick entered the aircraft where they

were greeted by Santiago with a warm smile. The interior had no rows of seats, only the most elegant leather couches and coffee tables with ornate cabriole legs. There were plush curtains at the windows and a large plasma screen. No expense had been spared in this plane, no doubt paid for with drug money.

In the comfy first-class seats, Dimitri and Nick took a load off and enjoyed the long flight away from imminent danger. There were no deadly booby traps here, no police or cartel to avoid. When they'd been in the air for a couple of airs and he was sure he wouldn't be disturbed, Dimitri extracted the hefty gray keystone from the damp duffel bag and laid it on the table in front of him, next to a dark briefcase and complimentary laptop.

Once he opened the briefcase, Dimitri smiled. Carlos had come through.

He booted up the laptop and opened his daughter's Instagram page, flicking through the images of his wife and child that were posted there.

He rubbed the screen with his index finger lovingly, once again overcome by sadness at their untimely deaths. The emotional pain he usually held in seeped out of him, and the tears flowed down his cheeks. He felt completely empty without them, but now he was a step closer. He had the keystone, and nobody was going to stop him from using it.

Chapter 26

Julien's Aircraft
Stationary on Easter Island

Boyce entered his boss's Gulfstream G550As as the first stars appeared in the evening sky. He crossed his heart as he stepped over the threshold and smiled stiffly at the cheerful flight attendant he was fond of but didn't have the balls to ask out.

Joey had been given clean clothes, medication and had his injuries tended to before being put to bed in one of the eighteen leather passenger seats that retracted horizontally for sleeping. Boyce patted his friend sympathetically on the arm and walked further in to find Julien exiting the cockpit with a worried expression on his face.

'What's wrong?' Boyce asked the man he idolized like a father figure.

'The captain needs a destination.'

'And . . . what's the problem?'

'Well, we need to know if Dimitri was successful

in finding the keystone. We haven't discussed this yet. We need to talk to Marie and figure out our next step, because believe me, Dimitri would have planned his.'

Boyce about-faced and they both went to find Marie, who was sitting in a daze in the window seat of a pair of chairs facing another pair. Julien sat across from Marie, his long limbs stretched out in the open space. Boyce remembered Julien once mentioning how much he loved this plane and its generous legroom. Boyce took the seat beside him.

Marie sat, tired-eyed and slumped over in her chair, with cuts and bruises that ran down her arms. She gazed blankly out the window until she was interrupted by the flight attendant, who handed her what appeared to be her second Kit-Kat chocolate bar. The first open wrapper was still on the empty seat beside her, accompanied by a half-drunk bottle of water and some clean clothes to change into.

'Sorry to bother you, Marie,' Julien said softly. 'Before you sleep, I need to ask you some questions.'

Marie took an exhausted breath and looked up at Julien's imposing frame. Despite sitting by his side, Boyce felt squeezed, Julien's broad shoulders creeping into his own personal space.

'You okay?' Boyce asked Marie.

'I am,' she said with a smile. 'But I'm feeling pretty awful with the nausea.'

'Nausea?' Boyce asked with surprise.

'Oh . . . I'm pregnant,' she told him.

'That's amazing news!' Boyce exclaimed.

'Congratulations to the both of you,' Julien said warmly.

'Wow, when this kid grows up, he or she's going to really be something, with amazing role models like you guys guiding the way,' Boyce said with genuine happiness.

'I have no doubt your knowledge of the world and what you have seen will be passed down to a bright young child,' Julien added.

Marie smiled, took another bite of her chocolate bar, and turned to Boyce. 'It sure helps having the best godfather in the world by our side.'

Boyce cherished the sentiment and returned a loving smile and a wink. He had never felt such love for a couple as he did for Marie and Joey. He was happy to have met them both, even though it had been under a dire circumstance, one that had left him boat-less and homeless. They had shared dangerous situations on multiple continents, and their bond had only strengthened through all of it.

'Marie,' said Julien, 'I need to know what happened here and if Dimitri has the keystone.'

'He does have a stone,' Marie informed him, taking a sip of her bottled water to wash down the mouthful of chocolate she was chewing.

Julien shrugged his shoulders. 'So, he has the key to activate the Stargate,' he muttered in a dejected tone. 'We have no choice now but to head to Egypt and try to stop him before he triggers it.'

'He has a huge head start,' said Boyce. 'We won't be able to stop him. Should I make the call and blockade the Sphinx with men?'

'Hang on,' Marie said with a smile. 'I told you he

has *a* keystone, but what you don't know is that it's not the *actual* red dolerite one. Trust me . . . he won't be able to activate anything.'

'I don't follow,' said Julien with a confused expression. 'What are you saying?'

'I went into the last cave alone, and found the red dolerite stone surrounded by four gray basalt stones. They were all cut in the same triangular shape and displayed like a flower arrangement.'

'And?' questioned Julien.

'Hoping Dimitri wasn't a stickler for detail, I handed him the wrong one.'

'So, he has a basalt stone?'

'Yes, sir, that's correct.'

'What happened to the red keystone?' asked Boyce with a frown.

'It was buried deep within the rubble when the cave system collapsed,' said Marie as she pointed out the window. 'Plus I saw it shatter into pieces before I got the hell out of there. Good luck trying to find it now. It would be like finding a needle in a haystack.'

Julien sat back in his seat with a half-smile. 'You gave him a dud,' he said happily.

'That's freaking awesome,' said Boyce with a laugh. 'You're a genius.'

Julien's levity was short-lived. He sat forward in his chair. 'This is not over, though, not in the slightest. You took away the only chance Dimitri believes he has to be able to see his family again. I think this will end unpleasantly when he discovers he was duped – we just backed a rabid dog into a corner, and he's going to bite back when he finds out. God help those in his path then.'

Chapter 27

**Deep Beneath the Great Pyramid of Giza,
Cairo, Egypt, 5:00 pm Local Time**

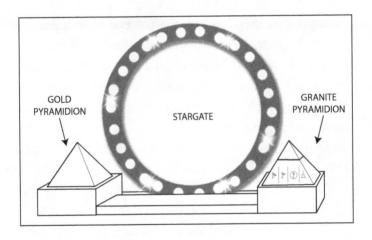

Dimitri and Nick stood at the end of the line, in the last secret chamber that housed a smoothly rendered limestone pyramid deep inside the Seventh Wonder of the Ancient World; the Great Pyramid of Giza. But this time, Dimitri held in his hand the all-important keystone as he walked inside the hollow shrine and fronted the Stargate.

Standing there, taking in its astonishing glory, Dimitri thought about the repercussions that were inevitable if word got out about this place. All religions around the world would crumble into dust. The panic that would ensue would create hysteria on all corners of the planet. The question of whether humans were the only sentient beings in the universe was not a question anymore. It was answered, and this revelation had rocked Dimitri to his core the first time he had stepped foot in this ethereal place.

One of his primary assignments working under Julien had been to help document all the artefacts found within the Hall of Records. The entire complex under the general's command was like Fort Knox, and it needed to be. All items had been carefully tagged and catalogued and moved to a secret location in Egypt, funded by entrepreneur Elliott Magnus. Right here, somewhere in this cave system, was where the ancient blue vase had been discovered, the one that had led him to Easter Island.

Now Dimitri stood feet away from the Stargate, about to initiate the portal he had been assigned to protect.

The hollow wheel-shaped structure was thirty feet tall but only twenty inches deep. It held upright by its indented limestone base, which gripped it like a vise. The material from which it was constructed was solid and sturdy and had a gunmetal-gray surface.

'So, this is it?' Nick said with open arms and a troubled expression, taking it all in. His expression had remained troublingly blank the entire way through this incredible maze, which Dimitri had told him was titled the Walk of Souls.

'What now?' asked Nick.

'Time to meet our makers,' said Dimitri, reverentially slotting the key into its shallow allocated slot. The stone fit snugly, and Dimitri inhaled as he stepped back, unsure what would happen next. He had read reports on the activation of the Stargate but had never had the pleasure of seeing it come to life.

Nick hovered his hand over his holster where a new gold-plated Beretta 92 pistol resided, compliments of Carlos. Dimitri carried an identical weapon.

Waiting patiently, Nick tapped his finger on the gun.

One minute of silence ensued.

'How come it's not working?' Nick asked. 'Is this thing supposed to light up or something?'

'We have to wait, be patient.'

Two minutes passed.

Three.

Five.

'Bro?' Nick said in question.

'Fuck! Fuck!' Dimitri exploded, punching the air impotently, the frustration erupting from him. 'I don't understand,' he said vehemently. 'The gate should activate.'

'Perhaps the portal *is* active and we just can't see it,' said Nick, tossing his flashlight through the circle only to see it crash-land on the opposite side.

'Any other grand ideas?' Dimitri said, irritated.

'I don't know, maybe try to insert the stone again into its hole.'

Dimitri stepped up, extracted the triangular prism–shaped basalt stone, and saw a shadow that was cast by the bottom end of the metallic circular frame. At first, he thought it could be a rat lurking in the darkness. He inserted the keystone back into its slot, and saw the shadow again.

'What's wrong?' asked Nick, who had read Dimitri's puzzled face.

'Two sliding doors,' said Dimitri, perplexed. 'They are built to hold something within the Stargates core.'

'What do you mean? Is there anything inside?'

Dimitri leaned over to investigate the secret compartment. 'Nothing in this one,' he said, feeling around with his left hand. 'Looks like if there was something inside, it's been taken.' He shifted to the next opening and his face lit up.

'What is it?' asked Nick, seeing Dimitri's delighted expression.

'There's something here.' He reached in and secured a shiny, dense object the size of a hardback novel, about sixteen by nine inches. He held the item with two hands, feeling the considerable weight in his palms.

Nick approached from behind as Dimitri rubbed the dust away and his eyes widened.

'It's a tablet made of solid gold,' he said in a wonder-filled tone. 'It's incredibly heavy, too, must weigh twenty pounds.'

'Are they hieroglyphics?' asked Nick curiously.

'Yeah.'

'I wonder what they say.'

Dimitri continued to study the object.

'Must be worth a pretty penny,' Nick continued. 'Hey, bro, just a thought. Why don't we forget about all this crap and sell it and find an island somewhere to retire on?'

'That's not the reason I'm here, Nick,' Dimitri spat. 'I'm here for my wife and child. No money in the world will satisfy me.'

'I know,' said Nick, dropping his head despondently.

'I never forced you to join me on this quest,' said Dimitri, trying to lock eyes with him. 'You're doing this of your own free will.'

'I know,' Nick said again, but sounding angry now.

For a moment, Dimitri merely stared at him, his expression unreadable. He felt torn. He knew his brother-in-law would do anything he said, whether he really wanted to or not. Nick was loyal, and he was family. But something in his gut was telling him Nick didn't belong on this journey. Dimitri needed to face this alone. The tablet was Nick's way out. He could sell it, make some money, and live large someplace.

'So, what do we do now?' said Nick, snapping Dimitri out of his reverie. 'The keystone you have doesn't seem to work. It just opens up two stupid trapdoors. Don't you think that's weird? Is it possible Marie could have given us the wrong stone? Or was the whole Easter Island cave meant to mislead us from the start? I guess we'll never know . . . Marie did swim into the last cave alone – we never did see what it actually looked like. Maybe there were other keystones there.'

It was an offhand comment from Nick, but the more

Dimitri considered it, the more he thought Nick had hit the nail on the head. The idea trundled through his brain like a train with no intention of stopping. Marie was no dummy. She was an educated and calculating woman who had been through this ordeal before.

'I think she played us,' Dimitri said in a whisper. He clenched his fists so hard that veins popped out on his temple.

'At least we weren't left empty-handed,' said Nick. 'See here,' he pointed at the golden tablet in Dimitri's hand, 'these markings look like planets in our solar system, and there's an image of the Stargate in it, too.'

Dimitri followed Nick's gaze. 'You're right, this plaque will be worth millions to the right buyer. Once the text is translated, I'm sure it will reveal more of our past and conceivably our future, who knows?'

Dimitri laid the tablet down on the ground, and Nick's eyes followed the shimmering gold like an excited child on Christmas morning.

Dimitri shrugged and took a breath. 'I understand you don't really want to be here, Nick, and that's okay.'

Nick looked up at him sharply. 'What do you mean? What are you saying?'

'I have decided that we'll need to part ways. I will enter the Stargate when I get the correct keystone, and you will disappear a rich man with that golden artefact.'

'But isn't it our destiny to go through the Stargate?' Nick asked in an injured tone.

'No, Nick, it's *my* destiny. I love you, Nick, like a brother, but you can't keep doing what I say. You need to carve your own path.'

Nick shook his head while continuing to gaze at the ground. 'Do you have a plan?'

'I might have one that can benefit the both of us. It involves you getting rich and me doing what I came here to do. But first, it means you have to do one more thing for me. Something that will garner the attention I rightfully deserve. It's time to turn up the heat in this place.'

Chapter 28

Sphinx, Giza Plateau, Cairo, Egypt, 6:00 pm Local Time

Nick's footsteps crunched over loose rocks and sand as he made his way back to the entrance: the right paw of the Sphinx, from which the vast network of tunnels snaked their way to the Stargate.

Nick saw his handiwork spread throughout the narrow passage. Four dead Egyptian soldiers lay slaughtered in the most brutal of ways, as evidenced by the bloody fingerprints smeared all over the limestone walls. It wouldn't have mattered if there'd been four or eight on patrol a couple of hours ago; no army was stopping Nick and his brother-in-law from accessing the dark void that would lead them to the ultimate prize.

The purposely installed caged door, which was supposed to stop stickybeaks from entering, was as he'd left it; pried open and the locks broken. He stepped outside onto the Giza Plateau and the fresh, inviting air filled his lungs. He craned his head to see that the blue haze of day had disappeared, revealing the first glimpse of stars.

He turned to look up at the beast guarding the promised land. The creature's paw was twice his height and longer than a city bus. In the far distance, three pyramids dominated the landscape as they rose silently in the dark sky. A sense of gratitude fell over him when he recalled why our forefathers had erected these mammoth structures.

He feared the unknown, it puzzled him, but he wasn't going to lose sleep over it. Humans were not the only species out there in the universe, he knew that now. But he didn't think that this mattered, unless the aliens decided they wanted to invade Earth. And why would they want to do that? Why would a far superior alien race come all the way from their planet just to destroy a primitive species? And wouldn't they have done it by now, if they'd wanted to?

Nick laughed at the ludicrousness of the idea as he glanced around, preparing himself for his next task. His brother-in-law's last parting gift awaited him;

the priceless golden tablet he could sell to the highest bidder. But first, he needed to get his hands dirty.

A group of tourists, probably the last of the day, was walking nearby, and several of them had noticed Nick emerging from the right forefoot of the Sphinx. Not being something they'd expected to see, it caught their attention and they were pointing and whispering.

'Hey, did you see that man,' said a young English-accented sightseer. Her tone was enthusiastic and eager. 'He came out of the *floor*.'

'Oh my God,' said another in surprise.

'Hello, everyone,' Nick said out loud as he brushed away the dust from his pants. 'Welcome to Giza. I know you're probably at the end of your tour, but you're in for a treat! Trust me, you haven't seen anything yet. Come down in here, and I will give you a personal tour and show you what *really* lies beneath the sands of Egypt.' Nick flashed an open arm at the entrance like he was in a game show, a broad smile on his face, but he didn't get the response he was searching for.

'What tour company is this?' asked an Arab man with heavily accented English.

'What difference does it make?' Nick replied playfully, still waving his hand at the hole. 'I'm offering you a complimentary history lesson.'

'I don't know,' said a woman dubiously. 'Nothing here is free. I've already been harassed by ten kids who offered me supposedly free gifts, only to have their much taller and scarier-looking brother come and collect.'

The tourists stood fast. It was evident from the expressions on their faces that they didn't trust, Nick.

It was dark, after all. Who would follow anyone down a gloomy, unlit passage, especially in a dangerous country like Egypt? Maybe if it were daylight, he would have had a better reception, Nick thought.

Never one to have much patience, Nick decided to up the ante and try another approach – one he had far more faith in. He extracted his gold-plated Beretta 92 pistol, concealed under his dark singlet, and flashed a sarcastic smile.

Dread suddenly washed over the many faces.

An American-accented woman shouted, 'He's got a gun!' and ducked low for cover before bolting in the opposite direction.

'Gun!'

Screams of panic and despair fell over the thirty or so travelers, who began jostling to escape.

It was chaos and anarchy in all directions.

A father aggressively directed his children out of the way.

A group of Asians fell over each other in a panicked state.

'Terrorist!' screamed another.

'*Yalla! Yalla!*'

A local bearded man wearing a black beanie, who appeared to be in his mid-forties, decided to confront Nick. His eyes were focused, his mouth shut, displaying his unshaved jawline. His dark features bore a serious scowl.

A fight was coming, and Nick welcomed it with a grin. 'Finally,' he whispered to himself, holding his ground. His armed hand relaxed and pointed downward to the crushed limestone sand beneath his feet.

Nick felt the adrenaline course through him as the man approached.

The broad man wore an orange polo shirt with East Delta Travel emblazoned across it. 'I'm sick of you terrorists,' he said, charging fearlessly.

Nick quickly surmised that the man must have been a bus driver or tour operator who had previously witnessed the catastrophic events on the Giza Plateau, where a double-decker filled with tourists was bombed. This unarmed man seemed to be after revenge. Why on earth would he be willing to attack a man with a gun? The answer was simple: another massacre would have sent him broke. The past killings would have crippled his business. Frightened people had taken Egypt off their list of must-see destinations.

The stranger roared as he approached.

Nick appreciated his heroism, but he wasn't going to give the man the upper hand. Without the slightest hesitation, he raised his arm again, took aim, and pulled the trigger.

The man jolted and fell backwards, and when Nick walked to him, he heard a gurgling sound that indicated that the man was choking on his own blood. The Egyptian's eyes flickered closed just as Nick bent down and pulled off his beanie.

Straightening up, Nick placed the dark beanie over his own head and then gazed out across the vast site, which was now like an empty movie set. He darted his eyes to a line of tour buses. 'Bingo,' he breathed.

Three vehicles' lights were on, but only one had its doors shut.

Nick advanced with his stylish, gold-plated handgun at the ready. The fresh air was warm and quiet, and there was no wind. The only sounds he could hear were his own footsteps crunching over the rocky sand. When he reached the bus, he banged the sidewall of the carriage hard, and was rewarded by the cries of frightened children inside.

Jackpot.

He strolled over to the driver's side window and reached inside, releasing the bus's hydraulic front sliding doors. The sound of weeping children increased in volume. He stepped onboard to see a dozen or so tourists from all walks of life hiding under their seats. He was gratified to see that they all looked petrified at the sight of him.

He found a pen on the floor, picked it up and removed the beanie from his head.

'Hello, people,' he said pleasantly, as he stabbed holes into his beanie to form eye holes. 'I'm only going to say this once, so listen carefully. If you all want to live you need to come with me.' He paused for dramatic effect. 'You are all here in Egypt to see the wonders of this place – the Sphinx, the pyramids – right? Well, then, it's your lucky day, because you will all get to see things that are not normally accessible to the common folk. I will take you deep inside the underground caves to the Hall of Records, and even further. What you will see tonight will blow your mind, and change your outlook on life forever. Now, you will follow me, in single file, and if anyone decides to run, you will die, and so will the person standing beside you. I don't care if it's your mother, father, or child. I will put a hole in their head. If you want to live, make sure you do what I say and just sit back and enjoy the ride.'

Chapter 29

'Breaking news live from Cairo,' reported polished and trusted Egyptian anchorman Mohammed Mohyedin. He wore a tailored navy single-breasted suit and a sharp red tie, which set off his combed dark, wavy hair nicely. Together with his cameraman, he was positioned at a high vantage point that overlooked the Sphinx and its enclosure.

Tonight, it seemed he was going to deliver the story of the century.

'Moments ago, we received news of a hostage situation deep within the Great Sphinx. Yes, you heard that right. A group of hostages has been forced at gunpoint into a cave system below the structure, through an entrance beside the right paw of the Sphinx, which is a location at which many historians believed there to be a network of secret tunnels. It looks as if these theories have now proved true.'

The cameraman turned the camera away from Mohammed and zoomed in on the opening in the ground among the timber floors around the Sphinx's paw, then slowly panned back to the host.

'The man behind this hostage situation has been identified as Dimitri Panos, a former employee of the French intelligence agency DGSE, where he obtained the rank of major. He is known by his peers to be a ruthless and dangerous individual with high-level combat skills. He is working with an accomplice, but the identity of this individual is currently unknown. Footage shows him wearing a balaclava to hide his face. We are uncertain if any demands have yet been made, but we do know that four guards were found dead, their bodies mutilated, near the entrance.

'We also know that eighteen unharmed hostages have been taken, and they have been guided inside this vast underground network of tunnels here on the Giza Plateau.'

Mohammed touched his earpiece and stopped to listen, concentration written over his face.

'I've been given instructions,' he said, stopping to hear some more. 'We have been given approval by the authorities to show footage sent to us by the perpetrator, Dimitri Panos. It is a little disturbing, so now would be the time to switch channels if kids are present. Here we go.'

The stream started. It showed a line of prisoners holding hands in a giant chain entering the limestone-walled tunnels. Some of the young children cried as they stepped deeper into the darkness, lit sporadically by portable lights emitting an orange hue.

In the narrow corridor, a male hostage began to argue with the man concealed behind his mask, and suddenly, the screen abruptly cut to the Al Jazeera News station logo. 'Oh my God,' blurted Mohammed.

Seconds later, the edit cut back to the detainees in a straight-line formation. Many of them were sobbing now. In the distance, there was a blurry view of a body left behind, executed, it appeared, for his disobedience.

Leaving seventeen hostages.

The camera panned around, showing the captives stepping into an expansive open space. Then the person holding the camera turned it on themselves, and Dimitri Panos, the mastermind, came into view. He fumbled, positioning the cell about a foot from his rough, unshaven face.

'Tonight, I will reveal the truth to the people,' he said with a mischievous smirk. 'Look at this place, it's enormous.' He swung the phone slowly around to show the vastness of the site.

'Did you know this place was discovered a year ago? Of course you didn't,' he answered his own question. 'Did you know this super cavern was filled with treasures that were relocated to a secret location? Yes, people. A treasure trove piled sky-high with ancient artefacts, gold, you name it,' he said theatrically.

'The Egyptians have been kept in the dark for way

too long, and tonight I want to give something back to them. The secrets of Egypt belong to the people, and I will expose one of many, right now.'

He gestured with his free hand to one side and said, 'Welcome to the Hall of Records! This is the subject of one of the stories told by many historians and conspiracy theorists, which until now have always been debunked and kept hidden by the men in power.'

He strolled amid the enormous columns, which dwarfed him. Part of Nefertiti's legs could be seen, but not enough to make out clearly. An empty bookshelf came into view, but the viewer had no way of knowing that it was constructed from cedar that could only have been found and imported from Lebanon at the time.

'Lost texts said to have been stored in the Hall of Records were found in this exact spot,' Dimitri said, gesturing to it. 'Now, they lie in a secluded vault somewhere, protected from prying eyes, and they tell the stories of our ancestors and the beginning of time. Can you imagine what they could unveil?' His eyes widened, and his head nodded dramatically as he let this fact sink in.

Sounds of fear and confusion continued to echo in the background.

'So, you might be wondering why I am doing this. Why take innocent people down here?' He paused and flapped his hand at the petrified tourists, who were huddling together like sheep in a rainswept paddock. 'The answer to that question is simple: there is more inside this place. Much, much more, but for now, the Hall of Records is all I'm willing to show you.'

He moved his face so close you could see his pupils dilate. 'I'm after something.' His eyes were focused on a single spot on his phone. 'The hostages will all be let go when I get my hands on a particular item. It's a key. If you're listening, Julien, and I know you will be, then you know what I'm talking about. I need your young friends to bring the correct key to me, or I will kill everyone and turn this country and the rest of the world upside down. You have my number; I'm expecting your call.'

The recording ended and the feed redirected to Mohammed, who stood still, lost for words.

'Wow. Let's hope the man named in the video is listening and delivers this mysterious key. The lives of eigh– seventeen innocent hostages depend on it. What I'm wondering is, what key is he talking about, and most importantly, what door does it open? We'll keep you apprised of any further developments, live as they unfold. This is Mohammed Mohyedin, Al Jazeera News.'

Chapter 30

Gulfstream G550 Aircraft, North Atlantic Ocean

Joey woke up to a loud commotion within the plane. His heavy eyes adjusted to the group gathering towards the front end of the cabin. He steadied himself, trying to comprehend what was going on around him. When he rose from his comfortable bed, a headache began pounding at the back of his skull and he had to close his eyes momentarily against the pain. Touching it gingerly, he found it covered in bandages but with no obvious signs of bleeding, although there was blood dried in his hair.

The events of the last few hours came rushing back to him. The anxious wait for Marie to return. Her quick wit had outsmarted Dimitri, and they now had the upper hand, but the win had been short-lived. The sound of multiple explosions had caught him off guard. As if rocked by an unimaginable force, the floor had realigned itself, and the cave ceiling had come crashing down. Joey had been sent sprawling in the chaos, his bare torso a bleeding mess. He vaguely recalled being smacked in the back of the head by the collapsing ceiling, which had blurred his vision to the point of seeing stars. And then it had knocked him out cold.

Shaking off the flashback, he looked outside the window to see thick gray clouds at what he presumed was thirty thousand feet. He slid into the blue-carpeted aisle and staggered towards the noisy group ahead, gritting his teeth against the searing fiery bursts of pain pulsating from his bandaged wound. The sound of arguing intensified as he quietly snuck up and found himself standing behind the group. This included Boyce, Marie, Julien, and his crew, and they were all standing around a television screen that was mounted high up on the wall.

The captain was also present, and judging by the pitch in his voice, what they were about to watch wasn't going to be pleasant. 'Here we go,' he said, exhaling a breath before he pressed the 'play' button.

Cries of fear, shock, and disgust arose as Dimitri's live stream from the Hall of Records played out.

Marie's jaw dropped, her shoulders slumping in defeat, while Boyce frowned angrily, and his face tensed.

Julien's expression was one of absolute disdain. 'This has now turned to shit!' he said, switching off the monitor. 'Dimitri has shown way too much to the public. Everything we tried to protect will be undone by that one video.'

'I'm sure Hazim is shaking in his boots right now,' said Marie, dropping numbly back into her seat.

'He'll be facing enormous pressure and public scrutiny for deciding to keep the Hall of Records a secret,' Boyce said.

'Do you think Dimitri will stop there?' Marie leaned forward in her chair. 'Or do you think his plan is to reveal that we're not alone?'

'He's on a death wish,' said Julien. 'He has no conscience.'

'Something needs to be done before he takes them through the Walk of Souls,' said Boyce. 'Once the press sees video footage of the internal pyramid and the Stargate … Ahh, shit, man, all bets are off.'

'So, we give him what he wants.' Julien stood with downcast eyes. 'We need to shut him up, make sure that doesn't happen.'

'You're forgetting one thing,' Marie said quietly. 'The keystone was crushed and buried beneath a heap of rubble back on Easter Island. We can't go back.'

'We can dig for it,' Julien said, a purposeful look written on his face.

'Hang on,' said Marie, digging into her pants pocket and extracting a small object. 'I think this is a piece of the red dolerite.' She flicked it onto the table in front of her, and it came to a stop inches away from the captain's arm.

All eyes darted to the coin-sized piece of red stone in wonder.

'To organize a dig back on Easter Island with the appropriate machinery would take weeks and you might just end up finding it smashed in pieces anyway – if you find it at all.' Marie turned to Julien. 'Do we have the time, and do we take the risk that it still works, knowing it's been damaged? It could be in a thousand pieces.'

Julien rubbed his forehead thoughtfully.

Joey understood how the general operated and how he would have felt hearing this news. He was a man who always had a plan of attack.

'We have no choice. We must act,' Julien finally said, his voice uncharacteristically emotional.

'Wait . . . it's possible there's another keystone somewhere in Angkor Wat,' said Marie, catching the general's attention. 'But trying to search the temple complex, which is one of the largest religious monuments in the world, might also take weeks or months that we don't have. We're talking about looking through one hundred and sixty two hectares to find the imprint of a double-spiral symbol. It could be anywhere.'

'What else do we do, then?' Boyce sounded frustrated; he was clearly out of ideas. 'We can't just sit around and do nothing. There is too much at stake. The last thing we want is mass hysteria.'

'I know what to do.' Joey stepped forward, coughing and wincing against the pain this caused.

'Well, look who's back on his feet,' said Boyce with his typically boyish smile.

Marie flashed him a wink.

'What do you suggest?' asked Julien, cutting the pleasantries. 'Time is of the essence.'

'If it's a keystone he wants,' said Joey confidently, 'then let's give him one.'

'How?' Open-palmed, Julien shrugged. 'What do you mean? We've just been discussing this.'

'We go after the keystone we found back in Egypt a year ago,' Joey said boldly. 'The original one.'

'Ahh …' Boyce murmured, seeming to understand where Joey was going with this.

'Am I missing something?' asked Julien. 'I thought the initial keystone was destroyed on your first venture.' Julien's gaze darted over to Boyce, who looked the other way. 'I read it in your report.'

'That paper was not entirely accurate.' Marie bit her lip, looking guilty.

'Which part?' asked Julien incredulously, his voice rising.

'Well, to make sure no other person laid their hands on the keystone that could activate the Stargate, we all …' Boyce indicated with his finger to include Marie and Joey, 'us three … made a pact with each other to relinquish it and we tossed it out of the helicopter off the coast of Santorini.'

Julien let out a whimper-laugh. 'How the hell are we going to find that now? Don't you think the Easter Island one – or even the one at Angkor Wat – might be easier to locate than one lying somewhere on the seabed in the Mediterranean Sea?!'

'That's true,' said Joey. 'But at least we know the one in Santorini is intact.'

'Did you happen to obtain coordinates when you dropped it?' asked Julien with no small amount of sarcasm.

'No, sir,' answered Boyce.

'Well, then, the answer is no!' Julien said forcefully

before turning to face the captain. 'Turn this plane back to Easter Island. We take our chances that the stone when recovered will still work.'

The captain nodded his head, and the second he moved past the table to get to the cockpit, the most unexpected and peculiar thing happened, capturing everyone's attention.

The sliver of red dolerite that lay on the table seemed to leap into the air as the captain passed, and became stuck to his stainless-steel watch.

'Holy crap,' Boyce said, pointing to the captain's wrist. 'It's magnetic! This changes everything, sir. We can use giant magnets to locate the stone. That would make the stone off Santorini much easier to find.'

The relief among the group was almost palpable.

'Okay, then,' Julien said, his voice much calmer now.

'Wait a minute. Before we fly to the Greek island on a diving expedition,' said Joey with a grave expression, 'Julien, you need to make an important phone call.'

Chapter 31

The Hall of Records, Cairo, Egypt, 7:30 pm Local Time

From nowhere came the sound of an old-fashioned telephone so authentic that the hostages scanned the room for an antique. Dimitri grinned and answered after the fifth ring, letting his former boss sweat a little, having seen his caller ID.

'Hello, you have reached the temple of King Tut, how may I direct your call?' joked Dimitri to a petrified crowd resting against the limestone walls.

Nick flashed him a grin as he continued to pace up and down the line of hostages, keeping them at bay.

'I'm glad you still have your sense of humor,' replied Julien dryly. 'But it looks like you've lost your freaking mind.'

'My dear old friend, it's a shame it has come to this, but—'

'But nothing!' barked Julien. 'I need you to relax and not act on emotion. Too many people have already died. This needs to stop now.'

'They are just casualties of war.'

'Whose war?' roared Julien.

'My war,' said Dimitri coldly. 'And in my war, we play by my rules – do you understand?'

Julien took a breath. 'Okay, what now?'

'Firstly, tell Marie she hurt my feelings.'

Julien exhaled sharply. 'I see the stone she gave you didn't work.'

'No, it didn't,' said Dimitri, irritated. 'Maybe I should kill someone for it.'

'No, don't do that. Listen, we are on our way to find you the right keystone.'

'What do you mean *find* me it?' His voice was disgruntled and direct. 'What happened to the one on Easter Island? The one your female Houdini should possess.'

'Well, if you hadn't decided to blow up the entire site, this could have been easily rectified.'

Dimitri stood with his cell hard up against his ear, puzzled. 'What happened?'

'The keystone was crushed before Marie could grab it.'

Dimitri sighed in exasperation.

'We are currently on a mission to retrieve another,' Julien continued.

'The one in Angkor Wat?'

'No, there is another one.'

'How is there another one? The markings on the wall clearly depicted three sites. Egypt, Easter Island, and Angkor Wat!'

'We are heading towards the Greek island of Santorini. It appears the original keystone that was found in Egypt was tossed into the water off the coast. Somehow that fact slipped Boyce's mind when he was writing his report.'

Dimitri could hear the sarcasm in Julien's voice. He laughed, knowing it would have taken balls for the youngster to keep this secret from a man many feared.

'How long will this take?' asked Dimitri. 'I have hostages, and I'm feeling trigger happy – one has already paid the price.'

Nick smiled at his comment.

'I need a couple of days. I'm sure it will be worth your while in the end.' Julien paused, then continued, 'I know that deep inside you is a man I once called my friend. I understand the pain you feel for losing your family, but if you reveal the Stargate to the world, it will cause mayhem.'

Dimitri stood quiet as a mix of emotions tumbled through him, but nothing was going to deter him from the task at hand.

'You have twenty-four hours and no more,' he said coldly. 'Lucky for you Greece and Egypt share the same time zone, so I will start my stopwatch as of now.'

T minus twenty-four hours.

'But it will take us hours just to arrive in Santorini,' said Julien angrily. 'It's not enough time.'

'I don't care. This is my game, my rules, remember. One hostage will be killed every hour after that. So, if I run down to my last captive, I will have no choice but to send a second video to the media. One I have pre-recorded that shows the inner sanctum and its purpose. I suggest you act swiftly. Time is ticking, and you *will* get me that stone, unless you want the world to know we are not alone in the universe.'

'Okay, Dimitri,' said Julien in a flat voice. 'I will contact you when I have it.'

'I'll be waiting.'

'And what happens if your phone runs out of battery?'

'I have a portable power-bank charger. I'm good to go.'

'Okay, fine.'

'When you're done with all this chit-chatting, can you organize someone to bring us some food and water? Unless you want my pawns down here to die from dehydration and hunger.'

He cut the phone dead.

Chapter 32

The DGSE Gulfstream Aircraft touched down at Thira International Airport, located 124 miles south-east of Greece's mainland. With its reputation for dazzling panoramas, romantic sunsets and volcanic sandy beaches recognizable around the world, it was hardly surprising the island of Santorini featured on so many travelers' bucket lists. But this was no holiday. The clock had started, and they now had twenty hours before the first hostage would be executed.

Two dark, polished four-wheel drives met the aircraft with precision timing, their headlights blinding those emerging from the plane. Three armed men in complete military attire stood motionlessly around their vehicles, and their presence was explained when another man stepped from the first vehicle. In his perfectly fitting, expensive-looking suit, it was clear this stocky man was someone of importance.

'Looks like our escorts are here,' said Julien, who led the entire crew down the stairs with open arms and a growing smile. 'Hey, *malaka*!' he shouted jokingly over to the stocky man.

The stranger laughed at the general's comment. As he approached they saw he was about the same age as the general with dark, curly hair and a twelve o'clock shadow, but his grin was as wide as Julien's.

Boyce was intrigued. It was a rare sight to see the general so happy; usually his customary grave expression seemed cemented on his face. It reminded Boyce that Julien was not a machine who only lived for the drama of work. He was like everyone else. He had friends; he just happened also to hold one of the most important positions in the known world.

As Boyce moved away from the plane, the cold, which had appeared mild at first, started numbing his face. It was winter in this part of the world, after all, he reminded himself.

'It's been far too long, my friend,' said the Greek-accented man. He reached forward and pulled Julien towards him into a warm embrace, after which he held his shoulders at arm's length.

'It sure has, Kypros,' Julien said. 'I'm sorry it has to be under these circumstances and at this time of night.'

'No problem at all,' said Kypros. 'Don't be stupid … You came to Santorini at the best time of year. Tourists stop coming in December and a lot of the locals go back to Greece for work. We will be at the marina in no time. *Ahte pame*,' he finished in his native Hellenic language.

'Joey and Marie, you two take the other vehicle.' Julien pointed loosely over to the second SUV. 'Boyce, you come with me.'

They all climbed in and immediately the BMWs accelerated sharply away, leaving skid marks behind on the tarmac.

The first thing Boyce appreciated was the heated air-conditioning. But he soon became aware of the strong smell of Kypros's cologne. He pinched his nose, and Julien observed his reaction and gave a tiny smile, as if he too found the scent overpowering. Looking around the plush interior Boyce admired the white leather seats and expansive sunroof, thankfully closed against the cold, although the fresh air might have given them some relief from the cologne's fragrance.

'How do you know each other?' Boyce asked, no longer able to contain his curiosity.

'Let's just say I saved your boss on numerous classified occasions,' Kypros replied quietly, as if lost in his own thoughts.

'We go way back,' said Julien.

Kypros smiled and scanned Boyce up and down. 'He's a little young to be operational, surely?'

Julien's response was a small sigh.

'I'm sure if Julien has taken you under his wing, he has seen the potential within you. Trust me, boy, you couldn't be in better hands.'

'I know,' said Boyce, staring at the stranger in the front passenger seat. 'I'm lucky to have him in my life.'

As the two men chatted, Boyce noted that Kypros didn't seem to have a cynical bone in his body; he seemed always high-spirited, polite, with an exuberant nature. *How could such a lightweight have saved the general?* Boyce wondered. In that instant, Kypros's demeanor turned serious and he started to discuss their current dilemma, and Boyce knew it to be true.

'All arrangements have been made and funded, giving us an open checkbook to go about our business,' Kypros informed them. 'We have three operational submersibles that have been rigged with giant magnets as you requested. And we have been searching for the keystone since the moment you first alerted us. Utilizing the record of the previous chopper's fly-over path, taken in late April of 2018, we have compiled reports of where the stone could have drifted and might have landed off the coast.'

'So, you know of the keystone?' asked Boyce, wondering how many other people had been privileged with this information.

'Of course I know about the key, I'm Greek.' Kypros laughed ebulliently. 'I know everything.'

'But you still wear a Christian cross around your neck,' Boyce pointed out shrewdly.

'I like this kid,' said Kypros with a wide grin. 'He's observant.'

'How are you mapping the sea floor?' asked Julien, ignoring the banter between the two.

'We're using high-end GPS technology that tracks our location. This is so we don't comb over the same surface twice. It's an amazing piece of software that runs the subs manually without the need for human interference. This program was also created by a talented man who lives on the mainland.' Kypros smiled proudly. 'Are you Greek?' he asked Boyce. 'You look Greek.'

'No, sir, I'm French.'

'Ah, I'm so sorry,' he replied with a roaring laugh. 'Nobody's perfect.'

'He does that to everybody.' Julien was trying to hold in a smile. 'Cheeky bastard.'

'No, he's a cheeky *malaka* who uses way too much cologne,' Boyce blurted out, and the car erupted with raucous laughter. Even Julien couldn't keep a straight face.

'I *really* like this kid,' said Kypros once he'd calmed down. His earnest face returned to business. 'I have a speedboat waiting that will take us out to the ship. Will all four of you be coming on board?'

'Is the Artemis suite still available?' asked Julien.

'Of course,' answered Kypros. 'Always available for you.'

Julien inclined his head, pleased. 'Can we contact the BMW behind us?'

A call was made across the inbuilt car system.

'Hi, Joey and Marie, it's Julien. Considering what you two have been through, I have decided to let you both sit this one out.'

'What do you mean?' asked Joey through the speaker phone. 'You might need our help.'

'I appreciate that, Joey, but you are dealing with a concussion and your wife is pregnant,' Julien reasoned. 'I'm going to send you to an amazing villa so you two can relax. You can treat it like a second honeymoon. Rest, and when we find the keystone, I promise I will keep you informed.'

Kypros then spoke in Greek to the two drivers before ending the call, and the vehicles broke away in different directions.

Not long into the drive, the road began to wind up a cliff road into some hills, where Boyce could make out goats, grass, and rocks on one side of the car. But on the other were breathtaking scenic vistas of the sea reflected by the moonlight. Boyce imagined that in the daylight, the Mediterranean water would be an ultramarine blue, deep and rich like he had seen on TV.

'Not long now,' said Kypros as they started their descent and entered Port Athinios, located at the bottom of an enormous cliff that looked like it belonged in a *Jurassic Park*–themed movie.

When the car drew to a stop Boyce exited and stretched his legs, and spotted a throng of fishing boats tied up against a jetty.

Julien glanced at his watch with raised eyebrows.

'The boat is waiting,' said Kypros, showing the way.

Boyce and Julien were ushered to a twenty-foot-long, mean-looking speedboat equipped with a single 150-horsepower Mercury engine and giant spotlights that were blinding.

The three men hurried onto the vessel where a man stood waiting holding onto the mahogany steering wheel.

Boyce sat down on one of the many weather-resistant swivel seats and braced himself as the engine roared to life, leaving him grasping at his chair. The wind gushed through his hair as the boat cut through the water like a knife. Soon, the island became a distant blur. All that mattered now was to continue to move forward in the hope of finding the long-lost secret keystone.

Chapter 33

Naval Ship, Santorini Waters,
12:30 am, T Minus 19 Hours

After a short trip out to sea, a grand naval ship appeared in front of them, dwarfing anything in its vicinity. The vessel was a dark shade of gray with spotlights that circled its perimeter. Before the speedboat moored onto the larger vessel's docking station, Boyce craned his neck to take in the grandeur of the ex-warship.

'Welcome aboard my ship,' chirped Kypros with open arms.

'This is *your* ship?' Boyce said in awe, now understanding the seniority of the man.

'Come on, *malaka*, let's go,' said Kypros with a joyful laugh that continued as he climbed the stepladder. 'I have a lot to show you both.'

Julien followed with Boyce behind him, still gazing up at the ancient rusting metal before him. Up close he could see that the paint was peeling and blistering like a bad sunburn. The lifeboats were hanging on rusted chains, and the noisy, vibrating engines rattled everything that wasn't strapped down, but there was no denying this ship was as strong as they came. Capable of landing aircraft, launching missiles, and all the other necessary functions of war. In this particular scenario, it had transported three submersibles on a search mission to find a rare magnetic artefact.

'Where are we going?' asked the general, close behind his old friend.

'Computer room,' said Kypros, leading the way. 'It's on the upper deck.'

After a few levels, they found themselves ducking and entering through a single-hinged, weather-tight, stainless-steel door. Once through, they found themselves in an open space literally covered in tech gear: blue cables, dim lighting, numerous workstation consoles, radar and sonar repeater displays, electronic devices in different sizes, and LED monitors mounted all over the walls.

'The CIC,' said Julien.

Boyce frowned.

'Sorry,' said Julien. 'It stands for Combat Information Center.'

Boyce nodded and thought that this must be what it was like to be in a NASA control center.

'This tactical room is now a search-and-rescue base,' said Kypros, who spoke to a well-groomed navy officer in dark-blue attire, who was waiting patiently to be of service. 'Report, Lieutenant?'

The lieutenant stepped forward, and Boyce saw that his sleeve rank insignia was emblazoned in gold.

'Nothing definitive yet, sir,' he said in perfect English, presumably for the guests' benefit, Boyce thought. 'We've picked up some shipwreck debris, but nothing of significance. The submersibles have already covered a wide area, and we continue to rotate the three around the clock.'

'What do you mean, rotate?' asked Julien, his eyes focused on one of the monitors that was beeping and showcasing two flashing dots.

The lieutenant was given the nod from Kypros to proceed and he indicated an iPad displaying three graphs, with submersibles one, two and three clearly labeled. 'These vessels are powered by diesel petrol, so we run two at a time while we fuel the third, then we swap them when the next runs out of diesel, which is every two hours.'

'Kypros was saying these pods are controlled via a software program?' asked Julien.

'Software created by a Greek man,' interjected Boyce, receiving an exhaled gasp of laughter from Kypros and a puzzled expression from the lieutenant.

'I *like* this kid,' said Kypros.

'That is correct, sir,' the officer answered Julien's question. 'Everything is automated and managed from this control room. The pods run themselves and have anti-collision sensors to make sure they do not run into any unexpected rock formations or large objects in their path.'

'What happens when shipwrecks are in the way?' asked Julien.

'They will correct their course and divert around any

obstacle,' the lieutenant answered confidently. 'We are able to use the most sophisticated technology at our disposal now that Magnus Industries has funded us.'

Boyce raised an eyebrow at again hearing the billionaire's name and his interest in all this, but chose to keep his mouth shut. The last thing he wanted to do was upset the lieutenant, who was keeping a wary eye on him.

'I still can't believe no one is driving them down there,' said Julien with a shake of his head. 'Modern technology, eh?'

The lieutenant moved to a screen showing the internal view of two submersibles in motion, respectively labeled pods One and Two. 'As you can see here, each vehicle carries two passengers for observation purposes only. Pod Two is flying solo.'

'Impressive,' replied Boyce, observing the steering wheel turn itself.

Seconds later, Kypros coughed and broke the silence. 'Did you and Boyce want to go under?' he asked with a smile. 'We'll have a fueled submersible ready to deploy in about thirty minutes if you're interested. All you have to do is sit back and enjoy the ride, and with any luck the magnets will pick up our prize.'

Boyce took in a sharp breath and swallowed uncomfortably at the thought.

He glanced over at his boss, and judging by the grin on Julien's face, he already knew what the answer would be.

Chapter 34

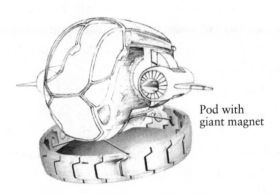

Pod with
giant magnet

The small compartment was made from thick steel that was able to resist the 1000 atmospheres of pressure at ocean depths. The rest of the horizontal column was made from a material called syntactic foam – a solid made mostly of hollow micro-balloons – giving it enough buoyancy to float back up to the surface. The sub had so many lights and cameras that it was like an underwater TV studio. Where the robotic arms would normally have resided, were now large circular magnets that would attract any dense metal that came across its path.

The pod submerged into the freezing water using a railing apparatus that was built onto the ship like a water amusement park ride. Julien's face lit up as they sank into the pitch-black sea. The twelve-thruster propulsion system launched them into a controlled downward descent.

Boyce covered his eyes with his hands and continued to shake his head.

'Take a look, Boyce,' encouraged Julien, knowing the younger man was completely out of his comfort zone. 'Isn't this one of the reasons you joined my team, so you can experience things like this? It's another world down here.'

Boyce peeked through his shaking fingers and sucked in a shallow breath. 'Look, I love boats, but I like to stay *above* the surface,' he said tightly. 'Plus I can't see anything. There's nothing but darkness down here.'

'You'll be alright,' Julien comforted him with a smile.

In the deep with the brine flowing past, there was freedom. Julien absolutely loved the sea and everything it had to offer. There was something about getting so far away from the bustling world that increased his sense of connection to it. The sea held so many secrets, so many treasures and stories yet to be explored and discovered.

The spotlights mounted on the submersible were their only eyes within the marine caldera.

'I just hope we find this keystone.' Boyce's voice

trembled slightly, along with the knee he couldn't stop bouncing up and down. 'It could be anywhere.'

Julien ignored the comment, his eyes glued to his plexiglass observation window. Even in the safety of the metal box, he could feel the temperature of the water drop, bringing goosebumps to his skin.

'Hello, this is the lieutenant,' spoke a voice from the inbuilt intercom mounted on the dashboard. 'You'll be hitting the sandy bedrock in twenty seconds.'

A low rumbling sound suddenly materialized around them.

'What's that?' Boyce practically jumped out of his skin, his eyes darting around in fright.

'Stay calm,' informed the officer, 'it's just the pressure from being thirteen hundred feet below sea level. Nothing to worry about.'

Julien admired the ever-changing panoramas that showed themselves in the light from the pod's spotlights. He initially fought to hold in his smile, but it was impossible, and he succumbed to the beauty before him.

The sea floor came into view.

Nearby was a rocky wall that seemed as tall as a skyscraper, broken up by fissures and caves. A school of blue-spotted stingray appeared out of the dark and sped right by as the sub maneuvered around the rock formation and approached the seabed.

'Preparing to lock and connect,' said the voice over the intercom. 'Five seconds.'

Like in a science fiction movie, the pod's thrusters came alive and adjusted the vessel to hover inches above the dark volcanic sand. A pinging sound increased in speed as the sub aligned itself on a course that was predetermined by the computer's GPS system.

'Three …

'Two …

'One …

'We have a lock, and the magnets have been activated,' the lieutenant told them. 'Good luck, gentlemen, sit back and enjoy the ride.'

'Here we go,' said Julien as the capsule accelerated at the speed of three knots, 3.5 miles per hour, displayed on the front console.

'If you glance at your two o'clock,' said the lieutenant, 'you'll see dim lights in the distance. That is Pod Two.'

Both Julien and Boyce turned squinting eyes in the direction the lieutenant had indicated.

'Pod Two?' repeated Boyce. 'Isn't that the unmanned one that's completely computer operated?'

'Don't worry, Boyce,' said the lieutenant. 'It's on another defined path that will not interfere with yours.'

'Great,' Boyce winced, rolling his eyes at Julien.

Julien proceeded to observe the monitors that scanned the floor as the beams from the submersible scared away the fish, leaving ripples in the dark sand.

'It's like finding a needle in a haystack,' Boyce complained. 'We could spend weeks down here.'

'Maybe next time you don't hide things from me,' Julien said scathingly. He leaned back uneasily, his mouth forming a pensive frown. 'We could have searched for it a year ago if you'd just told me you'd thrown it overboard.'

'And that's why we wanted to dispose of it,' said Boyce. 'It was a joint decision to do so. Humans can't help themselves. Someone would have sought it out to use it. I'm sure of it.' Boyce paused for a moment, then continued, 'You should be thanking me for keeping you uninformed. Can you imagine if Dimitri had known of the existence of this keystone, and that you had it in your possession? The Easter Island expedition would have been unnecessary. He could have stolen the stone from you and activated the Stargate without you even knowing until it was too late. At least we have some chance of stopping him now.'

Julien thought about it for a second. Boyce did have a point.

'You're right,' he told his young friend. 'But at least the entire world might still be in the dark. Now it's in the hands of a lunatic who's planning to reveal what we've tried so hard to keep secret.' Julien sat back in his seat. 'This is why we can't fail and must find the stone.'

Two long hours passed with nothing to report, and the lieutenant informed them it was time to return for refueling. The pod automatically realigned itself and started to ascend. Julien sat stiffly, his mouth set in a thin line while the magnitude of the situation swept over him. His shoulders were slumped, and his bleary eyes downcast. A saddened realization washed over him that they were coming up empty-handed.

This was going to end catastrophically for everyone.

Chapter 35

The empty shell that was the Hall of Records was lit up by rows of fluorescent tubes that were powered by multiple generators. Even though the enormous limestone cavern was flooded with overhead lighting, Dimitri found himself a dark corner in which to shut his tired eyes.

He left Nick in charge. His brother-in-law was given the task of keeping a close eye on the seventeen hostages while they lay together quiet and scared out of their minds. Five were children under the age of ten, who were now bundled up against each other, fast asleep. There was one boy in his late teens, almost a man, who needed to shave his overgrown stubble mustache. Two were overprotective women with peering eyes wearing hijabs, the traditional headscarves worn by Muslim women to cover their hair and neck, leaving the face visible. Nine were middle-aged men from all over the world. Half of them appeared to be of Middle Eastern appearance wearing the *ghutra*, a square white headscarf kept in place with a rope band.

There was absolute stillness in the eerie cave. Dimitri only realized he had fallen asleep when he was woken by an abrupt beeping sound. His eyes flew open, and he immediately rose to his feet and out of the shadows to rejoin Nick.

'We have visitors,' reported Nick, presenting the iPhone that was connected to a live surveillance feed, courtesy of the drug lord, Carlos. Two men, one carrying pizza boxes, the other carrying a large, clear-plastic-covered carton of water bottles, entered the secret tunnel. 'What do you think?'

Dimitri took back his cell and studied the footage. He observed the men's mannerisms, how they interacted, and how they carried themselves. Even though four dead soldiers lay in their path, it didn't seem to faze them. One of them gave a tiny nod of his head, and that's when Dimitri knew they were law-enforcement agents.

'We have food and water coming, but these men are officers,' warned Dimitri quietly. 'Nick, get ready; put on your balaclava.'

'I hate this thing,' said Nick grumpily, reaching into his jeans back pocket where he had shoved the lacerated beanie.

'As I told you before, I don't care if they see my face. I'm on a one-way trip, but for you … If you want to sell that gold tablet and live it up large somewhere, you need to stay anonymous.'

Nick slid on his headgear to reveal three uneven cuts for his eyes and mouth. He drew out his pistol and hid in the darkness of a corner, ready to pounce when needed.

Dimitri strode over and sat amongst the hostages, who turned to face him with widening eyes. He was outnumbered by the men in the group by nine to one, but he was armed, and they were not. 'Let's not forget who is in charge here,' he said in a soft tone so as not to wake the sleeping children.

Then in full view of the hostages, he extracted his golden Beretta and trained it on a young, innocent girl still napping, his finger loosely up against the trigger. Dimitri settled in and waited for his guests to arrive.

Minutes later, two men emerged, and the aroma of hot pizza engulfed the area.

Dimitri held his gun a little more firmly now. It was time to play.

'Don't shoot!' said the shorter of the two men, who were dressed in matching branded pizza company T-shirts. The second stood slightly behind the first. 'We have brought you food and water.'

'Yes, we can smell the mozzarella from here,' said Dimitri, eyeballing the men with a grin. 'Place the boxes and water on that low stone wall,' he ordered, pointing to a raised platform with a V-shaped groove cut into it that ran the length of the hallway. He knew it was a fire-channel wall used to bring light and warmth into the cold, dark complex.

'Where is your accomplice?' said the second man, the taller of the two, his eyes on the hostages. Dimitri guessed he was trying to gather intelligence to relay back to his superiors.

'Why do you care?' asked Dimitri lightly. 'Aren't you just the pizza-delivery boys?' His voice was dripping with scorn.

'Yes,' the man replied, more uncertainly this time.

'Listen to me carefully,' said Dimitri, fondling his semiautomatic in his right hand to make sure they could see he was armed. 'I wasn't born yesterday, and I've killed many men. I suggest you don't try anything foolish. Leave the food and water, back away and evacuate the same way you came in. What I'm doing here tonight has nothing to do with you.'

The shorter man moved his free left hand up to suggest he meant no trouble and slid the pile of boxes closer to the hostages, ignoring Dimitri's previous request. He gave a grim smile, and then, to Dimitri's surprise, he told the men and women everything was going to be okay.

Dimitri locked on to him with calculating eyes.

'Here ... take a slice,' the man said to the captives that were still awake. 'It's the best pizza in Cairo, some believe the best in the world.'

'Stop it!' warned Dimitri, his grip tightening on his pistol.

'I'm just helping.'

'Don't!' Dimitri shot back.

The man began to open the lid of the top box in the stack, but before he could reach inside, he staggered backwards and fell to the floor.

The gunshot cracked through the air as loud as thunder. The bullet had entered the man's chest and he now lay holding his gaping wound, fighting to stay alive, gasping for breath.

The five children woke up trembling and weeping, petrified. 'Mumma,' one cried, while another simply screamed, pure terror in his eyes.

The barrel of the Beretta blew smoke as Dimitri shifted it to the dead man's towering partner. He moved his hand with lightning speed to find his concealed weapon. It was as if it played out in slow motion for Dimitri as the carton of water bottles dropped to the floor.

'Die, motherfucker!' Nick roared, storming in with his gun held aloft. Four shots struck the officer's torso, the bullets hitting within inches of each other for the perfect assassination. The force propelled the officer backwards in an awkward cartwheel and ended his life before he had time to react.

Hunched together with their heads bowed, the hostages continued to weep.

Dimitri stood up aggressively. 'Quiet!' he ordered, approaching the man he had shot, who was still fighting for his life. The hole in his chest oozed with dark, congealing blood and the distinctive smell Dimitri had become accustomed to in his line of work.

'You had a choice. I told you to leave the pizzas and walk away,' he said, standing above the dying man, shaking his head in disapproval. 'But you decided to be brave ... You elected to test my wrath. Now you will die.'

Blood gushed with sickening relentlessness from the man's chest. His fingers scrabbled wetly over the wound, and his face turned paler by the second. He gulped blood that now flowed out of his mouth until a few moments later, he succumbed and his body went slack.

Dimitri withdrew the firearm concealed within the cardboard box and took a slice of pizza, stretching the cheesy topping away. He took a bite and closed his eyes approvingly. 'It truly is tasty,' he said, devouring it while the hostages stood and watched. The fear in their eyes was apparent, and that was exactly what he wanted from them. If they thought he was a madman, they would think twice before trying to defy his orders, or worse, trying to escape.

'It's been a long night,' said Dimitri, frisbeeing some of the boxes towards the hostages, who grabbed them eagerly. Then he tore into the carton of water and separated a couple of bottles for Nick and himself before passing those, too, on to his captives. 'But best in the world?' he said in a voice heavy with sarcasm. 'I don't think so.'

Nick picked up the firearm from the mutilated officer he'd shot and joined Dimitri away from the pack. He removed his balaclava and shoveled a warm slice of pizza into his mouth, liberally smearing tomato sauce over his lips.

'We need to talk about our insurance policy,' said Dimitri quietly. 'You realize the hostages have seen your face.'

'Soon they all will be dead, brother,' replied Nick.

'But if we do get to that point, maybe we spare the children.'

Nick gave his brother-in-law a hard glare. 'You really are getting soft in your old age.'

Dimitri didn't answer and turned to see the young, hungry mouths devour their last supper. A sadness came over him, knowing these kids were probably eating their last meal inside this cold, dingy place.

But they were the casualties of war.

Chapter 36

After a torturous two hours that had left them empty-handed, Boyce and Julien went to their rooms to get some much-needed sleep. Kypros and the lieutenant assured them that the search would continue through the night and their help was not needed.

Julien found his bed, a narrow bunk that left his long legs dangling off the end.

Boyce wanted nothing more than to lie down and be enveloped by warmth and silence. Still dressed in his military greens, he shrugged off his boots and fell into bed. The instant he laid his head on the pillow, he fell fast asleep, and his dreams took over.

Boyce was in a world where the sky was consumed by an orange glow. Two full-shaped moons hung in the distance, and the landscape was an ever-receding hill of grass and trees. The image blurred to a church-like cavern where a gigantic golden medallion depicting the sun god Atum was raised high with the support of thick bulky ropes. The strangers gathering around him were clearly not human, and they spoke a strange dialect. Their large heads were elongated, and as they approached him, Boyce's vision began to swim.

He blinked his eyes, and an eerie feeling washed over him as he found he was now walking through dark catacombs. Bending over to move through the low-ceilinged space, he discovered a scroll that was written in the native Egyptian hieroglyphics. This parchment had lain dormant for a millennium. The humidity and small insects had done their job, making it virtually unreadable.

The scene blurred again, and now his sight was filled with the murky shapes of flickering lights and he was being transported by a dodecahedron-like vehicle that hovered an inch off the ground. Outside he could see an urbanized metropolis that was flooded by a sea of people. These people shared the same unusually shaped skull, and they all seemed to be heading in different directions, in a place where buildings pierced the sky and were alien and astonishing in their architecture.

He passed through an area where concentric rings alternated between water and land. The water served as canals and helped form natural defenses that would make an invasion extremely difficult. In the innermost circle were palaces and temples that most likely honored the all-important sun god. In addition to the magnificent architectural structures, a network of bridges and tunnels linked the rings of land.

It was a breathtakingly beautiful sight to behold.

It was the lost city of Atlantis.

Boyce heard a crackling sound, and in the distance, the sound of clanking metal drifted away into nothing. The landscape now turned from a lush and healthy green-blue to a dry and desolate orange-brown. A dry wind blew sand into his face. Boyce stepped towards the rolling sandy hills as the sun's rays fell upon him, and there discovered not one, not three, but eight colossal pyramids. Each had their own obelisks lined up in perfect symmetry as identification markers that were the mysterious ancient graveyard used solely for teleportation purposes.

Now the Stargate, glistening like the surface of a pool held vertically, filled his vision. Boyce advanced to face it, and with an outstretched hand, the ring's energy reached out, surrounded him, and took him whole. He was sucked into the vortex.

Chapter 37

Naval Ship, Santorini Waters, 11:30 am, T Minus 8 Hours

Buzz … Buzz … Buzz …

Boyce opened his eyes and breathed long and slow, leaving the vestiges of the nightmare behind. It would be easier to recover if he had not lived through those experiences, but he seemed incapable of letting them go. He wiped the sweat from his forehead and looked through his port window, where he saw that the sun had risen. It took a moment for him to ascertain his surroundings. He was on a ship and could feel the gently swaying sea around him. He leaned over to pick up his cell, which was continuing to vibrate on the blue-carpeted floor, and found Joey on the other end of the line.

'Hey, brother, how's it going?' asked Joey in his casual American accent. 'I never heard from you, and I'm starting to worry, and so is Marie.'

'What time is it?' asked Boyce, rubbing his sleepy

eyes, still dressed in his military attire.

'It's eleven-thirty,' said Joey, and Boyce could hear his anxiety in his voice. 'What's going on, man? Tell me something.'

'Holy shit, I must have slept in,' Boyce muttered under his breath. 'I crashed at three-thirty this morning.' He thought about the time for a moment before blurting out, 'That means we have only eight hours before Dimitri starts killing hostages.'

'That's why I'm calling you,' said Joey. 'We're getting restless. Where's Julien, is he with you?'

Boyce's eyes shot to the general's empty bunk bed. 'No, he's not here.'

'With any luck, he might have found the keystone,' Joey said hopefully.

'Hang on,' said Boyce, quickly putting on his boots and leaving the room, still clutching his cell in his hand. He retraced his steps of the night before to the upper level, where he entered the busy computer CIC room to see flickering lights, accompanied by a familiar scent.

'Good morning, Boyce,' said the ever affable Kypros. 'You look like you need a strong Greek coffee, my friend.'

'I sure do,' said Boyce with a warm grin that changed instantly when he noticed the TV monitor depicting the interior of Pod One. 'Julien is down there,' he said, anxious to see the general's profile. 'We still haven't found it?'

'No.' Kypros lowered his head. 'We haven't found the stone. This is Julien's second dive this morning.

He insisted on going under as soon as he got up, even after having had only a few hours of sleep.' Kypros paused for a moment as Boyce stared at the display apprehensively. 'He sure is a persistent man.'

'I totally understand why,' shot back Boyce. 'We have single digits remaining on the clock before the lunatic in Egypt starts knocking off hostages, one per hour ... Time is critical.'

'We still have some time, son,' said Kypros, placing a comforting hand on his shoulder. 'Don't worry, we will find it before that happens.'

Boyce sighed and wandered absently towards the outer deck and the fresh breeze that blew across the Mediterranean Sea. He placed the phone up against his ear to his friend, who was eagerly awaiting a response. 'It doesn't look good, Joey ... Doesn't look good at all.'

Chapter 38

The Hall of Records, Cairo, Egypt, Time Runs Out, 7:30 pm

Dimitri stared at his altimeter stopwatch as the timer hit zero and erupted into a beeping sound. He cracked the knuckles of both hands and turned off the noise, which had caught the hostages' attention. Their eyes widened, and their breathing became ragged. Their hands twitched, and some of them started crying.

'Who will it be?' Dimitri said evenly, stepping over the empty scattered pizza boxes among the loose limestone debris. 'Someone must die.'

Nick walked behind him, holding the officer's nine-millimeter, while his own Beretta was tucked away in its holster, and the hostages cringed at the sight of him.

'How about you?' asked Nick, stopping and pressing the barrel of his gun up against the chest of a man with a receding hairline. 'Should we kill you first?'

'No! No! Please, don't!' the man begged, before

dropping to his knees and covering his head with trembling hands. 'I don't want to die.'

All grew deathly silent. Even the querulous children who had been bickering and sulking only seconds ago were now pressed under the arms of their protective mothers and not making a sound.

'I'm sorry, but one person must die,' said Dimitri, toying with them. 'Any suggestions on who goes first? Don't worry, there will be another in an hour's time.'

The silence echoed in the cavern as the seconds ticked by.

'Perhaps we should execute the oldest first and work our way down,' suggested Nick.

'Fabulous idea,' said Dimitri with a dramatic nod of his head. 'Now, who's the oldest person here?'

The ideal candidates were among the nine men. Two were definite contenders with wrinkled skin and gray-white hair around their balding, mottled scalps.

'Which of you will it be?' asked Dimitri, indicating the two men, who stared at each other hopelessly with sunken eyes.

Nick advanced and slowly raised his weapon to point at the two men, who swallowed hard and found themselves standing alone as the prisoners moved away from imminent danger.

'Close the kids' eyes,' ordered Dimitri.

'Do you know each other?' asked Nick.

'Please don't kill us,' said one of the men who possessed a beak-like nose. His voice shook. 'We have known each other for forty years.'

'We are long-time friends,' said the second man.

'It's only fair that one of you dies,' said Dimitri. 'You both have lived long lives. I'm sorry it has come to this for you. So, who will it be?' he asked, staring deep into the eyes of the two experienced souls.

Paralyzed with fear, the man with the crooked nose pointed with a shaky finger. 'I'm so sorry, Anjem,' he said, then turned back to Dimitri. 'He is the older one. He's seventy-five, and I'm seventy-two!'

'How could you?' said Anjem, the betrayal written over his face.

Dimitri's eyes narrowed. 'Thank you for making it so much easier for me to decide,' he said, turning to face Nick, who was waiting to receive instructions. '*Scotóse afton pou éhi megalo stóma,*' he said.

Nick smiled, aimed his weapon, and depressed the trigger without any remorse. The tattletale took a close-range bullet in the heart. It tore effortlessly through his soft human tissue, perforating his vital organ, and the sound reverberated in the vast, empty shell that was the Hall of Records. Killed instantly, the old man fell to the floor amongst the pizza boxes, his mouth ajar, his eyes still open, freezing the shocked expression that would not now be erased from his face.

A puddle of urine spread around the miserable Anjem, who knew he had escaped death only temporarily.

'That's disgusting,' said Nick, pushing him away to return to the rest of the group.

Dimitri held up his hand and waited for everyone to turn to face him. He was the dictator making all the rules, just as he saw fit. 'One thing I despise more than anything else in the world is a tattletale,' he said, shifting to Anjem, who was still trying to catch his breath. 'In an hour, Anjem, you will join your friend in death, so don't get too comfortable.'

Chapter 39

Submersible, Santorini Waters,
7:35 pm

'Attention, Pod One. Julien, do you read?' the lieutenant's voice erupted through the internal speakers mounted on the computer console.

'Yes, Lieutenant,' responded Julien. 'I read you loud and clear, what's up?'

'We've just received a message that has come in on your cell, sir. It appears to be from Dimitri.'

'It's not good, sir,' said another distinctive young voice.

'Boyce?' Julien asked.

'Yes, sir, it's me.'

'What the hell is going on up there, tell me straight.'

'Dimitri has executed his second hostage,' Boyce said in a deflated voice. 'Every hour from now on, sir, one life will be lost.'

'Hang on, I will patch the communication through to your sub's monitor,' said the lieutenant. 'So you can see what we are seeing up here.'

Moments later the message appeared on the screen, accompanied by a photo of an old man with a bullet in his chest.

The text read: *Now you have sixteen hostages left … Time is ticking …*

Every word stung, fueling the fire that burned inside of Julien. His fists clenched and his jaw ached from grinding his teeth so hard. Then he exploded, punching the solid metallic wall that surrounded him. 'I'm going to kill him,' he burst out.

'Remain calm,' cautioned the lieutenant. 'Don't forget you're thirteen hundred feet below the surface. The last thing you want to do down there is damage the only thing keeping you alive.'

The general exhaled a long breath and leaned back in his chair. He took a moment and stared into the dark ocean; the only place in the world he felt completely at ease. His mind took in the rhythmic percussion of the sub's propulsion system, and a blurry vision of a boy fluttered into his line of sight. He blinked his eyes, but the boy's face was still there and as clear as day.

'You're not real,' he said in a whisper, knowing it was his imagination playing games with him. It was an image that had come to him for forty years. A nightmare he could never escape.

'Ezra,' he murmured, reaching forward to touch the perspex panel that separated them. 'I'm so sorry I wasn't there for you,' he finished with a sadness that could never be healed.

'Sir, what did you say?' asked the lieutenant. 'Please repeat?'

Julien didn't respond, still staring out into the darkness of the abyss.

'I think he's hallucinating,' said Boyce. 'How long has he been under?'

'He's been down all morning,' informed the lieutenant. 'He insisted on going under with each new deployment.'

'I think you should bring him up, he's had enough,' said Boyce firmly. 'He's talking about a boy called Ezra. A boy who was murdered a long time ago by men who called themselves the Guardians of Egypt.'

Julien muted the volume that was coming from above. His mind tried to make sense of the image he thought he could see amid the bubbles. Squinting, he tried to find Ezra again, and his thoughts traveled back in time to the tragedy that had taken place beneath the Red Sea.

Muffled gunshots were heard below sea level. Ezra panicked, and a plume of bubbles escaped his mouth. Julien kept the regulator in Ezra's mouth and tried to keep him calm. The rhythmic sound of breathing intensified for both of them as they knelt on the seabed and waited. Something substantial penetrated the water above.

It was Ezra's father, who had been gunned down and tossed into sea as though he was nothing. Julien could see tears of anguish through Ezra's face mask. Julien comforted the kid with an embrace and checked his diving watch. They still had enough air; they just needed to wait it out in the hope that the murderers above would leave the scene.

And that's when everything turned to shit.

Anchored brick-sized objects entered the water all around them. Julien's eyes grew wide with fear. As one dropped behind Ezra, Julien realized they were explosive devices. He tried to yank the teen away to safety, but it was too late. One after the other they exploded, and the underwater world was turned upside down.

Ezra was pushed with incredible pressure to the seabed and collided with the ground, his scuba-gear mask and breathing apparatus smashed into pieces. Julien tried to reach him, but the boy was sucked into a whirlpool of currents and pulled in the opposite direction. As he drifted out of Julien's line of sight his body grew still, and Julien never saw him again.

Julien felt responsible for Ezra, his teenage friend who'd had an infectious smile and shared a passion for diving, a love he would never be able to pursue; could never now explore. This time, sixteen lives were at stake, hostages who were at the mercy of a crazed man and who would inevitably end up dead if they didn't intervene. Not to mention the lives that might be lost, and the utter turmoil and devastation that would ensure, if Dimitri decided to release the tape to the world that revealed the Stargate.

Julien had no problem handling the strain of his job. He was used to dealing with terrorists and murderers, but this was different. The stress of the situation spread through his mind, and he found himself inhaling deep, desperate breaths. He was coherent enough to realize that the pressurized air within this pod seemed to have taken its toll on him and unleashed many mixed emotions that had been buried for far too long.

The sonar pulses continued as the submersible ceased its course and realigned itself back to base. A sad realization washed over Julien; he was once again coming to the surface empty-handed. He felt defeated, and the fatigue was engraved on his worn face, as he awaited the inevitable disappointment.

Without warning, like a heavy brick hitting the bonnet of a car, the sub struck something hard and the instrumentation panel flickered ominously on and off.

Startled, Julien rudely pulled out of his reverie. His brain stuttered for a second, every part of him going on pause while his thoughts caught up.

'What in the hell was that?' he gasped, the shock only just registering within his mind. 'Lieutenant, something hit me.'

No answer.

'Lieutenant, do you read?' he said again, even as he realized why the communications had ceased. He quickly turned the comms back on and increased the volume to reveal the unexpected sound of joyful clapping and cheering.

'What's going on up there?' asked Julien, baffled by the merriment.

The brief outburst of laughter was quickly brought under control.

'We found it!' shouted Boyce, ecstatic. 'You found it, sir.'

'Look at your camera monitor,' the lieutenant said.

Julien leaned forward in his chair and saw an indistinct, milky cloud of bubbles on the screen. When the vision cleared he saw the triangular-shaped dolerite stone stuck up against one of the large circular magnets. 'The red keystone,' he muttered under his breath with a widening grin.

Julien sat up straight, his eyes bright once again. He tapped the camera above his head. 'Well done, everyone. Lieutenant, get me the hell out of this thing,' he said. 'I need to call this asshole ASAP.'

Chapter 40

The Anonymous Call,
7:50 pm

Kypros strolled along the deck of the navy ship, keeping a weather eye on things as the seas turned an eerie gray-green and a cold southerly swept through his dark, curly hair.

'Where are you going, sir?' the lieutenant called out. 'We're just about to have our first meeting.'

'I'll be there in a minute. I just need to make a quick phone call.'

The lieutenant nodded his head and left the superior officer alone.

Kypros dialed a number found in his contact list, and after a couple of rings, it was answered with a polite hello.

'Yes, it's me. I just wanted to inform you we have located the keystone.'

'That's fantastic news,' said the mysterious man on the other end. 'Um ... so you have it in your possession?'

'That's correct, sir.'

'This is the stone that will activate the Stargate?'

'Yes, sir, it is,' said Kypros, relieved to be able to deliver good news to someone who did not take bad news well. 'It's actually the original dolerite that was utilized to initiate the portal a year ago.'

'You've done well, Kypros.'

'Thank you, sir.'

'Now that we have both parts – the key, and the gateway between worlds – we can study and break down the advanced technology that was used to build them and propel our society forward into the future.'

'We have one tiny problem,' said Kypros, pausing before delivering the name. 'Dimitri Panos.'

'Yes, he's been all over the news. I wouldn't worry about him.'

'He has hostages and wants to use the keystone. We are formulating a plan now.'

'I understand … Do what must be done. I cannot be seen to be involved in any way.'

'Yes, sir. Don't worry, when this is over the key and the Stargate will be handed over to you.'

'Thanks for keeping me updated.'

'That's the least I can do for you, sir.'

Kypros ended the call.

Chapter 41

Naval Ship, Santorini Waters,
8:00 pm

On the bridge of the ship, Julien stood and waited. His phone and the keystone lay on a table behind the captain's chair which was normally used to roll out maps and plot new courses.

The phone's speaker was activated so all could listen. Kypros, the lieutenant, Boyce, and two soldiers with broad shoulders paid close attention as Julien put the call through.

After five long rings that seemed to go forever, Dimitri answered.

'I hope you have good news for me, Julien. I'm not in the mood for old-time banter.'

'We found the keystone as promised,' Julien said gravely. 'Now, you need to stop the killing of innocent hostages if we are to trade.'

'And how do I know you're not lying? That this isn't just another ruse of yours to buy more time?'

'Hang on,' Julien replied, raising his handheld device. He took a quick photo of the stone, then texted the image to Dimitri. A long pause followed as Dimitri checked his cell to identify that the red dolerite was in fact real.

'*To éhi*,' Dimitri said in Greek, his voice filled with excitement.

'I delivered my end of the bargain,' reiterated Julien as he returned the phone to the table.

'Yes, you sure have.'

'I will be in Egypt in around two hours.'

'Excellent, I'll be waiting. I have one more request from you.'

'What's that?'

'Make sure you and the three musketeers deliver me the keystone personally.'

'I can't do that.'

'Yes, you can, or there is no deal.'

'Hasn't there been enough death, Dimitri?'

'Having them here ensures my safety. Julien, I know how you operate. I was your second-in-command for a long time. No tricks, no backup team, nothing. If I see anyone else enter the cave ... well, I'm sure you can use your vivid imagination.'

Chapter 42

Artemis Suite Villa, Santorini,
8:15 pm

Footsteps sounded outside the villa's freshly painted blue door. A loud double knock caused Joey to slide off his bed and turn to Marie, whose expression was grim.

'I didn't order room service,' she warned, still tucked up under the thick woolen blankets in their luxurious king-sized bed.

'Neither did I,' Joey breathed, on high alert.

'Be careful,' she whispered.

Joey cautiously approached the door, picking up a timber lamp on the way to arm himself. The tiles under his feet were cool, even though he wore thick cotton socks. He peeked through the peephole, and his shoulders relaxed.

'False alarm,' he said, opening the door to see two worried faces staring right back at him. 'It's Boyce and Julien.'

'What's with the lamp?' joked Boyce as Joey opened

the door to let them in. 'Don't you think it's a little too late to be decorating?'

'What are you guys doing here?' Joey asked as they stepped inside the room to greet Marie, who had climbed out of bed and put on a thick robe. 'Please tell me you found it?' asked Joey as he shut the door behind them.

Julien rolled his backpack forward, extracted the red keystone, and held it up high for Joey and Marie to see.

'Holy shit, you *did* find it,' Marie blurted out, her mouth agape at the welcome surprise. 'That's fantastic.'

'So why the sad face?' asked Joey, reading Julien's negative body language as he slouched up against the wall. 'Does Dimitri know you have it?' Joey placed the lamp back on its table then turned towards the two men.

'He does, and he has demanded that we four deliver it to him personally,' Julien informed him apologetically.

'He just wants to kill us all,' said Joey. 'Marie's pregnant; I can't put her through all that again.'

'Well, that explains your depressed faces,' said Marie.

'He thinks by having us all there it will secure his own freedom,' said Boyce.

Joey looked to Julien, who towered over him. He knew without a doubt that despite the difficult circumstances, Julien would have a plan of attack. The general lived for these situations, and Joey trusted this time wouldn't be any different. 'What's on your mind, sir, what do we do?' he asked.

Julien leaned away from the rendered white surface

and stood tall. 'I think we give Dimitri what he desires,' he said, sounding defeated. 'Let's give him the keystone,' he finished.

'Are you out of your mind?' Marie practically shouted, turning to face Boyce, who shrugged his shoulders. 'That's crazy.'

'But we can't let him activate the Stargate!' said Joey, confused.

'Don't forget that the last time the portal was activated, Cairo went into darkness,' Marie reminded the general. 'Not to mention this time we have news vans parked all over the Giza Plateau. Reporters will work out the connection, that whatever was down there was the reason for the blackout.'

Joey turned back to face the older man with the scar over his temple.

'There is no denying he has us in a precarious position,' said Julien, taking a seat on one of the many cane chairs that circled a glass dining table. 'We can't prevent him from revealing the truth,' he added, tapping a finger on the glass in front of him.

'We have to assume Dimitri will show the world the Stargate,' said Boyce. 'There is no way to know for sure if he has organized an automated email to be transmitted to a third party. A video could surface even if we got lucky and killed the bastard.'

'So, he has total control either way.' Marie frowned. 'Whether or not we give him the keystone, the world will most likely discover the secret that was kept hidden for centuries.'

'So why deliver him the stone at all?' said Joey. 'Let

the people find out there is a Stargate. If it can't be initiated, who cares if they know?'

'We can't just let sixteen innocent lives be taken,' said Julien. 'I couldn't live with myself if I didn't try to stop that.'

'I thought there were seventeen hostages?' asked Marie.

Boyce shook his head. 'He executed his second hostage and sent us a photo to brag about it.'

'The problem is not Dimitri,' said Julien. 'It's the goddamn Stargate. I suggest we flush him out, pretend to hand over the keystone, then blow up the portal.'

'Eliminate the threat,' concurred Boyce.

'And how do we accomplish that?' asked Joey.

Julien took a moment, and Joey watched the general fold his arms across his broad chest. His mouth formed a rigid grimace, and he tapped his foot nervously before he opened his mouth to speak. 'I have no clue.'

Chapter 43

The Hall of Records, Cairo, Egypt,
8:30 pm

Nick roamed the narrow hall in deep thought, carrying the backpack that would change his life forever. He found a toppled-over limestone block and dug into his bag to retrieve the golden tablet. He rested it on the smooth surface and ran his finger across the indented hieroglyphics, clearing away the dust to reveal its glistening shine.

Out of nowhere, a heavy hand landed on his shoulder and Nick flinched. He snapped round ready for a fight, fists squeezed, expression hard.

'What are you doing?' asked a familiar, authoritative, deep voice.

'Shit, Dimitri, you startled the hell out of me.' Nick's heartbeat slowed down once more.

'Never take your eyes off the hostages,' warned Dimitri, fixing his brother-in-law with his penetrating gaze. 'I need you to stay sharp down here. Julien will never give you a second chance.'

'Sorry, that won't happen again.'

Dimitri nudged his head towards the group leaning up against each other like cows in an abattoir waiting yard. 'It's been another hour. Time to execute the old man; what was his name again?'

'Anjem,' answered Nick, disinterested.

'Did you want to do it or do you want me to?' Dimitri asked evenly, almost casually.

Nick rolled his eyes at his brother-in-law's First World problems and turned to the solid piece of gold in front of him. 'I wonder what this inscription reads?' He changed the subject, leaning in to take a closer look at the strange circular shapes. Something about it was mesmerizing and made him want to touch it.

'This thing was concealed within the Stargate's frame,' said Dimitri. 'So, if I were a betting man, I would guess the ancient text might explain the gate's true purpose and who developed it, maybe even reveal the whereabouts of other gates.'

'There can't be another Stargate,' said Nick, straightening his back. 'The one here in Egypt is in the exact center of Earth's landmass. We know that's why they built the Great Pyramid here.'

'I see you also read Boyce's report.'

Nick nodded his head and squeezed the tablet back into his backpack protectively. 'You still haven't told me your plan that will help me escape this place unseen when you succeed.'

'Hey, what's wrong?' asked Dimitri, placing two hands against his brother-in-law's shoulders. 'Why are you stressing now?'

'I just want to be prepared.' Nick frowned as he ran the palm of his hand over his right eyebrow, which he often did when he was stressed.

'Have I ever let you down before, brother?'

'No, but—'

'Trust me. I have your back. I will always have your back. When this is all done and dusted, the Stargate will cause a blackout in the city and plunge it into darkness. That's how you will walk out of this place unnoticed. The chaos that will be going on outside will provide ample cover for your dumb ass.'

Nick raised a brow at that.

'But first, we need to set a trap for the true danger that is coming. It's simple, Nick … grab the keystone, ignite the portal, and kill all the witnesses.'

'Just like that?'

'Yep.'

'And the tablet?'

'That's the easy part.' Dimitri exhaled a satisfied breath and gave his brother-in-law a friendly nudge. 'If you want to read the inscription before you sell it, go to Hazim: the Director of the Ministry of Antiquities here in Egypt. He has a program on his phone that can be used to scan and translate ancient texts. The bastard stole it from Youssef.'

'Yes, I remember reading his name,' said Nick, brows drawn together. 'Wasn't he the man who discovered the secret key in Tutankhamun's mask that led them here? What did happen to him? Boyce wasn't specific in his report.'

'Let's just say he was eaten by a pissed-off crocodile.'

Nick, who was holding in an anxious breath, exhaled and finally gave a smile. Dimitri had a plan. He was always combat-ready. He was the smartest and most calculating man Nick knew. A reassuring feeling spread right through him.

'Ready to end this shit and start a new life for yourself?'

'Yes, let's do this.'

'Small steps, Nick, small steps. First … put a bullet in another witness's head. We can't have them thinking we've gone soft.'

'Consider it done.'

Chapter 44

Cairo International Airport, Egypt,
11:00 pm

After a short flight south over the Mediterranean Sea, the Gulfstream G550 aircraft touched down at Cairo's International Airport. This time Kypros, the lieutenant, and two of his officers accompanied Joey, Marie, Boyce, and the general. The two officers stood broad-shouldered, their eyes fixed on Julien, who would lead the team. It was as if they didn't trust anyone. They had a grave, concentrated expression over their faces and never smiled, and this made Marie wary of them.

A briefing was announced before the plane taxied to a stop and everyone gathered around. An arsenal of guns, bullets, explosive devices, and tactical supplies was spread over a considerably long foldout wooden table for all to see.

'Gee, you guys don't muck around, do you,' said Joey, rubbing his hands together delightedly and looking like a child in a candy store.

Unease blossomed within Marie. She was staring at the hazardous explosives that were clearly labeled C-4. 'How are we going to get all that into the country and past customs?' she asked.

'We have high-ranking officials that have granted us a safe passage,' answered Julien. 'Everything has been prearranged, isn't that right, Kypros?'

'Yes, of course,' Kypros said. 'Our connections here go way back.'

Marie flashed a smile, but the anxiety continued to manifest below her masked grin.

'Don't forget, this is Egypt,' said Boyce. 'Everyone here can be bought with Benjamin Franklins.'

'So, who's going in first?' asked Joey, gesturing over to the officers in their navy-blue uniforms. 'How are we going to do this? What's the plan to take this guy out? I'm hoping one of you two is a professional sniper so we can end this quickly?'

The soldiers didn't say a word.

Julien glanced at Kypros, who raised an eyebrow and followed through with a nod. It was as if they had pre-agreed on how tonight would go down, leaving Marie, Joey, and Boyce in the dark.

'What's going on?' Marie asked, not liking the body language. 'Like Joey said, what's our strategy?'

Julien looked each of them in the eye, which reassured Marie somewhat. 'If it were anyone else, yes, the best ploy would be to strike hard at the enemy, but this is no ordinary person,' he said. 'This is Dimitri, a highly intelligent major. We can't overlook the fact that he was trained under me. He knows all my tactical moves and defenses.' He paused for a moment just as the door to the aircraft was opened. 'If I were him, I would have hidden cameras concealed within the network of tunnels, and that's why the four of us need to go it alone.'

Julien turned to Joey, Marie, and Boyce, who didn't take the news so well.

'That's your plan?' barked Joey in disbelief.

Boyce frowned at his boss. 'You're sending us on a suicide mission!' he accused. 'Why do this alone? We have veterans here who can help us!'

'Hang on, before you all get touchy, let me remind you that every hour we wait, another hostage dies. We are approaching 11:30 pm. There are many innocent lives counting on us,' said Julien with conviction. 'Dimitri specifically mentioned on our call that no one else was to enter. If we risked trying it, we would be jeopardizing the lives of all those people.'

'So instead you endanger *our* lives,' Marie shot back, dumbfounded.

'Come on, that's unfair,' said Julien quietly.

'How do we know Dimitri hasn't killed all the hostages already?' asked Joey, folding his arms.

'It's his only bargaining chip,' said Kypros in a sharp tone. 'He won't kill them all; he would be stupid to do that.'

Boyce sighed heavily.

'We can do this,' Julien said encouragingly, never one to show fear. 'Kypros and his team will secure the outer perimeter. I will personally take out Dimitri and his accomplice, and all you three have to do is use the

C-4 to blow up the Stargate.' His hand signaled over to the device that was interconnected with wires.

'Oh, easy,' Joey joked sarcastically.

'Is it essential to blow up the portal?' Kypros asked mildly.

'It must be done,' said Julien, and Kypros hesitantly nodded his head and his gaze shifted away from Julien.

'Don't forget, we outnumber them down there and we have more firepower. The odds are in our favor,' Julien said reassuringly. 'Let's gear up. Lieutenant, did you want to take it from here?'

The decorated officer stepped forward and delivered a brief explanation on how to use the Heckler & Koch nine-millimeter full-sized sixteen-round pistol. He handed Joey, Boyce, and Marie one each, along with a fresh clip. Marie weighed the polymer frame in her hand, and comfortably slid it into her jeans. A couple of years ago, she had been repelled by guns. Fast-forward to today, and although she still didn't much like them, she was able to handle a gun as easily as she would her cell phone.

The meeting ended, and they were ushered out of the plane and down the airstairs. Inside the enormous hangar, two dark four-wheel drives were waiting. In front of them were two police vehicles with red-and-blue lights flashing, geared up to escort them.

A soldier put three canvas backpacks inside the trunk of the second SUV, and moving quickly, the group climbed in the cars and were on their way to the Giza Plateau. The cars sped along on the right-hand side of the road, and in the comfort of the plush air-conditioned vehicle, Marie's mind traveled back to the first time she had visited Cairo. As she gazed out of her window, she saw that even in winter, the air was thick with a *haze* that seemed never to lift.

'I can't believe we've been roped into this again,' Joey said quietly.

'We sure have been on a roller-coaster ride this past couple of years,' agreed Marie, touching her stomach. Her priorities had now shifted to the baby growing inside of her.

Boyce didn't say a word; his silence a sure sign of his anxiety. He always had something to say.

Joey squeezed Marie's hand and held it firmly the entire way.

After a short twenty-minute drive without traffic, the pyramids rose up into the night sky before them. All three triangular-shaped prisms stood like sentinels, dominating the skyline. Even though she had seen the large structures before, there was something mystical about them that transported her back in time to a vast desert landscape once ruled by the ancient pharaohs.

The vehicle bounced up and down as they diverted to the flat causeway that led to the Sphinx. The sound of the crushed rocks and loose debris under the tires sounded loud in their ears as they were directed past a plethora of news vans with their headlights on. The reporters lined the stretch of sand and spoke into their microphones, expecting to capture an exclusive as they filmed the SUVs passing through.

They reached their destination away from prying eyes and exited the vehicles to see the enormous limestone mythical creature with the body of a lion and the head of a human only a hundred feet away.

The same soldier removed the three backpacks from the trunk and placed one over Joey's worried shoulders. 'I don't want to alarm you,' he said. 'But you have the explosive equipment in your bag.'

Joey nodded but felt his heart rate increase.

'It's harmless to carry,' the private informed him. 'It's not armed. The trigger switch is in the bag.'

'Tell me again?' asked Joey with raised, trembling hands. 'Just a refresher.'

'The device is run by a control arm. Think of it as a square computer joystick. On it is a small stainless-steel toggle lever. When you flick this on, you will see six red flashing lights. These indicate the bomb is armed with the six C-4 blocks you will place on the target. Make sure you give yourself a secure clearing then depress the trigger. That's all there is to it.'

'Thanks,' said Joey, once again swallowing hard. 'I love it when the world is literally on my shoulders.'

Boyce couldn't help but chuckle at his comment. 'You've never failed us before. I'm sure you will come up with the goods again.'

Marie took in an audible deep breath as she was also given a canvas backpack. 'What's in this?' she asked.

'In your bag, there are winding flashlights that don't require batteries, flares, and medical supplies,' said the soldier. 'Better to be prepared.'

'You won't need the flashlights,' said Julien, stepping forward as the last bag was handed to Boyce. 'You will be carrying the keystone,' he told Boyce soberly.

'Remember, we are taking the stone to prove to Dimitri that we have brought it in good faith, but we risk everything if he gets hold of it. We must keep this away from him at all costs.'

Boyce nodded and they shared a fist bump.

'Good luck to you all,' said Kypros, pressing his hands together. 'I will be praying for your safe return.'

Marie winked at Joey, who pulled her close for one last embrace. Then, hands locked together, they approached the giant paw of the Sphinx that was lit up by the moonlight. Their journey into this godforsaken place was about to begin – again. This time Marie hoped it wouldn't go as badly wrong as it had the first time. Hope was all she had.

Chapter 45

Disgruntled Hostages
11:38 pm

Nick nudged the twelve remaining hostages down to their knees in the last secret chamber. They were all trembling, their chests heaving for breath. After a short conversation with his brother-in-law, Nick nodded his head and once again approached his anxiously waiting audience.

'I told you before that you would all see things that would blow your mind,' said Nick, holding his hands open and using a persuasive, engaging voice. 'Was I wrong?'

No one answered.

He paced in front of them, and they lowered their heads, like beaten dogs.

Nick suddenly slapped a man over his head, for no reason than for his own enjoyment, and the victim barked back in Arabic. Taking pleasure from this reaction, Nick drew his spare pistol, reaped from one of the so-called pizza delivery men. He swung the hilt of the weapon unexpectedly and sent the man crashing to the limestone floor, holding his battered skull.

'Leave him alone, you monster,' cried a woman in a navy hijab.

Nick addressed the woman, who had frightened children wrapped around her. 'What is your name?' he asked her.

'Aya,' she replied proudly, craning her neck to take in his much taller frame.

'Well, Aya, I have a question for you.'

Aya's watery eyes grew wide, clearly dreading what was to come.

'I need your hijab.'

'I can't give you that,' Aya said, shaking her head from side to side. 'I wear my headscarf because of my religious beliefs.'

'I need your hijab, too.' Nick pointed to the other woman standing a few feet away.

'No!' she immediately said in her limited English and thick accent, but she seemed to understand what he was after. 'I'm a Muslim.'

'I'm not asking you both, I'm telling you!' said Nick with a deep scowl meant to intimidate them.

'Sorry, I will never give you this,' Aya protested between clenched teeth.

Nick held in a smile and didn't hesitate, jabbing her in the nose with his gun, leaving behind a trail of blood that ran down her mouth. The children holding on to her screamed.

Aya struggled to remain upright, probably held

up by the crying kids clinging to her. She grasped her hands at her gushing nostrils to stem the bleeding. Her eyes were watery, and she appeared to sway from side to side.

'Give me this thing,' Nick roared with an outstretched hand, snatching the garment off her head to reveal her long, dark, curly hair, while she burst into tears.

'I can't believe you religious freaks,' spat Nick, holding the material in his hand. 'All religions have been invented by man for the sole purpose of controlling people. It dates back to the beginning of time. Look at this place – who do you think built it? If you want to believe in someone, believe in our ancestors who created this place.'

Nick shrugged his shoulders and swung his gun towards the other terrified Middle Eastern woman. 'Your turn,' he said, waiting. 'Allah won't mind,' he taunted.

Despite her sore face, Aya spoke out in Arabic.

The other woman nodded somberly. Slowly she removed the cloth from her head and fell to the ground, praying in her native tongue, repeating a passage over and over.

Nick neared two men with shiny bald heads. 'Don't lose these,' he said, handing the two hijabs to them. 'You will need them later on. Don't ask, just do what I say.'

The men hesitantly took the garments and continued to stare down at the ground.

With the pistol still in his hand, Nick sauntered back along the row of hostages, gazing upwards as he did so. He found his target, aimed and unloaded one complete round at the three spotlights. The bullets collided with the globes, and as they smashed, shards of glass rained down. Darkness once again fell upon an area in the super cavern, just as Dimitri had wanted. The stage was now set for what would be the ultimate showdown.

Chapter 46

The Sphinx Entrance

Marie felt humble as she stood between the creature's paws, each twice her height and about the size of a railroad passenger car. The Sphinx was carved from a single stone, and gave the impression that it was ready to lunge viciously at any intruder, yet at the same time taunting, daring that intruder to come nearer to the necropolis of Giza.

Déjà vu struck her when she spotted the opening in the timber deck. Her mind traveled back to Youssef and his thugs escorting them into the unknown, hoping to find the Last Secret Chamber and its precious treasure kept hidden for centuries; a wealth she now knew was the Stargate.

In the darkness, fast approaching midnight, Marie frowned and wondered why Julien had said that no flashlights were needed. She dug her hand into her backpack and handed Boyce a flare. He ignited it and was first to enter the tunnel system with caution.

A cheaply constructed wooden ladder led them below ground.

'I can't believe we're doing this again,' she said to Joey, who never left her side. 'The thought of this place creeps me out.'

'You'll be okay,' said Joey. 'This time we have the muscle on our side calling the shots. We're in excellent hands.'

'True, but at the end of this path is the devil himself,' muttered Marie, following the incandescent light that cut through the blackness, avoiding the loose stones that littered the entire floor. 'God, I hope Julien is prepared.'

The general entered last. His boots crunched on the soft sand underfoot as he jumped down from the ladder. The steely expression on his face told Marie he was no Boy Scout; he was the real deal, and under his leadership, they would be victorious.

Marie, Joey, and Boyce faced the limestone wall depicting the tri-spiral shape that symbolized the creation of the universe: a symbol found throughout the known world in relics of many ancient civilizations. But this was not just any cave drawing. It was an indented keyhole that opened a secret passage within the sandy bedrock. But the key that lay flush inside its groove was missing.

Grooved Symbol   Tri-Spiral Key

'With all this commotion, we didn't stop to think that we don't have the tri-spiral key,' Joey said nervously, as Julien advanced from behind.

'Hang on,' Marie said, darting her gaze to the floor, where a single solid boulder the size of a household door had once resided. Before she could vocalize what she saw, Boyce beat her to it.

'We don't need a key,' Boyce told them, moving the light of the flare over the lip of the hole. 'There's a metal brace holding the entranceway open.'

'I could have told you that,' said Julien. 'You'll see many changes down here.'

The incandescent flare in the teen's hand revealed another purpose-built ladder and a box-shaped room about eight feet under them.

A sudden putrid smell struck everyone in the face.

'What the hell is that?' Boyce blurted, pinching his nostrils. 'Joey, did you fart?'

'No, man.' Joey shook his head but smiled at the juvenile comment.

'No, that smells like ...' said Julien, pushing them aside. 'I'm going in first.' He extracted his Heckler & Koch, squared his shoulders and steadied his weapon before jumping the rest of the way. 'It's the four dead guards we saw in the Al Jazeera Live news report,' he warned the team above.

'Could be a trap,' Joey said, following the general down with his pistol raised.

The examination was unnecessary. A grotesque crimson was sprayed all over the smoothly rendered walls. You didn't need to be an expert to see the men weren't breathing. Following the two men down through the entrance, Marie looked away from the corpses and held her nose against the lingering stench of death.

Julien kneeled and removed a piece of plywood that had been placed over a hole in the ground, and an unexpected beam of light lifted from the surface.

'There are lights down there,' Joey blurted out in surprise. 'That's why we don't need flashlights.'

Julien nodded his head. 'This place has been part of a military operation for over a year now,' he explained.

'Can we please move on from this spot,' Marie said, gagging, her right hand cupped over her mouth as she found the precipitous descending stone steps that would take them further into the caves.

Julien nodded, and led the way down the steps.

The temperature dropped as they entered the underground chamber, sending a violent chill down Marie's spine. The passageway, barely ten feet high, had a slight decline to it, so the further they trudged into the vast tunnel system beneath the Sphinx, the deeper below ground they descended.

'The lights lead all the way to the Stargate,' said Julien. 'We have installed safe passageways and platforms throughout that avoid all the booby traps. As long as we stick to the ascribed path and follow the yellow tape and traffic cones, we'll be fine.'

Fifteen feet in and the walls suddenly came alive with richly colored drawings depicting ancient Greek and Egyptian battle scenes. With ample light illuminating them, Marie took a moment to appreciate the artwork, as the art historian in her demanded.

'I remember you,' said Joey, touching the wall where a tremendous sun motif was displayed. The ornate yellow image had sixteen separate pieces forming the sunrays, each of which extended outward to a sharp point.

'The symbol of Alexander the Great,' Marie supplied proudly.

'Yes, the man whose bones lie in Saint Mark's Basilica.' Boyce winked at Joey; they were among a privileged few who knew this.

'You sure have been through a lot, you three,' said Julien.

The artistry of the paintings made it seem like they were walking in a church with intricate stained-glass windows. The Greek art morphed into Egyptian, with side profiles of men and women giving offerings to their god. The sun image was always a focal point as they prayed and worshiped it.

They came across a man spread-eagled on the floor with a bullet hole in his skull.

'We've found the first dead hostage,' Boyce said as Marie pinched her nose.

Julien left the poor man behind as he trod further inside.

Three hundred and fifty feet into the subterranean system they reached the end of the tunnel, and Julien pressed a thick finger over his mouth, motioning them to keep quiet. 'This is where the hostages were filmed in the video,' he whispered. 'We need to be careful.'

Joey and Boyce extracted their Heckler & Koch pistols and exhaled slowly.

'I don't hear anyone,' said Boyce in a soft voice.

'You move when I move,' ordered Julien as they approached a flight of steps that they knew led to a long, expansive but narrow super cavern.

As they carefully mounted the steps, the cave stretched away from them, but this time, the whole hundred yards was lit up with enormous spotlights. His gun held firmly in his hand, Joey flashed a smile in Marie's direction, and she reciprocated with a nod. Then the wonder of the place overtook her afresh. Once again, she felt humbled by the grandness and scale that was the Hall of Records.

Chapter 47

The Hall of Records
11:45 pm

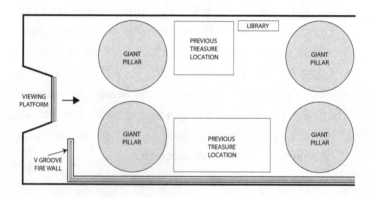

The vast chamber was the size of a football field, three stories high, but with a narrow thirty-foot width. Two pairs of monolithic pillars, strategically placed in the center of the room, divided the area into sections. Its ingenious design stopped your line of sight until you walked around them.

And when you did, Marie remembered, a treasure trove awaited, piled up to about the size of an Olympic swimming pool. Crown jewels, diamonds, silver plates, Egyptian statues, chalices, and countless sacred artefacts. Not to mention a rotting twenty-foot-long cedar timber bookshelf that housed books from the lost library of Alexander the Great. These included rolled-up papyrus scrolls, stone tablets, and texts that dated back to the beginning of time.

Marie's heart raced in her chest as they slowly and cautiously headed to the first massive column, which was ten feet wide with a five-foot gap on either side to walk through. She had never forgotten the site, and she knew the image would be embedded eternally in her mind.

The group was suddenly confronted by two colossal figures on either side of the hall, carved into the limestone bedrock. Marie knew the unmistakable illustrations to be Akhenaten and his beautiful wife, Nefertiti. Their presence made Marie feel like she was entering a place of fundamental importance.

She gazed up at the queen and her elongated head, aware that she was the one who had tried to hide this place from existence, secreting a key inside Tutankhamun's death mask that would open the doors to the Walk of Souls; a mask that was discovered to hold hieroglyphic text beneath Tut's name, marked there by an earlier individual.

His mother, Nefertiti, was its true owner.

'Our planet and the people in it owe this woman everything,' Marie murmured reverentially, rubbing her own belly, knowing she would have done the same thing for the safety of her own child.

'We sure do,' whispered Boyce as Julien edged ahead

of the group with his gun raised. He leaned up against the pillar and then stepped quickly into the open beyond it, ready to kill first and ask questions later.

'We're not alone, there are four men down,' Julien warned quietly, directing Joey to where he wanted him. 'Back me up.'

Joey approached fast on the general's opposite side. 'Careful,' he whispered, training his weapon on the four bodies just in case.

Julien nudged the men with his boot then kneeled down to check for a pulse. Moments later, he stood back up, shook his head, and lowered his gun. Marie and Boyce, who hung back a safe distance away, received the okay signal to progress. Marie's shoulders relaxed, and so did her rapidly beating heart.

'These two aren't hostages; they were undercover agents,' said Julien, glancing at an empty pizza box lying near the bodies.

'Why have they been laid out across each other to form a diamond shape?' asked Joey, now joined by Marie and Boyce, who were busily scanning the site.

'It's a keystone pattern,' explained Julien, surveying the crime scene. 'Seems like Dimitri has left us a note on a stick.' He grimly indicated a vertical staff, which rose up from between the bodies with a piece of paper impaled on it like a marshmallow on a skewer.

'He's playing with us, sir,' said Boyce. 'He's letting us know who is in charge down here.'

'He *thinks* he's in command down here,' retorted Julien in an authoritative tone. 'Joey, I need you to peek past the second set of pillars and cover the entrance to the Walk of Souls. Shoot anything that exits from it.'

'No problem,' answered Joey, handling his Heckler & Koch like an expert and moving with rapid speed.

'This guy is crazy,' said Boyce. 'He's leaving us breadcrumbs to follow, like Hansel and Gretel.'

'You have no idea,' Julien muttered as he carefully stepped over the bodies and carefully retrieved the note.

'Where are all the treasures in here?' Marie asked as he did so. 'This place looks like an empty parking lot now.'

'Hazim, the head of the Ministry of Antiquities, moved all the items to a secret location,' answered Boyce. 'He has a team working around the clock, cataloguing and analyzing the items.'

'I can't believe they even took the old rotten bookshelf,' said Marie before she was interrupted by Julien, who looked up from the paper and sighed deeply, meeting her gaze.

'What's wrong?' asked Marie, waiting. 'What does it say?'

He shook his head angrily. Then he flipped the paper around so they could all read the black text.

Follow the yellow brick road through the Walk of Souls and to the Last Secret Chamber. Your hostages await you at the Stargate. Time is ticking! ☺

Chapter 48

The Walk of Souls
12:00 am

Joey worked his way cautiously forward around the second set of pillars to cover the opening to the Walk of Souls. With both hands grasping his Heckler & Koch, he stopped short and noticed that the god of the underworld was still there. His eyes took in the replica of the Sphinx, shaped in the body of Anubis and carved out of solid black granite.

Even though he had seen it before, it took his breath away to see it in the blaze of overhead lighting. At half the size of its limestone twin guarding the Giza Plateau, it was still an impressive sculpture, one he knew had been wrought by a much older pre-dynastic civilization and not by Pharaoh Khafre, who had ruled in the fourth dynasty. This was a fact that would never see the light of day; one he would take with him to his grave.

'I don't remember it being so beautiful,' said Boyce, advancing from the rear and admiring the statue's reflective surface. Marie joined him, clearly mesmerized by its craftsmanship. 'At least we don't need to climb on it this time,' Boyce added, nodding towards the open passageway where the Walk of Souls began. 'No key needed.'

Joey scanned the area between the God-like creature's detailed paws, which comprised a set of stairs leading to the entrance in question. The huge granite doorway had moved upwards, into the rock, and was now secured there by an enormous steel plate. The modern-day contraption had stopped the load from falling and kept the entrance accessible to all who wanted to enter.

'Let's go,' Julien ordered, heading towards the entrance. With his back to the wall, he leaned over and peeked inside, his weapon at the ready. 'Coast is clear,' he said, waving a hand for them to join him.

Joey approached the steps, but he was frantically sifting through details in his mind. Something was missing here … Then, as quick as a flash, it came to him. The two sarcophagi that had previously lain here were gone. The shape of the funeral boxes had left a rectangular indentation in the rock.

In one of the coffins had lain Saint Mark the Evangelist: the person who had died as a martyr and was dragged through the streets of Alexandria with a rope around his neck. The man who had been honored with the Patriarchal Basilica, commonly known as Saint Mark's Basilica in Venice, which was said to house his remains. Another supposed fact that Joey knew not to be true.

Also, in the casket that had borne the religious cross, the saint had concealed and protected the almighty holy chalice, the cup Jesus and his disciples had used in the Last Supper. Joey had decided to leave this agate vessel on Planet X when he gave it to a bearded man who had helped them establish their course back home. The fact that this elderly man had had no idea what he was presented with had made Joey all the more certain that he was doing the right thing. No human on Earth deserved the glory of being in possession of the chalice.

But they had more immediate issues to deal with, so Joey decided to put the missing sarcophagi out of his mind. He pressed himself up against the hard surface adjacent to Julien.

Marie and Boyce trailed behind, tilting their heads upwards to face the enormous animal, both visibly in awe of their surroundings.

'Make sure to stay on the prescribed route to avoid the dangers,' Julien reminded them before ducking his head and entering the cave, gun first.

'Here we go,' said Joey, exhaling one last deep breath before signaling to Marie to follow and entering the cave beyond.

The first thing he saw was lines of electrical cables mounted along the wall. The floor was lined with four-inch-wide yellow pipes. They were similar to the fire hoses used by firefighters, which could produce a liquid velocity of six feet per second.

Out in front, Julien raked his eyes back and forth as they proceeded down the lit tunnel. The group moved in silence, which amplified the crackling sound of their footsteps.

'Those aren't loose rocks we're stepping on,' Marie said, cringing as she walked close beside Joey.

'Human skulls,' Joey said grimly while his boots crunched down on the scattered bones. 'At least this time, babe, you're wearing shoes,' Joey teased his squeamish wife.

'Don't worry, they won't bite,' Julien whispered back to them over his shoulder as suspiciously life-like noises could be heard rattling amongst the debris.

After a few yards, the hallway widened into a bright, tall box with a single arched tunnel up ahead.

'You will notice all the open spaces have been fixed with overhead lighting,' said Julien as they stepped into the box-like room. They were met by the penetrating stare of hundreds of hominid skulls stacked on ledges all over the walls.

'Our team went to exceptional lengths to safeguard this place.' Julien gestured to bricks and golden traffic cones encircling a hidden trigger stone; a trap that had left the current head of Egyptian Antiquities permanently in a wheelchair.

'Yes, let's avoid that trap,' cautioned Joey, remembering the roar that had come out of Hazim's lungs as the solid mass had crashed down on his leg, snapping his foot like a toothpick.

A hundred feet further in, the next hallway broadened into a large area that resembled the apse of St Peter's Basilica.

'Jump stones,' Marie said, joining the men at the

edge of the pit. A place where the floor fell straight down: a seventy-foot devil's drop. But this time was different; a bridge had been erected over the twelve tree-like pillars, delivering a safe passage across.

'This is too easy.' Boyce chuckled, leaning over the side to take a peek.

'I wonder if Nader is still down there,' Joey said sarcastically, remembering one of his three former kidnappers and the way he had been able to trick the man and turn the odds back in their favor.

'We are not here to relive your previous encounters,' said Julien, slowing to a complete stop. 'But the answer to your question is no. Nader is not down there. His body and many others were collected and buried. Let's keep moving, it's not far now. There are hostages and armed men at the end of this, don't forget.'

Boyce looked into Joey's blue eyes and gave him a wink. 'What you did here was genius,' he said with an impudent smile. 'That asshole got what was coming to him.' The two shared a fist bump.

The square tunnel widened into a tall but narrow cavity, rising about twenty-eight feet high but extending a hundred yards into the distance. It was similar to the grand gallery within the Great Pyramid, and the walls were built from thick limestone blocks that were smooth to the touch.

'The Orion steps,' Marie recalled as they came across a tombstone twenty feet inside the mammoth corridor. 'I remember this,' she breathed, her expression a mixture of concern and excitement rolled into one.

Emblazoned on the stone's flat façade was an image

of three pyramids taken from a top-down perspective. It was representative of the form of Orion's Belt.

'The last time I was here I nearly got crushed by the falling ceiling,' said Joey, looking up to see the giant rollers spaced out along the tight cavern.

'You mean you were nearly squashed like a pancake,' quipped Boyce.

'That's why we need to stay on the path as indicated,' Julien reminded them. 'We've had a plethora of teams working down here and we haven't once had an incident. So I think we'll be okay. Just step on the designated Orion symbol, and it's a piece of cake.'

'This is Joey you're talking about,' smirked Boyce. 'Trouble seems to follow him wherever he goes.'

Joey shot his friend a half-smile.

'He's not lying about that,' said Marie, playing along. 'It would be nice to have a normal life one day. Go to the beach, maybe have dinner and go see a movie. I'm not asking for much, am I?'

Joey shrugged his shoulders and lifted his hands as if to say, *What can I do?* He acknowledged Boyce was trying to be funny even under these dire circumstances. It was his coping mechanism for handling the stress that was building the closer they got to the Last Secret Chamber.

Guided by the pathway of cones, they stepped over the Orion constellation square tiles and zigzagged comfortably to a narrow ledge that had once abutted the end of the press about to crush whoever was left behind.

'Down we go,' said Julien, indicating the deep well-like passage that was the next stage of the journey, with its high stepping stones descending around the walls in a spiral fashion.

'This is all looking very familiar,' said Marie dryly.

'The yellow pipes continue down?' asked Joey.

'They were installed to remove the water,' said Julien, careful with his own descent. 'So the Stargate would be easily accessible without needing to dive under each time to reach it.'

'Well, that's a silver lining to this situation,' said Marie, rubbing a hand through her hair. 'At least we're not going swimming. It's too cold to get wet, and I've seen enough cold water these past few days to last a lifetime.'

Minutes later, they reached the lower ledge where there had once been a pool of water covering the entrance to the next tunnel.

'I remember being the one to dive in first,' said Boyce as they descended further still to the very bottom, where an inch of water still remained. 'We would have been completely underwater now,' he finished, taking a breather and looking around.

'Eyes wide open,' Julien warned, darting his gaze left and right like the trained operative he was.

The sound of splashing footprints ensued as they made their way through the open entranceway. Different-sized rocks were scattered everywhere. Joey's eyes came alive when they entered the colossal man-made chamber beyond: the holy inner sanctum of Nefertiti's deadly labyrinth.

All of a sudden, Julien flashed an upright fist and they all stopped dead.

His body tensed and his gun was raised in the ready-to-fire position. 'We have men down,' he said in a gruff voice.

Joey and Boyce hoisted their weapons and hid behind a huge boulder, while Marie crouched down behind a small rock.

Julien approached the first victim, quietly and attentively. After a careful examination, he nodded his head once and gave the others the okay to approach. This process was repeated twice more; each body was spaced about thirty feet away from the last.

Marie shook her head and together with Boyce hovered over the first victim. 'There's a note on his chest,' she said, before reading it out loud for all to hear. '*Tick ... Tock ...*'

Joey stepped further. 'This one has one, too.' He snatched the note off the second dead man's bloody chest. '*Time is ticking ...*' he said with a downturned face.

Julien read the note from the third victim out loud. '*I see you.*'

'He's killed six hostages, and two undercover operatives,' said Joey, doing a quick count as he gazed down at the man's chest, where a single bullet had pierced his heart. 'This guy is a freaking homicidal maniac.'

'Yes, and he knows we're here,' said Boyce. 'He's been watching us.'

'We need to be alert at all times,' answered Julien. 'There's no telling what Dimitri is capable of and what he has in store for us. And never forget the fact that he's been trained by yours truly.'

'If I was a betting man,' said Boyce, patting the

general on his arm, 'I would choose you against him any day of the week.'

'Me too,' said Marie. 'You're the man.'

'You're a badass,' said Joey. 'He's probably shaking in his boots with the knowledge that you're with us.'

Julien flashed a smile and without saying a word motioned for the group to follow his lead. It appeared he was taken aback by their praise, but he knew deep down the battle was just about to begin.

Chapter 49

The Inner Sanctum

Lurking in the distance were two sets of enormous statues in the form of Anubis warriors: half-man with the head of a rabid dog. There was a stairway at the end of the cave, inviting Joey upwards to what was a stretch of sand. He entered cautiously, gun in hand. He remembered vividly how the quicksand in front of him had swallowed Marie and Boyce whole last time they were here. Boyce had only escaped due to Marie's selfless act of fishing him out of the semi-liquid surface. Joey could even still hear the screams of disbelief and panic as they had fought what had looked like a losing battle. Until finally, utilizing a pulley system Joey had concocted using the Anubis scepter as an anchor, Marie had emerged wheezing for air, spitting the dirty sand out of her mouth. Her entire body had been consumed by the thick mud while Boyce had been sucked in so deep, his palm had been the only part of his body still free of the goopy sand.

Shaking off the image, Joey now turned to Boyce, whose face was suddenly bitter, his fists pressed hard up against each other. He too must be remembering that fateful day, Joey thought.

'You okay?' Joey asked.

'I still have nightmares about this place,' said Boyce under his breath. 'I can't believe those assholes planned to leave me here to suffocate and die.'

'You survived, Boyce, and they didn't,' said Joey. 'Try to let it go, man.'

'I owe everything to you, Marie,' said Boyce, turning to give her a warm embrace. 'You risked your own life to save me. I love you so much.'

'I love you too, Boyce,' Marie replied, comforting the teen who had changed their lives in so many ways. 'You mean so much to us,' she said, looking deep into his teary eyes.

'Come on, let's go,' interrupted Julien with a wave of his hand. 'Stay on the path,' he said again as he trod over a newly constructed narrow timber bridge that was laid across the far left side of the dangerous liquid sand.

Yellow warning tape and traffic cones showed the way to a viewing platform, where they stopped for a moment and rested in contemplative silence.

Marie found comfort in the powerful reassuring arms of her husband, who rubbed her back soothingly.

'You okay?' Joey asked Boyce, who still looked upset. 'You need to put all that behind you, we have bigger fish to worry about now.'

Boyce exhaled a long sigh and nodded his head.

'This way,' said Julien as he moved up to the round entrance that had been created to resemble a gaping jaw.

Joey followed Julien into the corridor beyond, where they were hemmed in by perfectly arching sandstone walls. The yellow fire hoses and electrical cables seemed to continue deep within. The tubular passage sloped downwards, and Joey spotted the horizontal scratch lines that stretched away from him.

'Shit,' Joey spat with widening eyes. 'This tunnel is designed for a giant rolling boulder. We'll be crushed if we're in its path.'

'Relax,' Julien said evenly. 'Yes, it was devised that way, but I can assure you there are no moving parts to worry about anymore. All that has been taken care of.'

'Thank God for that,' said Marie, resting her hand over her abdomen. 'I'm not really in the mood to run for my life. The last time nearly killed me.'

'It seems like you're not in the mood to do anything,' joked Boyce. 'Don't want to swim, don't want to run ...' He paused as she flashed him a mischievous grin and told him playfully to shut up.

They reached the end of the shaft where the tracks banked to the right. Joey peered over the edge to see a hundred-foot drop where two long timber ladders had been permanently nailed into the wall.

'Look, Marie, we don't have to jump on the tree roots and climb down,' Joey teased. 'I wish it had been this easy the first time we were here. All that stress for nothing.'

'In hindsight,' Marie said with a sigh.

'Now, all we have to do is penetrate King Kong's door,' said Boyce.

Joey flashed a smile, happy that his young friend seemed to be back to his usual self.

Julien bent down on one knee and assessed the possible dangers. 'Eyes alert,' he said soberly. 'From now on, we're in Dimitri's domain, and we're going in blind.'

'How can we be sure Dimitri doesn't have a sniper to take us all out once we walk through?' asked Joey, dreading the possibility.

'I'm counting on the hunch that he won't act until he has the keystone,' said Julien, shifting to face Boyce, who was still wearing his backpack. 'Stay together, do what I say, and like I said before, keep your eyes open.'

Joey climbed down the ladder after the general. Marie and Boyce followed. They proceeded to the enormous thirty-foot-high cedar doors, and this time they'd been left ajar. It was the absolute end. They were standing at one corner of a massive cavern.

Joey had once again passed the test through the Walk of Souls and reached the end of the line – the Last Secret Chamber.

Only time would tell if he would be as lucky this time around.

Chapter 50

The Last Secret Chamber

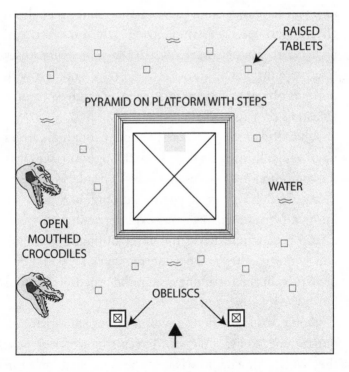

Julien and his team reached the perfectly square, massive super cavern. Exactly seven hundred and fifty-six feet wide, it matched the footprint of the Great

Pyramid itself. To know they were standing under the colossal foundation was truly mind-bending and surreal, magical even.

Joey took in the sight, craning his neck back as he strode down a ramp. Reaching the bottom he was confronted by two towering obelisks. The hieroglyphics and side-profile depictions of the king and queen worshiping the sun god were a common theme of the time.

Joey breathed in awe as they advanced into the airport hangar–sized chamber that had once been covered in knee-high water, giving it the appearance of a vast, flat lake. Now, thanks to the yellow fire hoses that were draped all over the floor, they were left with puddles of water only an inch deep, enough to cause a splash as they moved.

A handful of monoliths, each about a foot high, stood up proudly. Resting on their smooth upper surfaces was the sculpture of a man with a jackal's head.

'Anubis,' Marie whispered, keeping her distance, knowing from their previous experience that this was a trap that would flood the cave, ultimately sending you to the afterlife in the most tragic way. If you didn't drown from the incoming water, the crocodiles would finish the job.

'Don't touch them,' warned Julien with an outstretched hand. 'We still haven't figured out how they work. All we know is that the water channels run five miles, connecting this chamber to the Nile.'

'Yes,' said Joey, turning to face the eastern side of the cavern, where two large dinosaur-sized, open-mouthed crocodilian heads were carved in the bedrock. The site was quite confronting to behold, with the heads' razor-sharp teeth prominent as they rested above the shallow water. The tubular, dark aqueducts were dry as a bone this time. No controlled streams of liquid shot out from the creatures' jaws. 'The last thing we need is pissed-off Nile crocodiles,' he said. 'Trust me, we know. We've had firsthand experience.'

'Let's not relive that, please,' Marie said, coming alongside her husband.

'Still no sign of Dimitri,' said Boyce, scanning the open void with his pistol held in combat position.

'He's here,' said Julien. 'Trust me, he is here.'

At the center of the enormous space was a raised square platform flanked by stone stairs that ran downwards into the surrounding puddles. The platform's centerpiece was an impeccably rendered limestone monument. The structure appeared even more ethereal this time, with the overhead lighting illuminating its transparent crystal capstone.

It was a stupendous view to say the least.

Even though he'd seen it before, Boyce was awed afresh by its grandeur. 'The oldest Wonder of the World, we meet again,' he whispered, but loudly enough for Joey to hear.

Joey now had a deeper understanding of the monument's true purpose. It was evident the architects who had designed this underworld were not from this world. The logistics required to keep all that dead weight above – around 2.3 million stones, weighing between three and fifteen tons each – from toppling into this hollow space were mind-blowing. The creators of this place were from a planet where technology reigned supreme, and human civilization, even in the twenty-first century, was still in its infancy in comparison.

'Finally!' said a deep, accented voice that echoed in the quiet surroundings. 'Welcome ... You are now standing directly beneath the Great Pyramid of Giza.'

Marie gasped in shock.

Julien reacted to the voice by grabbing his gun with both hands and sidestepping quickly to pinpoint the source. 'Take cover,' he told the others briskly, gesturing for them to go low to the ground.

Marie, Boyce, and Joey hid behind a low monolith that bore the name Sobek, the Egyptian God of the Nile river.

'Be careful not to touch the surface,' Marie warned the men as they peered together up in Julien's direction with watchful eyes.

'We have a deal, Dimitri,' shouted Julien, placing a cautious foot up the first step and away from the water. 'We have your keystone as promised. Let the people go.'

'You're in no position to make deals, boss. I have the high ground. I have the advantage.'

'Show yourself.'

'Still trying to control the situation, aren't you? I guess some things never change. I suggest you throw away your pistol before the next person dies.'

Shuffling footfalls could be heard from the top of the platform somewhere near the base of the white Tura limestone pyramid.

Peering around the plinth, Joey inspected the pyramid's perimeter. His thoughts raced as he wondered what was making the shuffling sound. Julien lowered himself to one knee in a ready firing position as a line of captives began to move into view. They stopped at the top of the stairs, their hands behind their necks and shrouds covering what seemed to be the men's entire faces.

'Holy shit,' mouthed Marie, her face tight with anxiety.

'This doesn't look good,' added Boyce.

'Have you noticed that the spotlights above where they are standing have been blown out?' Joey said quietly, seeing the men and women in half-shadow. 'He is clever and calculating.'

There were five children among the hostages who looked to be under the age of ten, clinging to two females who must have been their mothers. The women's hair appeared to be tangled, and their faces were bruised and battered. Five of the hostages were men, two of whom had dark-blue cloths covering their faces – the women's hijabs, Joey guessed. The other three with white headscarves also covering their faces. Finally, there was a short teenage boy. Thirteen in all, at Joey's count. They stood frozen, at the mercy of a crazed man, the fear apparent in their pinched faces and trembling voices. They would have witnessed multiple murders from a person with no remorse or regard for human life.

Julien reacted, his Heckler & Koch held ready, waiting for Dimitri to show himself.

Minutes passed that felt like an eternity.

'This isn't going to be as easy as Julien had thought it would be,' Joey whispered, and Boyce nodded in agreement. Joey took a step back, his eyes filled with dread. 'I thought there were twelve hostages left?' he whispered to himself. 'Dimitri is up to something,' he said out loud. 'Let's just hope Julien didn't teach him everything he knows.'

Chapter 51

The Entrapment

The line of hostages stood anxiously waiting. On the one hand, they could see their salvation in the form of Julien; their only hope of survival. But on the other, they had to somehow escape the harsh and unyielding man who had the power to decide if they lived or died.

One of the women, who had dark frizzy hair, shuddered and glanced over her shoulder as a shadow approached her from behind. She froze, but the children cringed and squirmed, pressing up against her, and it was enough to give Julien the heads-up to Dimitri's arrival.

And just like that, Dimitri revealed himself, using the woman and children as cover. He rubbed his hands together in that classic way villains do with a bright, false smile.

'Let these people go, and we can do business,' Julien shouted, bringing up his Heckler & Koch in readiness.

Dimitri sighed, pausing for dramatic effect. 'I know

you better than that, Julien. You have never negotiated with scum before. I doubt you intend to start now.'

'You have murdered far too many innocent people,' said Julien. 'You are going down for this.'

'Show me the keystone!' Dimitri barked. 'Let's not bullshit each other. I want to initiate the portal and you want these peasants alive. We can both get what we want, if you're sensible.'

Julien glanced at his friends, who remained behind the cover of the plinth, low to the ground. 'Joey, unzip your bag and show him the contents.'

'But *I* have the keystone,' Boyce whispered with a confused, tight-lipped expression. 'I think he has mixed us up.'

'Joey!' Julien repeated firmly. 'Open *your* bag.'

Joey raised an eyebrow and removed the backpack from his shoulders, then proceeded to open the zipper. Still shielded by the wall, he slid the package over to one side to be viewed.

'I see you have brought destruction,' hissed Dimitri with a shake of his head. 'Clever boy.'

Julien hinted at a smile as he saw the odds nudge back into his favor. 'In all three backpacks, I have enough C-4 explosives to blow up this entire place. That will cause the Great Pyramid of Giza, with all its two million blocks, to come crashing down on us and crush the Stargate once and for all.'

'What?' Marie muttered, dumbfounded.

'He's bluffing,' said Boyce, shifting to face the general.

'He's trying to trick him,' said Joey.

'You wouldn't do that to your friends,' said Dimitri.

'It's not in your DNA.'

'I will do whatever it takes to keep this place a secret, and if that means sacrificing everyone here, then so be it.'

'There was never any common ground with you,' Dimitri said, scowling. 'Never a gray area. You go from one to a hundred in seconds.' He paused as if thinking hard. 'But I can do the same. I can play your game and call your bluff.'

Dimitri extracted his shiny gold-plated firearm and pointed it at the two men wearing blue headscarves over their hidden faces. He pressed the gun's barrel up against a cringing man's skull carrying a backpack, causing the victim to lean away from him.

Joey could only imagine the fear this poor person had to endure, knowing his life was about to end in the most brutal of ways.

'Don't do it,' Julien pleaded.

'Maybe I should kill two for the price of one. That will get your attention,' said Dimitri, now moving his pistol up against the second masked man.

'What will that prove?' yelled Julien, too far out of reach to take Dimitri out.

'It will prove I am crazy. You have until the count of three to give me what I want or suffer the consequences.'

Julien stopped to think, but Dimitri had started the countdown.

'One …

'Two …'

'Don't do it,' warned Julien, 'please.'

'Three …'

Bang!

'No!'

A single bullet was fired into the man's skull and the gun's report echoed inside the super cavern. Blood splattered inside the blue cloth, the garment catching most of the brain fragments. The man was killed on impact. His body fell limp and toppled down the limestone stairs until it hit the shallow water, leaving a flow of crimson that dispersed outwards.

The children screamed in panic, their terror obvious on their faces.

Julien looked with cold eyes at the homicidal maniac.

'You will run out of hostages soon,' Dimitri said boldly. 'It's your move, boss, and for the sake of the rest of them standing here in puddles of urine, I hope you decide wisely.'

Chapter 52

A Boy Named Ezra

Julien was conflicted. The man controlling the situation from the high ground wasn't the same man he once thought he knew. Julien wanted to beg, plead, get down on his knees and tell his old friend that initiating the Stargate was a fool's errand. It would create unnecessary pain and heartache, and would give him no answers. It would certainly not bring his wife and daughter back. But Julien knew the face he had seen meant business. This was no longer a rational man who might listen to reason. This was a man whose ears were closed and who had put up barriers in his mind. So, no matter what Julien wanted to say, it would just push him further away. The kind-hearted Dimitri Julien had once known was gone.

'I can do this all night,' Dimitri said grimly. 'I suggest that whoever is carrying my freaking keystone, reach into your bag and toss it to me. Right. Now.'

Joey glanced helplessly at Julien. The situation had turned into a stalemate.

'Maybe I can help with your decision-making,' Dimitri offered, aiming the cold barrel of his golden pistol along the line of terrified hostages. 'I have the perfect scenario to help you speed up the process.'

Julien frowned, his heartbeat pounding in his chest. Then he felt a jolt of complete horror when he saw Dimitri grab a young boy and pull him away from his mother. The distressed woman screamed, her tears running freely into a stream of blood that was seeping from her clearly broken nose.

'No,' Julien pleaded, his nightmares returning to him.

'Get down on your knees, boy!' Dimitri ordered, holding the boy by the thick curly hair that matched his mother's.

'You used to be a father, Dimitri! This is not you. Surely you would not kill a child in cold blood,' Julien said, starting to sweat. Flashbacks were beginning to invade his thoughts, and he fought to remain focused.

'How old are you, boy?' Dimitri asked the child, who was swaying on his knees as if he might faint.

'I'm eight,' the boy said weakly.

'Did you hear that, Julien!' yelled Dimitri, grinning insanely. 'He's younger than Ezra.'

Julien couldn't help it; he shuddered uncontrollably.

Boyce tried to catch his eye, but Julien turned away, feeling the weight of despair begin to settle over him. His dirty laundry was about to be aired, and that made him feel vulnerable. He felt like a failure, not someone who had attained the title of general.

'Boyce, are you hearing this?' Dimitri shouted, his eyes glittering. 'Did you know Julien had been seeing a shrink for decades after losing this Arab kid? It screwed him up entirely, trust me ... I read piles of reports on the matter. How he felt, and all the other juicy stuff he told his psychiatrist.' Dimitri paused for a moment, making sure everyone could hear it all.

'You're a monster,' Marie shouted back.

'I already got that from Aya, the boy's mother,' commented Dimitri, his evil smile growing. 'Boyce, are you still listening?'

'It's hard not to listen to your bullshit,' said Boyce angrily from behind the plinth.

'Did you know you were offered a job at the DGSE because of that stupid boy? Julien must have seen something in you that reminded him of Ezra.'

'Why are you telling me this shit?' asked Boyce. 'This doesn't change the fact that you're an asshole.'

'No, it doesn't,' Dimitri agreed. 'It just means Julien has a choice to make, and if he makes the wrong one, history will rear its ugly head yet again. How will Julien be able to process the death of an eight-year-old? That's the question.'

Aya begged for mercy for her child and was shut down with an evil stare.

'I will give you to the count of three,' Dimitri warned, and Julien knew he would go through with it to prove his point.

'One ...'

Aya begged Dimitri.

'Two ...'

'Okay ... okay ... you win!' Julien shouted, lowering

his gun and hurrying over to his three friends, who greeted him with perplexed faces.

'What are you doing, sir?' Boyce asked, confused.

'Boyce, hand me the keystone.'

'You're just going to give it to him?'

'I have no choice.'

'Yes . . . but tell me you have a plan,' urged Joey.

'I'm working on it,' Julien replied, exhaling a breath. 'Be prepared for anything, and stay alert,' he whispered.

Boyce handed him the red dolerite and dropped his backpack.

Julien held it aloft, yelling, 'I have it! I will toss you the keystone if you promise to let everyone go.'

'Yeah, yeah ... Give me the key first, or the kid is toast. You know I mean it.'

Julien approached the steps once more, and in an underarm movement rocked the item back and forward, then let it go. The stone ascended high, extremely high.

It was as if it was in slow motion, spinning in the air.

Dimitri reacted, moving forwards with open arms to catch it.

He was exposed.

Julien's ploy to get him out in the open was planned to perfection. He sucked in a breath, straightened his shoulders and raised his Heckler & Koch. His finger was prepared to depress the trigger for the kill shot that would take the lunatic down.

At that moment, as he squinted his left eye and squeezed the trigger, another gunshot ripped through the air. The sound was loud, but it didn't come from Julien's weapon.

Julien winced and grunted in pain.

A sharp, throbbing agony exploded in his shoulder. It was deep and warm, and he knew it too well. He scanned his body to witness his soaked sleeve, the liquid radiating rapidly outward. A reddened hole now oozed with dark blood, and the smell wafted across his face.

He was hit.

Julien lay his hand on the source of the blood flow as agony suddenly washed through him. He felt dizzy and bit his lip as he took a step back, dropped his weapon and tripped into the shallow water with a heavy splash.

Chapter 53

The Deceit

The water lapped softly around Julien's outstretched fingers. As he lifted it, he watched the droplets wash away his pain. He gathered himself and glanced upwards to see a faint line of smoke exiting from a tubular barrel.

The unknown assailant was one of the hostages.

No. That couldn't be right. Julien wondered if he was hallucinating.

A smug smile crept over the face that emerged from behind the navy-blue headscarf.

Julien cursed himself for his stupidity. Dimitri's accomplice had disguised himself as one of the hostages who was carrying a backpack.

'I see you met my brother-in-law, Nick,' Dimitri said scathingly, playing with the keystone he now held in his hands before tucking it in his back pocket. He peered over the edge of the platform as though he was the king on the hill with the military advantage.

'It's a pleasure to meet you,' Nick said smugly. 'Tell me, do I deserve an Oscar or what?'

'You deserve a punch in the head,' replied Joey. 'That's what you deserve.'

'The funny thing is,' said Dimitri with a satisfied smile, 'the idea to hide Nick as a hostage came to me when we were attacked by the two lying pizza men. It's amazing where you find your inspiration.'

Julien's frown lines grew more pronounced, and he clenched his jaw even tighter, the pent-up anger building deep within. Dimitri had outsmarted him, and that fact pissed him off. No one tricked the most decorated officer in the French intelligence. He eliminated problems, never caused them.

'Nick, can you do me the honor of finishing off the old man?'

'With pleasure,' Nick replied, aiming once more to fire.

Julien rotated his body to see Marie's eyes widen. He reached for his gun inches away beneath the crimson water, knowing what was coming. But he wasn't fast enough.

Gunshots rained from above.

He winced and closed his eyes, but felt no pain.

The shots had not been aimed at him.

Joey had pounced, launching himself over the monolith and letting loose a plethora of bullets in Nick and Dimitri's direction.

Boyce had quickly followed suit, causing everyone on the platform to duck for cover as shells zinged past them.

'Run!' Marie yelled to Julien, who locked eyes with her. He knew he would only get one chance.

Julien picked himself up, pressing one hand hard against his wound, and waded through the shallow water as fast as he could.

'He's getting away,' Dimitri yelled, but the covering fire was enough to allow Julien to escape, and he found himself on the western side of the pyramid and away from imminent danger.

The three male captives who wore the white *ghutra* headscarves had tried to use the chaos as an opportunity to escape by fleeing down the steep stairs.

'Where do you think you're going?' Nick called furiously after them, his tone filled with menace. From his high vantage point and sheltered position that was low to the ground, he swiftly aligned his golden Beretta and squeezed the trigger several times in rapid succession. All three men still on the upper end of the steps fell like video game characters, sending brain fragments spurting in every direction.

Marie turned away and vomited as Nick continued his offensive at Joey and Boyce. It was a maelstrom of terrified screams, an onslaught of relentless bullets and stone chips pinging off all surfaces and hitting the puddles of water.

'We're going to die,' Marie squealed, remaining huddled behind Sobek's plinth while Joey and Boyce took cover elsewhere.

Julien had lost copious amounts of blood, but he knew he couldn't just do nothing. These were his friends, and they were in grave danger. He had to find a way to strike back.

His mangled shoulder dripped a line of blood over

the far side of the limestone steps, he quietly reached the top of the platform that encircled the pyramid and started to creep along the structure's edge.

This was the real Seventh Wonder of the Ancient World.

It rose above him to one hundred and twenty feet, a quarter the size of the Great Pyramid. At the corner point where two planes of the pyramid met, he peered around to evaluate the situation.

The five young kids, teenage boy and two women were all that was left of the hostages. They were huddled together on the ground, weeping and shaking. He could see Nick hiding behind the hostages saying something to Dimitri. They were probably discussing their next move, but this time they wouldn't know what was coming.

Julien took a deep breath and composed himself. He shut his eyes, and used all his training, all his experience, to still his mind and focus. Seconds later, he opened his eyes wide. He had one clear objective. It was simple: take down these two fuckwits and end this once and for all.

Taking one last peek around the corner, he spotted Dimitri pluck the teenage boy out of the cluster of hostages. The fire from below resumed, so he used the teen as a shield. This seemed to have worked, because silence quickly returned, as if everyone was collectively holding their breath.

Julien saw Nick reloading his clip and cursing at the prisoners to not grow a brain and try anything.

This was it.

Julien gripped the handle of his firearm tightly with

his sticky, blood-soaked fingers, then bolted forwards, his weapon up and aimed.

Surprised by the sudden movement, Nick and Dimitri spun around and quickly ducked as Julien opened fire. The shots missed.

'It's Julien!' Dimitri cautioned his brother-in-law.

The hostages erupted into screams of panic as the shells hit the ground at Dimitri's feet and scattered like seeds of destruction.

Dimitri flashed Julien a look of pure loathing. He grabbed the teen by his neck and fired back to cover his brother-in-law, who he saw was now in a more compromised situation than he himself was.

Dimitri's shots flew over Julien's snow-white hair, too close for comfort, but the older man wasn't stopping for anything. His senses were sharpened with adrenaline, and his mind was oddly calm and clear. It was as if the moment was playing out in slow motion as he advanced on his enemy.

'Fall back!' Dimitri shouted to his partner. 'You're exposed.'

'I've got him,' Nick barked, continuing to engage. 'He's mine.'

'Don't be stupid,' warned Dimitri.

It was then that Julien's perseverance paid off.

Nick took a bullet in his neck, which sent him backwards, gulping blood. It was a professional hit, and Nick knew what it meant. The pain burned like fire. He stood up like a bewildered and possessed zombie, dropped his weapon, and grasped at his wound as despair closed in.

His eyes caught his brother-in-law's, and the realization that he was about to die crystallized in his mind. Black filled the edges of his vision and the only thing he could hear was his own heartbeat. His breath now came in ragged, shallow gasps.

He stumbled to the edge of the platform carrying his weighted backpack, where a bullet from Joey's pistol entered his spine, and any feeling he'd still had faded away to an icy numbness. His eyes rolled back into his head and his ravaged body dropped like a heavy sack of potatoes. As the momentum of the fall carried his bloodstained face into the shallow, stagnant water, the last thing he heard was Dimitri's cry for vengeance.

Chapter 54

The Confrontation

Dimitri raised his bloodshot eyes from his brother-in-law's dead corpse. His fingers curled tight around his gun, and all he could see in his mind was Julien's neck snapping. With burning rage hissing through his body, he let loose like a volcano erupting.

'I'm going to destroy you,' he screamed, digging the barrel of his gun into the spine of the teenager he was holding. 'Time for you to commence your counseling!'

'No!' yelled Julien. There was no mistaking the madman's intentions. This boy would never get to live out his teens and see adulthood.

Dimitri squeezed the trigger, and the teenager's back arched forward as the bullet entered, his eyes grew wide and bulged in shock, and his mouth fell open. His face fell slack as his heart stopped. His diminutive frame became limp and dropped where he stood.

A mother's cry of agony echoed in the vast space.

Joey and Boyce could be seen comforting Marie who continued to vomit.

Julien's glare narrowed, and the hatred was evident in his eyes. He tossed aside his pistol as he approached, the clip empty. This emboldened Dimitri, who knew he had two or three rounds left in his Beretta.

Julien was now ninety feet away and unarmed.

Eighty feet ...

Dimitri waiting for the clean shot. He aimed at the target fast approaching. He fired, and the general dove into a commando roll, dodging the incoming bullet. Regaining his momentum, Julien came out of the roll, wincing as he put pressure on his injured shoulder, and that was when the patiently waiting Dimitri pressed the trigger.

The bullet flew out of the chamber and hit the general with extreme precision, as it was meant to.

'Motherf—' cried Julien, looking down in shock at the second bullet hole in his upper torso. His face turned gray, revealing the agony he was feeling, but he continued to stagger forward.

'It's going to take more than two bullets to kill me,' Julien barked, though he could feel the strength draining from his limbs and his hands were trembling.

Dimitri flashed an evil grin, acknowledging the stubbornness of his former boss. *He wouldn't know defeat if it came over and slapped him in the face*, he thought with quiet admiration. The man was wounded, bleeding, but the old bastard persisted with his charge.

'You will never learn,' said Dimitri, lining up once

again for the final shot. 'Time to end you and go start up my Stargate.'

Sixty feet …

Fifty feet …

Julien was now in close range.

Dimitri pushed the trigger, and nothing happened. The clip was empty. To make matters worse, bullets now zinged at him from below, catching him off guard and causing him to run for cover – straight towards Julien.

Bang!

Julien's wounded shoulder collided with Dimitri's broad chest and the Greek's gun was flung out of his hands as they both fell in a rolling struggle among the remaining hostages. Seeing her chance, Aya instinctively seized hold of the children and made a run for it, as screams once more echoed within the super cavern. '*Yalla! Yalla!*' Aya yelled as the other Muslim woman followed her lead in an absolute panic.

'I'm going to kill you,' Julien growled as he grabbed Dimitri in a headlock and squeezed as hard as he could. 'Murderer,' he ground out through his clenched jaw.

Dimitri started seeing stars as his brain was deprived of oxygen. Even with two shells inside Julien, the old man was a beast in tactical combat, and Dimitri was about to face what so many feared, and what he had always dreaded: going toe to toe with the general.

Dimitri managed to sneak in an elbow in Julien's ribs, allowing him to free himself from the general's stranglehold and breathe. But it was a very brief respite. Julien came in hard with a right hook that sent Dimitri's nose to the floor.

First was the blackness, followed by an excruciating ringing noise, but Julien wasn't going to let him off that easy. He straddled Dimitri like a horse and continued to punch at his head, left and right.

Dimitri roared as the fiery bursts pulsated through his jaw. He pleaded for him to stop, but it was as if Julien couldn't hear through the red fog of his rage. Blood oozed out of numerous wounds in Dimitri's face, becoming a constant flow of crimson.

'You don't deserve to live,' Julien said, continuing to hammer down.

Through the onslaught, Dimitri heard mumbled sounds and recognized a woman's voice; it was Marie.

'He's had enough,' she said in an ice-cold voice. 'Julien, this is not you, stop it.'

Joey placed a hand on Julien's shoulder, and the general finally ceased his barrage of punches.

Julien gazed at his bloody fists and exhaled. 'We need to destroy the Stargate,' he insisted in the commanding voice Dimitri knew so well. 'Joey, set up the C-4,' he grunted now, finally acknowledging his wounds by placing his hands over them.

Dimitri watched all this from his swollen, barely open eyes. His mouth was full of blood. He rolled over, spitting, and pulled himself up on all fours. He could hardly see for all the blood running down his mangled face and into his eyes, but there was no mistaking what he'd heard.

'No!' he cried as three shadows now appeared over him. 'Not the Stargate,' he begged. Blinking his eyes uncontrollably, he managed to clear his vision slightly, but then he felt an unbearable pain right between the legs that sent him down for mercy in the fetal position.

'No one gives a rat's ass what you think,' said Boyce bluntly, keeping his gun trained on his captive. 'You don't look so tough now, do you.'

Chapter 55

The Plan

Marie took hold of Julien and assessed his torn body. 'You need immediate medical attention, you've been shot multiple times,' she said.

'Listen to me.' He coughed weakly, then turned to face Joey. 'Take the explosives in your backpack and blow it up,' he said vehemently.

'What about him?' Joey asked, pointing to the battered and defeated Dimitri still spitting blood out of his mouth.

'Don't worry about him,' Julien sniffed. 'We have a lot of catching up to do.'

Marie reached into her bag of supplies and found military-green, extra-large two-by-four-inch emergency bandages with adhesive strips. 'Here, sir,' she pleaded, moving in to place them over his bullet wounds. 'This will hopefully stem the flow and help stop the hemorrhaging.'

'Before we go do this,' said Joey, staring into Julien's

eyes with unease, 'I need to know. This isn't gonna be the death of me, is it?'

'Yeah,' interrupted Marie, taking a furtive step back. 'Earlier, you said the entire ceiling and the two million stone blocks from above would come crashing down.'

'No, I just said that to scare him,' said Julien, nodding his head in Dimitri's direction. 'There's only enough C-4 for a targeted explosion. Use your commonsense, though, and make sure you're far away from the Stargate before you blow it.'

'You can't do this,' moaned Dimitri as he tried to move, arching his back. 'My wife and child!'

'No one asked you!' Julien spat, knocking Dimitri's chest back down to the floor with a heavy boot in his spine.

'Is that the keystone?' Joey asked, pointing to Dimitri's backside.

'Yes, it is,' answered Julien sharply. 'If you do your job right, it won't matter. It will become just another piece of stone, nothing more.' He directed his index finger to the entrance. 'Now go!'

Joey acknowledged with a nod.

'Let's do this,' he said to Boyce, but Marie wouldn't be left behind.

'Marie, no,' Joey begged. 'You've had enough, you don't need to do this.'

'I'm not leaving you alone again. We stay together all the way,' she insisted and took off in a jog.

Joey and Boyce ran to catch up, and soon all three were jogging down the side of the square platform that led them to a man-sized opening into the smoothly rendered pyramid. A rectangular doorway the size of a backyard pool had been partially concealed by limestone bricks.

'You can really see the discoloration better under this lighting,' Marie said, rubbing her hand up against the wall where the brick pattern showed through. 'The new is clearly distinguishable from the old.'

'Must have been erected in a hurry,' Boyce called out.

'Here we go, just like old times,' Marie said, stepping over the broken debris.

'I'm still trying to forget the last time,' said Boyce, who had technically been the first person in the twentieth century to have entered the portal. 'Some things can never be erased from our minds,' he said. 'Trust me, I've tried.'

Inside the hollow pyramid, Joey glanced around in wonder as if seeing it again for the first time. 'The Last Secret Chamber Nefertiti tried to hide,' he said. 'Until we came along and discovered it and put the whole world at risk.'

'We kind of didn't have a choice,' Marie replied with a grim smile. 'We were being held at gunpoint.'

'I know,' said Joey, thinking about their wild adventures. 'We've been extremely lucky through all this.'

'And we'll be lucky again once you blow this thing to kingdom come,' said Boyce, leading the way to the feature in the room.

Joey scanned the space, which, like the exterior, was pyramidal. The base of the building was vast and square. Dolerite stones encircled its perimeter, like in graveyards of immense importance. At the pinnacle above, the underside of the crystal could be seen. It sat within the structure, like the stone in a diamond ring that was held in place with giant claws.

'At least we don't need to shine our flashlights on it to bring on natural light,' said Marie. 'This is going to be a walk in the park.'

'It appears everything inside this room is as we last saw it,' Boyce said, identifying the two nine-foot-tall pyramidions that sat on either side of the circular edifice. One of these was the golden capstone that had once sat atop the Great Pyramid of Giza, completing its perfectly aligned triangular form.

'Here is what we came for,' said Joey, standing a few feet away from the wheel-shaped structure that was the Stargate.

'The Stargate,' Boyce whispered, his expression one of awe and fear at the same time.

'Just being so close to it is giving me the creeps,' said Marie.

'You're not alone,' said Joey. 'Let's do this.' He reached for his backpack and carefully extracted the explosive device.

'Be careful,' Marie warned.

Six blocks of C-4 were embedded with magnets for easy placement on the gate's metallic surface. A thin blue wire was attached to all six pieces like a giant spider web and connecting the parts to a handheld trigger device.

'Here, let me help you,' said Boyce, slowly taking three bars with him, mindful of the wires dragging along the floor. He used the indentations in the

Stargate's circular frame to climb up with ease, and like vacuum cups, the magnets snapped in place on the structure.

Boyce positioned them evenly at one, three, and five o'clock.

'My turn,' said Marie, who copied her friend, placing the remaining three blocks on the opposite side of the gate to complete the setup: at seven, nine and eleven o'clock.

'Excellent,' Joey encouraged. 'Now come over here well out of the way,' he directed Boyce and Marie, while he uncoiled the wire and stretched it towards the doorway. 'It's time to end this,' Joey said as he turned to face his wife, who looked horrified. As Joey stepped through the entrance, he realized why. From the other side of the pyramid he could hear the sound of anguish. It appeared Julien was continuing his harsh punishment of his former colleague, and from what they could hear, he wasn't holding back.

Chapter 56

The Showdown

Staring into the jaws of defeat through swollen eyes, Dimitri lay helpless. His time was running out, and soon the Stargate would be nothing more than pieces of useless metal. This fact ignited something deep within him. He couldn't sit back and watch it unfold. He wasn't dead yet, and he was willing to fight to the death to prevent that from happening.

Gathering the last vestiges of his strength, he managed a solid scissor kick, which abruptly knocked Julien off his feet.

Julien's eyes widened, and his expression instantly went hard as he crash-landed on his backside. 'Ah!' he cried out in pain as he tried to break his fall.

Dimitri gave him a bloody grin. He found it fitting that his offensive move had been carried out on the man who wrote the book on attack drills.

'You're going to pay for that,' Julien groaned, pressing a hand against his back as he struggled up to his knees.

Dimitri reacted swiftly, springing to his feet as blood continuing to drip down his battered face. He didn't waste a moment, straddling Julien from behind. Dimitri squeezed his neck with all his might, knowing that if he had any chance of beating the general, he needed to fight dirty. So, he hung on with the vise that was his bulging biceps and didn't let go.

In a defensive action, Julien held on with both hands, his neck bent and his jaw clenched. The grunting sounds intensified as his airways were slowly crushed.

The adrenaline coursed through Dimitri as he fixed his eyes on the trained killer in front of him, and he allowed himself to enjoy the fact that he had him pinned down and fighting for his very breath, his very survival.

But Julien wasn't going to be so easy to kill. He elbowed Dimitri hard in his rib cage, forcing him to let go. In a battle to stay in front and on the offensive, they both pushed themselves to their feet and began to circle each other.

It was a stand-off from which there could only be one winner.

'I should have finished you when I had the chance,' said Julien, looking grim.

'Bring it,' replied Dimitri.

Julien took the advantage with his soaring height, and threw rapid jabs that seemed to come from nowhere.

Through a glaze of red, Dimitri blocked two of his punches, but one slid through his flailing hands and connected squarely with his nose. He reeled backwards from the power of the blow, and blood rained down from his nostrils.

'You will not stand in my way,' Dimitri growled, his fists clenched.

'And you will not stand in mine,' retorted Julien.

Dimitri charged and tackled Julien to the edge of the platform in a dog fight, where knees and elbows were thrown.

'I'm going to kill you!' Julien roared as he forcefully brought another hand into Dimitri's face, snapping his nose into a grotesquerie.

'Motherf—' Dimitri screamed in agony. But before Julien could get the upper hand again, he pummeled the general's body with his fists, taking handfuls of Julien's clothing in an attempt to wrestle him to the ground. 'You're not getting the better of me,' he grunted. 'Let's let fate decide.' He grabbed hold of Julien's shirt collar with hatred in his eyes and forced Julien down over the edge in a rolling struggle.

Their bodies tipped over the limestone steps.

Dimitri's perception of time distorted, everything slowed down until …

Splonk!

Julien hit the cold, shallow water first and his right shoulder dislocated on impact. He howled as pain ricocheted through his torn body. The boss man who towered above everyone and never accepted defeat was gravely injured. He had two bullets in his chest and a broken shoulder. He lay there like a wounded animal.

Dimitri found the strength to stand up and pulled the keystone from his jeans pocket. He dangled it in his left hand and advanced towards Julien, who hadn't moved.

'Time to die, old friend,' said Dimitri.

Julien spat at him, and as Dimitri bent down, he swung a punch that didn't go anywhere. Dimitri blocked it, holding Julien's arm at bay, then leaned in and followed through with a strong right hook to the general's jawline, connecting with a loud *crunch!*

The general's head hit the dirty water with a splash, but nevertheless he tried to use his left hand to drag his body away from his assailant.

'Why don't you just *die*?' asked Dimitri, moving in to straddle the older man's chest, where he ripped off one of the bandages. He proceeded to dig his finger into Julien's bullet wound and press deep into his flesh.

Julien howled for mercy. But then, with the last of his strength, he kicked out and managed to push Dimitri off him. Then he backed away in a crawl that was stopped when he came up against a knee-high monolith.

Dimitri advanced again, arms flexed as the emotions swirled inside him. 'I will be the man known and remembered for murdering the untouchable DGSE general.'

'If I'm going to die in this place,' Julien said, reaching with his left arm over the hieroglyphic that bore the name Sobek, the Egyptian God of the crocodile, 'then so will you.' Then he pounded down on it with a hard fist.

Instantly, a robust vibrating hum was heard, which built in intensity with each second.

'What have you done?' Dimitri's voice was filled with dread.

The ancient pressure system that connected the chamber with the Nile river had been activated.

An instant later, Dimitri spun around with wide eyes to see a burst of rushing water gush out of the giant crocodile mouth holes. The water level rose rapidly as water swirled around the monoliths on the cave floor. The God of the Nile had unleashed his fury into the super cavern once again.

With gritted teeth, Dimitri aimed a blow at Julien's skull that sent him face first into the water, unconscious. Then, knowing from the reports he'd read of the dangers he faced in the Nile water, Dimitri sprinted up the stairs to the limestone pyramid with the keystone in his hand.

Time was running out.

He hoped the Stargate had not yet been rigged with explosives.

He found two guns at the top of the platform. One had an empty cartridge, and the other was his brother-in-law's shiny golden Beretta. He picked them both up and bolted for the opening to the pyramid as the blood and sweat poured down his face.

He had the key. The Stargate was close. His destiny awaited, and all that was standing in his way now was Joey Peruggia and his band of misfits.

Chapter 57

The Threat

Joey swallowed hard at the sight of Dimitri fast approaching. Something had gone badly wrong, he realized. In Dimitri's hand was a golden gun. A wave of adrenaline flooded Joey's system, and his hands trembled while holding on to the detonator the major would surely be after.

'It's Dimitri!' Joey breathed.

Marie and Boyce turned, stunned.

'Relax!' Dimitri warned with both hands, suggesting he meant no harm, and joined them inside the holy sanctum. 'We can come to an agreement.'

Boyce reacted swiftly, lifting his Heckler & Koch. 'No way in hell I'm listening to you,' he said with a shake of his head.

The tension in the air escalated.

Marie approached Joey and hid behind his frame, extracting her own pistol.

'Put your weapon down!' Boyce instructed Dimitri with a trembling hand.

Dimitri didn't respond. Instead, he frowned and looked thoughtful, as though he was assessing the situation.

'Where is Julien?' asked Joey, waiting for an answer that didn't come.

'Did you kill him?' Boyce spat.

'Relax,' Dimitri said again, wiping the blood from his face. 'Let's not be irrational.'

'*Nothing* about this has been rational,' Marie responded bluntly. 'Drop your gun.'

'I see this as a one-way deal,' Dimitri replied quietly, ignoring her.

'It's the only deal,' said Boyce.

Joey flicked the switch to turn on the detonator device. It ignited six red lights on the controller, indicating all C-4 explosives on the circular structure were now armed. His thumb was an inch over the red button. 'I'm in control now, Dimitri, not you. If I have to blow us all to kingdom come to stop you, then I will.'

Dimitri lowered his head in defeat, like a child who has been told to go to his room. He tossed his gun to the ground, and it clunked to a stop a few feet away.

He was now unarmed.

Joey calmed his racing thoughts. He felt a stab of relief but understood he needed to keep focused. 'I can end it right now,' he said, hovering his thumb over the button that would blast the metallic framework to smithereens.

'Before you do,' said Dimitri, exhaling a deep breath. 'Let me pass … Let me redeem myself,' he pleaded with seeming sincerity.

'Redeem yourself,' Marie scoffed. 'You're a mass murderer. You've killed too many people in search of something that will never satisfy your hunger. Your family is dead, and there's nothing you can do to bring them back.'

'Family,' Dimitri said softly, turning to face Joey. 'One day, *you* will become a father, and only then will *you* understand the power of a father's love.' He paused for a moment, his swollen eyes seeming to grow sharper. 'God forbid if what happened to my family ever happened to you. And if it did, what lengths would you go to, to obtain the answers you seek?'

'It's a death wish,' replied Joey, trying to reason with the psychopath. 'I've been to the place you want to go to. Let me remind you that humans are the slaves on that planet. Yes, Dimitri ... the laborers. You will face our makers who evolved us thousands of years ago, but you know all this. You've read the report, and yet you still want to go? I don't understand you.'

'He has the keystone,' said Boyce, pointing to the triangular shape clearly visible bulging out of Dimitri's pants pocket. 'He's extremely dangerous, Joey, don't listen to a word he's saying. I suggest we end him now.'

'Hey, boy, shut up,' Dimitri barked, profound scorn and loathing in his voice. 'Boyce, if you squeeze the trigger you better kill me or else.'

'Oh, don't worry, I will,' said Boyce, like the well-trained operative he was.

'If it so happens that he misses, I won't,' added Marie, raising her own Heckler & Koch.

Dimitri grunted to himself and hit his jeans with

a fist to express his growing anger; the movement caught everyone's attention. 'I promise to whatever God is up there listening,' he said in an authoritative, rasping voice, both fists clenched, 'that if the Stargate is blown up before I have a chance to enter, I will kill you all in the most brutal of ways.' He stared at Joey with sheer fury on his face. 'This will include the unborn child inside your wife. Maybe then you will understand my pain.'

Joey swallowed hard and stopped to consider this building dilemma. On the one hand, blowing up the device would protect humanity's greatest secret. On the other, if by any chance Dimitri survived this shootout, everyone Joey loved would die tragically. He surmised that if Dimitri had fought off and survived Julien's wrath, what prospect did they have? He had to be careful. Dimitri was the most dangerous adversary he'd faced.

'Don't listen to him,' said Boyce, his wrist tightening. 'He's not killing anyone.' Boyce aimed for Dimitri's skull.

But there was one thing Boyce and Marie had momentarily forgotten about the major.

He had been taught by the best.

Chapter 58

The Victor

It all happened in the blink of an eye.

The tension in the air was at its peak.

Unexpectedly, Dimitri made a move, feinting to his right in an offensive. In doing so, he extracted the hidden Beretta that was tucked away in his sock.

Marie gasped, ill-prepared for what was happening.

Flabbergasted, Boyce fired his weapon, but missed the major entirely as he ducked out of the way.

Down low and like a trained assassin, Dimitri aimed at Boyce and fired, sending him reeling backwards and screaming, his hands pressed against a bullet wound in his shoulder. Instinctively, like a well-oiled killing machine, Dimitri turned and shot the weapon out of Marie's hand, leaving a gaping hole in her palm.

She screamed in agony and fell onto her backpack, clutching her hands together.

Joey looked down at the button, but before he had any time to react, he copped a bullet in his thigh, causing him to lose balance and fling the box up in the air.

Marie froze in a shocked, trancelike state. All three of them had been gunned down in a matter of seconds. The adrenaline surged through her like a bushfire.

Now back on two feet, Dimitri charged for the device that had fallen out of Joey's hands. It was making its way to the floor in an uncontrollable rolling spin.

He dove to save it from landing on the trigger.

The scene played out in slow motion and Marie could only watch in horror.

'No!' yelled Dimitri, as the box bounced on one edge, then another.

One more turn and . . .

Marie held in a breath.

Dimitri thrust himself forwards, and, in the nick of time, he salvaged the trigger device before the button was pushed. His face was a picture of utter relief and victory as he held it, rejoicing briefly in the moment. He immediately flicked the lever to the 'off' position, deactivating the six bright lights, and turned to Joey, who was grappling with his injured, likely broken leg.

'Time to die,' he said in a menacing tone. 'You three were given a chance.' He stepped towards Joey.

'No!' Marie cried, covering Joey's battered body with her own shredded hand, leaving streaks of blood over his clothing.

Dimitri trained his barrel on the two of them.

'One bullet is all I need to finish you both,' he teased.

Marie turned her face to Joey's chest, clinging to

him. If it were going to end this way, then she would die locked in the arms of the man she loved. Dimitri's shadow seemed to hover over them, and she heard Boyce moaning, fighting his own battle of survival.

Marie closed her eyes. She prayed to Jesus Christ, even though she knew all religions on Earth were utter nonsense, created by people who wanted control, power, and money. She had witnessed firsthand how humans had evolved as a species. She knew that we were not unique in our universe. We were evolved by beings from another planet, used as pawns for their own gain. But at this moment, in the grips of death, the Catholic faith imbued in her as a child comforted her.

Boyce grew quiet, and in the momentary silence, Marie heard footsteps treading away.

A loud *bang!* made her flinch, and she turned to see that Dimitri had destroyed the handheld trigger, and had yanked the wires out from their sockets, making it inoperable.

Dimitri was the victor tonight. He had the red dolerite keystone, and there was no one left to stop him from activating the portal. Even if she hadn't been pregnant, taking him on with a wounded hand would be sheer suicide. At least some hostages had escaped, Marie thought grimly.

With complete autonomy to roam free, Dimitri meandered over to Boyce and kicked him, for the fun of it.

Boyce yelped in agony.

'Your shooting skills are laughable,' Dimitri said

scathingly. 'I thought you said you wouldn't miss, and now I'm standing above you watching you suffer.'

'Please, don't,' Boyce spider-crawled into a corner taking deep, raspy breaths.

'Leave him alone,' Joey warned. 'He's just a kid.'

Dimitri snapped back to face Joey, and Marie steeled herself for what might come next as he approached again.

'Who's asking you?' Dimitri nudged Joey in the backside with his boot.

'Enough!' Marie yelled with her injured hand raised.

'Your wife is feisty,' said Dimitri. 'I like it.'

'Fuck you,' Joey barked.

'Now the big decision. Do I let you all live or die?'

Joey shrugged in defeat.

'What do you want from us?' Marie pleaded. 'You've won. It's time to do what you came here for.' She gestured to the Stargate. 'No one is stopping you. Do it. Your family is waiting.'

Chapter 59

The Stargate

'My family,' Dimitri repeated in a whisper, still hovering above Joey and Marie, who had never suffered the pain he'd had to endure. He looked up to face the Stargate that was standing tall in front of him. He thought about his wife, his daughter, and the reason he had begun this crazy adventure in the first place. It was all for them.

He lowered his gold-plated Beretta and nodded to himself.

He knew what he needed to do.

Boyce continued to moan in anguish.

Dimitri cast his gaze into Marie's hazel eyes, and she peered back into his. He expected to see terror, hopelessness, panic. Instead, he saw a sadness there.

'One day, you will understand why I did all this,' he told her softly. 'One day, you will look into your daughter's innocent eyes and want to keep her safe and protected.' He paused for a moment, remembering his daughter's infectious smile and laughter. He remembered the feel of his wife's warm skin against his body and wished he could tell her one more time that he loved her.

Then he forced himself to snap out of his reverie, and Marie was there waiting, and he could sense she felt his pain, his sorrow. 'Even though you see me as the devil himself, I'm not the bad guy in this story. I'm just on a spiritual quest in search of answers.'

'What answers?' asked Marie tiredly.

'I want to find God.'

'But we told you before. The creator you're searching for is an advanced civilization with large, elongated heads. Once you enter the portal, they will either kill you or force you to join the other human slaves that make up their labor force.'

'You don't believe in God, do you?' Dimitri asked.

'How can you believe in the divine when we *know* these beings evolved us?'

'And who evolved them?' countered Dimitri, catching Marie off guard. 'There is a God out there, Marie, never lose your faith.'

Marie was taken aback by his words.

Dimitri extracted the keystone from his pocket, gave her a goodbye nod, and turned back to the Stargate.

'He's letting us go,' Marie whispered, surprised.

'Yeah, but at what cost?' replied Joey.

Dimitri flashed Boyce a smirk, stepped up to the circular frame and inserted the stone into its fixture.

'Here we go again,' Marie muttered.

One long minute passed.

Then a zapping sound buzzed around the device in the center of the room. It was faint at first, but it soon began to build in intensity.

Boyce turned to it with fearful eyes.

Dimitri took a small step back, licking his lips.

The red dolerite stone was like a battery, which started an electromagnetic pulse. Short bursts of life in the form of lightning strikes hit the top of the golden capstone and then ran north to the giant crystal directly above. It was gathering and blending shimmering energy fields of power from the Great Pyramid's core structure. The beams that trickled out were thickening with an assortment of colors, mainly white, electric blue and turquoise.

Dimitri stood cautiously, looking slightly unsure. The rumbling sound coming from the ring shook the chamber with a deafening roar until …

Shhh, boom!

The Stargate blasted to life with a flash of cerulean light that illuminated the room, seeming to defy all the laws of gravity. The glow was almost blinding and created a ghostly waterfall within the gate's circumference. The dazzling energy of the structure was evident, making all those who stared at it feel small and insignificant. The Great Pyramid above, dormant and mysterious for so many centuries, was doing what it had been designed to do all along.

Chapter 60

The Darkness

A dazzling straight laser beam of white light suddenly blasted into the night sky from the apex of the Great Pyramid with a roaring *boom!* Cairo, a beautiful city that housed 19.5 million people, was once again sent back to the Stone Age.

No light.

No transportation.

No internet.

Chaos engulfed Egypt as it fell into darkness. Screams of panic and terror were heard through the streets. It wasn't long before fear turned quickly to violence and crime. Bricks were used to smash into stores and they were ransacked and robbed. Alarms did not buzz, and there were no police patrols, no ambulance sirens. The sound of screeching brakes echoed throughout the city, ending in a gridlock of smashes.

Bang! Bang! Bang!

The Al Jazeera live news helicopter hovering

above the Giza Plateau lost all electrical function and pitched to one side, dropping quickly to the ground. A billowing fireball heralded its end.

All computer devices, cell phones, including the camera crew filming nearby, were shut off, unable to record the wonder taking place before their stunned eyes.

In the anarchy before them, everyone turned to the bright light being emitted from the oldest of the Seven Wonders of the Ancient World. It was as if the Egyptian people were witnessing a religious phenomenon that was bigger than themselves.

Chapter 61

The Blinding Glow

The strategically positioned lights throughout the super cavern switched off, leaving the luminous force of the ring to take center stage.

With a raspy breath and a hand against his blood-soaked upper torso, Boyce observed Dimitri's silhouette as the madman's final wish came true.

Dimitri stretched out his hands as he approached the shimmering gate until he was an arm's length away from the turbulent energy field. His expression betrayed his awe and wonder. Then he touched his wristwatch as he stepped forward into the light to fulfill his destiny.

'Good riddance, you stupid man,' Boyce breathed with a shake of his head as Dimitri vanished into the shimmering light, disappearing the instant he touched the ring's inner vacuum.

Boyce turned to see his friends. 'Joey! Marie! He's gone,' he told them, the relief in his voice almost tangible. Boyce pushed himself up onto his feet and examined his wound, which went straight through to the other side. A relatively harmless flesh wound, he told himself thankfully, though nonetheless his clothes were soaked in crimson front and back. 'Man, I need to go to a hospital,' he told himself.

Marie began to cry tears of joy. This emotional roller-coaster ride had clearly taken its toll on her. She held on to Joey as they kissed and looked at each other lovingly. It was a brief moment between the two, and Boyce let them have it.

He neared the radiant glow that was like the sun, causing him to look away and blink uncontrollably. 'I need to remove the keystone,' he said, holding a hand up against his eyes.

'Be careful,' Marie said, ripping part of her sleeve with her uninjured hand to bandage her bullet wound.

Boyce wrapped his bloody fingers around the triangular shape and took a firm hold of it. Then he yanked the keystone out of its setting and fell backwards. Knowing that the shimmering light would continue for a short while, he held onto the keystone and approached his friends.

'We have one minute before this place turns completely pitch black,' Joey warned as Marie helped him to his feet, where he placed more weight on his unscathed leg.

As they headed towards the doorway, they all heard a loud splashing sound. They stopped, listening intently. The sound repeated itself in a rhythmic motion, like some type of Morse code.

'Julien!' Boyce murmured, and immediately started to follow the sound to its source.

'Where are you going?' Marie asked.

'Julien could still be alive.'

'Okay, go check,' answered Joey, 'but come back before it goes dark – we'll need to stay together to escape this shithole.'

Boyce acknowledged with a nod of his head.

'Wait!' Marie cried, digging into her pack of supplies. 'Here, you'll need this out there.' She tossed him a seven-inch battery free flashlight.

'Thanks,' Boyce replied, catching it. 'Here, take care of this,' he added, flinging her the red keystone. 'Make sure you put pressure on that to stop the bleeding,' he advised, darting his eyes to her bloody palm.

Marie nodded, and Boyce stepped out and into the darkness.

He cranked the winding lever on the flashlight and light shone out. He bolted down the square platform to the sound of rushing water. His rapid heartbeat pounded as his beam of light sabered through the dark void.

He proceeded to the edge of the stairs, where three dead bodies lay on the floor. One was the innocent teenager. Shocked by the sight of the boy's corpse, he shifted his beam to see four more bodies drifting in the water. His light came to a figure face down in the water carrying a backpack, it was Nick.

'Oh no!' he sighed, seeing the gallons of water gushing out of the aqueduct vents in the crocodile heads. The water level in the cavern had risen to waist height and didn't seem to be stopping anytime soon. He needed to warn the others before the Nile crocodiles were forced inside, blocking their only escape through the Walk of Souls.

Knowing Nick could possibly be holding spare guns and supplies to use against the angry crocodiles, he decided to quickly dart over and retrieve his bag. And when he looked inside, a golden tablet stared right back at him and it took his breath away. With no time to spare, he flung the backpack over his shoulders and continued his search.

'Julien!' he yelled, cupping his hands around his mouth.

'Over here,' croaked a shallow voice, and Boyce finally spotted Julien. He lay up against the edge of the stairs with two gunshots in his chest; wounds that appeared to be fatal blows close to his vital organs. Boyce rushed towards his friend, who was breathing erratically and coughing out copious amounts of blood.

'Oh no, you need help,' Boyce blurted as he took note of the sea of blood cascading from Julien's chest. 'We need to get you out of here, sir, before the crocs get a whiff and come in for the kill.'

'You too have been shot,' said Julien, upset. He was like a worried parent, always one to put everyone else's needs ahead of his own.

'I'm okay,' said Boyce shortly. 'Just a flesh wound. We need to get you inside the pyramid. Marie has a medical kit and bandages to stem the bleeding. You've lost a lot of blood.'

Boyce assisted the older man to his feet, wincing as he rested the general's weight on his much shorter frame.

'Hang in there, sir.'

The two hobbled together out of the water. Boyce used all the strength he could muster to carry the hefty tablet and the giant towards the bright light that was still blasting inside the inner sanctum.

'What happened?' Julien asked worriedly. 'The Stargate has been activated. Did we stop him?'

'Sorry, sir, we did not. He went through.'

Julien shook his head, clearly upset as they reached the doorway where Joey and Marie greeted him with a warm smile.

'Put him here,' Joey suggested.

Boyce leaned Julien up against the granite pyramidion that had once held the first keystones inside its secret compartment.

Julien slouched and peered over to the portal that was still ablaze, and then, just as spectacularly as it had come to life, it disappeared, and the hollow pyramid fell into utter blackness. The single winding flashlight still in Boyce's hand was their only source of light now.

Marie removed her backpack and dumped the contents on the floor to reveal two more light sticks, flashlights, scissors, an emergency supply kit, a flare gun and the red keystone, Boyce had given her. She passed Joey one of the flashlights and shoved the flare in her back jeans pocket. Then she began to treat the general's injuries by applying bandages to stop the bleeding.

'We need to blow it up,' Julien croaked. 'We must.'

'We can't, sir,' said Joey, wincing at the pain in his leg. 'Dimitri destroyed the trigger device and yanked the cables out of their sockets, so it's useless.'

'Useless to you three, maybe,' he hissed. 'Not to me.'

'What do you mean?' asked Joey, frowning. 'What do you propose?'

'Marie, hand me one of your light sticks,' said Julien, reaching out a hand.

Marie obliged.

'Boyce, take this and hover the stick a few inches away from the golden capstone,' instructed Julien. 'But please, do not touch it.'

Boyce did as the general asked, and as he closed in on the bright, shiny pyramidion, something magical happened.

A green hue started to emit from its core.

The three younger people gasped in astonishment as they peered at the sight before them.

'We have a source of power,' said Julien. 'The C-4 will work. It just means I will have to stay behind and blow it up manually.'

'What?' Boyce exhaled, stepping away from the pyramidion. 'No. There must be another way.'

'This is my destiny, Boyce. I know I cannot survive the injuries I've sustained. I will stay behind and end this.'

'No, don't say that, we just need to get you some urgent help,' Marie suggested. 'Kypros and his men are waiting outside.'

'No!' Julien said gruffly. 'It needs to be done now. There's no time. And I don't trust anybody apart from you, and you three are all badly injured. Look at Dimitri, he was a good man too, once. No man can be trusted with this thing, and I will make sure no one ever will be.'

'Are you sure?' Boyce said as a tear tracked down his face. The general was the closest thing Boyce had to a father in his life. And like all kids growing up, he knew he had to let go and become the man he was brought up to be.

In response, Julien just looked him in the eye and squeezed his hand.

'Grab me the cables torn away from the trigger device,' Julien said, struggling to stand and move beside the golden capstone, close but not close enough to touch it. 'I will need the scissors from your kit, and can you please ignite the light sticks.'

Joey cracked the light rods and they illuminated the space in a shade of green.

'Now, I need you all to flee,' said Julien. 'I'll give you as long as I can – a minute or two – before it goes up in flames.'

'You're an amazing man,' Marie murmured, shutting her eyes as she hugged him. 'God bless you.'

'It's been an honor and a pleasure,' Joey said, nodding his head and then taking a step back for Boyce to say his goodbyes.

'It has been my privilege to know you all,' replied Julien, turning to Boyce, who continued to rub his teary eyes. 'Especially you, Boyce.'

'I will never forget you and what you have done for me,' Boyce said with reverence and a quivering jaw. He pressed himself into the general's embrace and Julien, the man who could not be broken by emotion, began to weep.

'I love you, Boyce. It's been a crazy journey.'

'It sure has,' said Boyce, remembering the moments when the general had laughed at him, watched him cry and helped him through troubled times. He was the father figure in his life, who had taken him in and matured him into the man he was today.

The hug ended with a fist bump for old times' sake, and they smiled at each other.

'Now you all need to flee,' Julien told them gently, always the professional, looking at his wristwatch. 'You have one minute or so, starting now.'

As they made their way to the exit, Boyce picked up the red keystone and shoved it into his backpack. He soaked in the sight of the distinctive scar on the general's temple and the familiar snow-white hair before disappearing into the darkness with his friends, knowing he would never see him again.

Chapter 62

The Sacrifice

Julien sat alone, his thoughts dominated by a feeling of profound sadness. This was going to be his last act. His last attempt to make things right. He took a minute to calm his nerves and to give his friends the time they needed to get away from the cavern. He gazed up at the Stargate that Queen Nefertiti had promised to hide thousands of years ago to save her own son, Tutankhamun.

Fast-forward a few millennia, and the unconditional love of a parent remained true to this present day.

Dimitri, even though psychotic and deranged, did all this for his family.

Marie and Joey for their unborn child.

And me, for the boy I took in and saw as my own, Boyce.

Julien's eyes circled the quiet void in awe, marveling once more that the three pyramids on the Giza Plateau were aligned to the star constellation, Orion, created for the single purpose of producing energy to power the Stargate that was only feet away.

With the two green light sticks providing his only light source, he stepped into action, grabbing the series of wires that snaked up to the C-4 blocks. Using the medical scissors, he wound the loose, broken cables together and connected them as one. With fatigue engraved on his worn face, he hovered his shivering hand holding the bunch of wires up against the golden capstone, and waited for his idea to play out.

The anticipation created a nervous kind of energy in him, and sweat trickled down his forehead.

Hope spiked in Julien's chest as something started to happen.

Sparking static bounced off the end of the wires, as he had hoped it would. The pyramidion had absorbed enough energy to run multiple charges. All that was left to do was to touch the wires to the golden façade, and the charge alone would trigger the explosion.

Adrenaline flooded his system now. This was it. Never in a million years had he envisioned he would go out this way, but at least it was on his own terms. The scars on his body were a reminder of the long life he had enjoyed that had been filled with amazing adventures.

Julien had served his country proudly in the army. He had had a decorated career within the DGSE. And it was while doing this that he had been introduced to three of his favorite people in the world: Joey, Marie, and Boyce; an unlikely trio who had unearthed secrets that had been buried for eons.

They had discovered that the skeletal remains

in Saint Mark's Basilica in Venice were actually the bones of Alexander the Great. The Pope of Rome had acknowledged the findings to be correct, but a truce to keep it classified had been agreed upon.

Julien had been that man in the middle.

They had found the secret entrance at the right paw of the Sphinx that had led them to the Hall of Records, where a treasure trove of religious and ancient items had awaited. This included an Aswan bookshelf that was part of the Great Library of Alexandria.

Once again, Julien had been at the forefront of the effort to help safely transport the valuable artefacts to a secure location.

Then there was the momentous and earth-shattering revelation: the existence of the Stargate and its creator, another sentient society on another planet, known to humans as the lost city of Atlantis.

It had been a roller-coaster ride of ups and downs, and Julien was now about to write his last chapter. It was time to say goodbye, and his final act would be one for the good of humankind.

He took in a deep breath, closed his eyes, and smiled proudly as all the emotions of his rich and rewarding life flashed before him. He embraced the quiet moment alone, and let the joy and gratitude run through to his soul.

Julien opened his eyes, and with his bunched-up fist of wires, he slammed the golden capstone, and the electrical charge ignited on impact.

Kaboom!

* * *

Joey, Boyce, and Marie waded through the moat of water, luckily this time, avoiding any crocodiles in their path and reached a high vantage point that overlooked the super cavern, turning to the sound of the explosion.

'Holy shit!' Joey spat as the shock wave shook the entire site.

Marie's eyes widened.

Boyce swallowed hard and gripped the straps of his backpack tightly.

The three of them stood and watched from afar as the hollow pyramid caught most of the force of the blast and collapsed on itself, its limestone blocks thundering down in a heap of rubble. The crystal at the pyramid's apex crashed down, shattering into millions of pieces. The implosion created a billowing dust cloud that spread in every direction.

'He did it,' said Boyce, covering his mouth with a trembling hand as tears sprang to his eyes.

Marie comforted her friend with a hug. 'He sure did,' she said in her sisterly way. 'He will be sorely missed.'

'No one will ever know what he did for humanity,' said Boyce, his voice muffled by Marie's embrace.

'That is true,' she said with a comforting hand. 'But we'll never forget him.'

'I know it's premature, but if we have a boy …' said Joey, looking down at Marie's midsection.

'I like that,' Marie said with a sad smile. 'I like that a lot.'

'I'm sure he would have too,' said Boyce as they stepped inside the Walk of Souls with their flashlights and the single flare gun to find their way back to society.

Chapter 63

The Cover-up

Boyce was the first to see the clear starry sky in all its majesty. No artificial light interrupted its beauty; only the glow of burning fires could be seen in the distant background. But an instant after he emerged from the trapdoor near the Sphinx's paw, a swarm of soldiers surrounded him with M16 machine guns.

'Don't move!' a menacing voice shouted.

'Relax, it's me!' Boyce called, forcing both his hands aloft while wincing at the sharp pain coming from his wounded shoulder.

Marie helped Joey as he climbed the ladder. He was trying to put all his weight on one leg, using his arms as much as he could and sparing the other, injured, leg.

'We need medical assistance,' Marie called out as they got themselves through the trapdoor and collapsed on the decking. She pointed at Joey and held up the blood-stained hand she had wrapped in the ragged cloth.

'Don't move!' urged the armed soldier again in accented English.

'Hey, *malaka*, it's me, Boyce. Tell your men to back down before I lose my shit.'

The men in uniform smiled at his comment and relaxed their shoulders, which were heavy with weapons that could have spelled very bad news for the trio in any other situation. Their white teeth now glowed in the darkness.

Something was yelled briskly in Greek and a stocky male figure approached in the gloom. It was Kypros, and his men lowered their heavy firepower as he drew near.

'I'm so sorry, Boyce,' he said, catching his breath. 'In this instance,' he gestured vaguely to the darkness and chaos around them, 'we can't be too careful.'

'I understand,' replied Boyce while he pressed a hand up against the source of his agony.

'Where is Julien?' Kypros asked, his gaze scanning the surrounding area.

'Sorry, sir, he was killed in the explosion.'

'What explosion?'

Lowering his voice so the soldiers around them wouldn't hear, Boyce said, 'He sacrificed himself in order to blow up the Stargate.'

Even in the darkness, Boyce could feel the sadness that fell over the captain. They were old friends, and now Julien was gone.

'Can we get some medical help, please, sir?' asked Boyce, breaking the captain's silent reverie. 'As you can see, we've all been shot.'

'Of course,' replied Kypros, then proceeded to shout orders in his native language.

A soldier standing to attention turned and sprinted at the captain's request.

'So, the portal is gone and so is Julien?' Kypros asked once more, soaking in the unfortunate news.

'Yes, sir, I'm terribly sorry. The entire inner pyramid erupted, leaving behind nothing but a heap of rubble.'

Kypros nodded his head as if thinking deeply about it. 'I will take care of the mess here, Boyce. You and your friends go get fixed up.'

A man wearing a stethoscope approached the team, along with a group of nurses in scrubs uniform.

'Take care of my friends first,' Boyce gestured, as he watched them attend to Marie's hand and Joey's leg.

Kypros leaned in and tapped his shoulder gently. 'I know you lost a man who was like a father figure to you, Boyce. He was a close friend of mine and will be unbelievably missed. If there is anything I can do for you, don't hesitate to let me know. If you need a job, anything.'

'Thank you, but I think I might take my chances and move to America, maybe start a new career or something.'

'The offer is always there if you change your mind,' said Kypros, gripping his shoulder respectfully.

Moments later, a man in a motorized wheelchair rolled in. The way he forced his way through suggested he was a man of importance. He recognized Kypros and greeted him with a handshake.

Marie and Joey, still being treated, turned and smiled at the stranger.

'Hazim, is that you?' Marie called out in surprise.

Boyce squinted his eyes to see better. It was indeed him; the head of the Egyptian Ministry of Antiquities. The man who ran the show down here, who understood all of Egypt's deepest secrets and what lay hidden in its depths. Not so long ago, he too had shared an experience with the three of them that had left him incapacitated – permanently in a wheelchair, in fact – but on the bright side it had earned him a once-in-a-lifetime job.

'What have you three done now?' he joked as he greeted Boyce. 'We are in a blackout. I assume the Stargate has once again been activated?'

'Yes, sir, it was,' said Boyce with a shake of his head. 'But for the last time.'

'You mean until the next time,' Hazim countered.

'No, sir, it's all over ... Never to be used again. Julien made sure of it. He blew it up.'

Hazim turned to scan the group. 'Where is Julien?' he asked, frowning.

'He's gone, sir. He sacrificed his life to set off the bomb.'

Hazim looked stricken, sincerely saddened by the loss, and darted his eyes up to the Great Pyramid that dominated the skyline. 'He's lucky it didn't come crashing down,' he said, nodding towards it. 'Can you imagine the political nightmare . . .?'

'It was a controlled detonation,' Boyce informed him. 'Your Great Pyramid is safe.'

Kypros stood quietly.

'Julien Bonnet was an honorable man and he will be immensely missed,' said Hazim.

'He sure will be,' answered Boyce.

'Hang on, what about Dimitri?' asked Kypros, jumping in. 'I forgot to ask you about him due to all the commotion. Was he killed?'

'He is with his family now,' replied Boyce. 'You don't need to worry about him anymore, he is in a place that is far, far away.'

'So, he's still alive,' shot back Kypros, dreading the thought. 'He entered the Stargate?'

'Yes, but—'

'What's stopping him from coming back?' Hazim said quickly. 'You all returned, via Stonehenge. Isn't that the return route?'

'Yes, sir, but we had the Earth blue keystone with us on entry,' informed Boyce. 'There is no blue stone on Planet X. Dimitri is not coming back, trust me. You will never see him again. He was on a death wish anyway. He was a father struggling with the death of his wife and child. He felt that in doing this, it would bring him salvation.'

'I just hope you're right, and there isn't another stone somewhere stashed on that planet,' said Kypros in an unsettled tone. 'I would hate to think Julien's death was in vain.'

The doctor called out for Boyce to be treated.

Boyce told the doctor that he was going to be there in a minute and rolled the backpack off his back. 'I have something for you to add to your collection,' he said, placing it on Hazim's lap.

'What's in this?' asked Hazim, feeling the outside of the bag with excited hands.

'Inside, you will find the red dolerite keystone, and an added bonus: a gold tablet carved with ancient hieroglyphics. Dimitri and his wingman, his brother-in-law Nick, must have found it, as this was Nick's backpack. It will be interesting to discover what the text might reveal. Perhaps something important ... who knows? I think you're the best person to keep it safe.'

'Thank you,' Hazim said, taking possession of the priceless artefact.

Kypros and Hazim said their goodbyes and walked away to have their own private chat. It appeared they were putting together a story to deliver to the press – a logistical nightmare Boyce was glad he wasn't a part of.

Boyce reported to the waiting doctor and, in mid-treatment, Joey and Marie came over to him, the relief and gratitude shining from their faces. Boyce gazed upwards at the moonlight, and relished the feeling of the fresh night air on his skin.

'How are you doing, buddy?' asked Joey. 'You look like shit.'

Boyce laughed. 'You don't look any better,' he teased back.

'That's your second bullet wound in a couple of years,' said Marie. 'You're such a badass.'

Boyce sighed. Young though he was, he knew his body couldn't take many more hits. 'I was wondering,' he said, gazing at his best friends in all the world. 'Can I come and stay at your beach house?' He flinched as antiseptic was applied to his wound. 'I've decided that now Julien is gone, there is no point in me staying on with the DGSE. I'm thinking I might want to make a go of it in America.'

'Of course you can stay with us,' said Marie, smiling broadly and giving him a fist bump.

'The team will be together at last,' said Joey, grinning. 'We need to form a save-the-world club or something.'

Marie shook her head at his comment.

'One big happy family,' Boyce said, feeling the love and a flush of optimism about his future. 'Or at least until our next crazy adventure ...' He paused with a cheeky grin. 'The birth of my godchild, Julien – or Juliet? – Peruggia.'

Chapter 64

The Informant

Kypros sauntered over to his BMW as the sounds of joy erupted all around him. Lights had begun to flutter back to life across Cairo in a rolling progression. It was as if the city had been brought back from the Dark Ages to the twenty-first century once again.

As the electricity grid flooded back to life, the city manifested in the distance as a welcome white-yellow glow. The car headlights shone against each other. Alarms were heard wailing as they went off belatedly, and the overhead streetlights showed the way once more.

The camera crews seemed to have gained a resurgence of energy as their equipment became operational again, but their efforts to get close to the action near the Sphinx were short-lived as a plethora of armed soldiers refused to take any shit from anybody.

Kypros climbed into his vehicle and shut his door, gazing out of his grimy window to make sure no one was in earshot. He took a breath and exhaled it in a loud sigh of anxiety. He needed to make the call. Tapping his foot nervously, he managed to calm himself enough to be able to reach into his glove compartment to find a working cell phone.

After a quick search, he dialed the number with the Los Angeles extension and waited for the man on the other end to answer.

'I was expecting your call, Kypros,' said the man with the robust German accent. 'It's been all over the news.'

'Sorry to bother you, sir, but we have a small problem.'

'I don't like problems, Kypros. I like solving them,' said the man in an authoritative but calm tone. 'Go on, tell me, what's wrong?'

Kypros hesitated and then spoke honestly. 'The Stargate has been destroyed.'

A moment of silence ensued.

'Are you there, sir?' Kypros asked.

'Yes, I'm still here. Hmm ... it's a setback, definitely. But not the end of the world.'

'I'm sorry I failed you.'

'If I had a dollar for every time I failed, I would be a billionaire.' The man laughed at his own reply.

'What do we do now?'

'We continue as planned, Kypros ... On the positive side, my pet project has progressed exactly as hoped and I have identified the planet our makers derived from.'

'Are you talking about Planet X?'

'Yes.'

Kypros paused to think. 'How? Where?'

'It is in the Orion Nebula eight hundred light years away.'

'How do you know this?'

'Let's just say I gave a gift to someone and it has paid off in spades.'

Chapter 65

Angkor Wat,
Ta Prohm

It was dawn, and the tourists were on an adventure with their tour guide that had begun with a drive into the jungle. This was followed by a walk by torchlight through the wilderness, listening to the caws and chatter of the parrots and monkeys in the canopy overhead. Before they realized it, the holidaymakers were in the grounds of the temple. As the warm glow of daybreak filtered through the canopy, the mist gradually lifted and highlighted the temple's moss-covered pinnacles and courtyards.

They were standing at the Ta Prohm Temple, which had been left undisturbed since it was first discovered in the early nineteenth century. The giant creeper fig trees remained, partly pulling the structure down, and partly propping it up. The roots of the towering trees spilled over the ramparts like the tentacles of a gigantic octopus, with the leaves cloaking the temple casting a greenish hue, creating an otherworldly ambience.

As the tourists moved on, unbeknown to them, a thick root had, over time, displaced a section of stone from the ground. The sand blew away in the morning breeze to reveal a deeply indented marking.

It was a double-spiral symbol.

If one happened to have the key to open it, it would reveal a secret doorway that would lead to an underground chamber.

Hardly anyone knew that this was the last of the three places on Earth where a red dolerite keystone was hidden, laid to rest by our ancestors, the last point on the triangle shape the locations made on the Earth's surface. This was a stone that now posed no immediate danger to humanity if it were found. Julien had made sure of it, by eliminating the one and only Stargate on *our* planet.

Chapter 66

The Golden Tablet

The ceiling light still illuminated the windowless office that was Hazim's hidden laboratory. A swivel chair sat to one side near a bookshelf bursting with books, but the large glass desk that was also used as a light table was the feature in the room. Laid out in an organized fashion, there was an open notebook, a cell phone, a lamp, a stack of papers and a forty-three-inch touchscreen TV, sitting on its own universal table stand.

Hazim entered his office, turned the switch to ignite the table light, and carefully placed the hefty golden tablet down to be examined. A small red light on a security camera mounted above his head suddenly turned on and he noticed it. Since being at this facility, Hazim had had the feeling that he was being watched. Needing some background noise to help settle his nerves, Hazim touched the screen and let one of his favorite YouTube-recommended videos play. Lately, he had been watching footage of the advancements his newfound partner, Elliott Magnus, and his company, Magnus Industries, had made into space travel.

Hazim's face was now a blur of white light as he leaned over to study the hieroglyphics, running his finger along the grooves. His eyes glinted as he stared at the symbols. He picked up the cell phone that rested on the table and opened a program that was designed by the late Youssef Omar. Even though Youssef had been a murderous maniac, and the reason Hazim would never walk again, he had done one thing right in creating an ingenious translating app, which Hazim utilized all the time.

He scanned the golden plaque using the phone's inbuilt camera, and a female voice began to speak in her eccentric English accent. The software had been designed to deliver the translation using deciphered words in the simplest form.

After evacuating the unstable red planet (Mars), situated fourth in line from its star (Sun), we discovered a third planet from the sun (Earth), located 183 million miles away. The blue world is double the size of the red planet, and its atmosphere is perfectly intact, providing protection, free oxygen, and oceans of water, perfect for life and reproduction.

In the name of our mighty god Atum, we discovered a new intelligent species inhabiting this planet (Homo erectus). We adjusted their DNA and evolved these creatures to be ruled and used for our building and farming needs. With each passing year, they helped us construct the beacons that would allow us to travel to our homeland within the Orion constellation (Planet X).

This message is to warn our people that we have abandoned the desolate red planet that has become a graveyard for our population. The Stargate will remain active there. The purple (Mars) keystone should never be used to travel there unless you wish your last days of life to be spent in peace among our ancestors. End of translation.

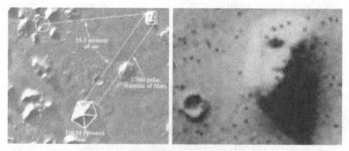

Giant face and Pyramids found on Mars

Hazim glanced up from the tablet in utter amazement. He bit his bottom lip, took a breath, and opened his mouth to speak. It all made sense to him now. 'There is a Stargate on Mars,' he said aloud in the empty room. 'They used Mars as a graveyard.'

Hazim glanced at a charismatic man on the TV monitor, a man who had high cheekbones, blondish-brown hair and blue eyes. It was the billionaire entrepreneur who gladly funded this entire place in secret, one of the many projects he had a personal interest in. He was the man in the shadows, pulling strings to obtain all the knowledge he could of Earth's deepest secrets.

Hazim pursed his lips disapprovingly. 'Now I know why you want to send people to Mars so much,' he muttered, before stopping to listen to the YouTube channel playing in the background.

Elliott Magnus/ NASA Press Conference – December 15, 2019

I want to help make humanity a space-exploring civilization. This … um … will be a long-held dream for a lot of people, especially me, and Magnus Industries. Within five years, we aim to send the first people to Mars to establish a self-sustaining city. With the help of our partner, NASA, I promise you that I will do what I can to make it a reality. It all starts with great minds that think alike.

Not many people know about our own history and the involvement of Nazi scientists who transformed NASA into what it is today. Wernher von Braun was one of those pioneers, a high-ranking official under Hitler and Himmler's regime, who led us to the moon before the Soviet Union. It began with sixteen hundred engineers and technicians under a secret program they called Operation Paperclip. And now I will lead by their example and take us further into space. We start with Mars and go on from there. The prize will be worth the effort, I assure you. Only then can we evolve ourselves and become the interstellar master race we have always been meant to be.

Books by Phil Philips

FORTUNE IN BLOOD
MONA LISA'S SECRET
LAST SECRET CHAMBER
LAST SECRET KEYSTONE
GUARDIANS OF EGYPT

ACKNOWLEDGMENTS

Foremost, I want to thank my strong and beautiful wife Marie who went through hell last year. She was diagnosed with breast cancer in late September 2018. Life was definitely put on pause for a while. I found myself not sleeping, worrying about what if? I changed my diet and joined the gym. So many mixed emotions catapulted into my mind at the time. I thought after this, I would put my writing aside, but instead used the anger, the passion into my storytelling. It became my release. Some people meditate, some go for long runs. I got lost in my story when everyone went to bed. It all started for me with a single question that kept repeating in my mind. What would a father/mother do for her children? – Anything… Everything…

This very statement I idolized with all the characters in this novel, and I hope you the reader enjoyed it and went along for the ride.

I also want to thank my two boys Alexander and Leonardo who continue to support me through this writing journey.

Since the story idolizes what a parent would do for their child, I want to thank my mom, whom this novel was dedicated to, for always being there for me and the family during tough times.

A special thank you once again goes out to my genius editors Brianne Collins and Alexandra Nahlous for giving this book life and making it the best it could possibly be.

Last of all to you, my dear reader, for picking up my book. I truly hope you have as much fun reading it as I did writing it. I would love to hear from you. I can be contacted via social media, or on my website: **philphilips.com**

ONE MORE THING …

If you loved the book and have a moment to spare, I would really appreciate a short review where you bought the book. Your help in spreading the word is gratefully appreciated, as it helps other readers discover the story.

MORE FICTION FROM PHIL PHILIPS

Mona Lisa's Secret

A Joey Peruggia Adventure Series Book 1

Joey is the great-grandson of Vincenzo Peruggia, the man who stole the original Mona Lisa in 1911. Along with his girlfriend, Marie, an art connoisseur, he stumbles across his father's secret room, and finds himself staring at what he thinks is a replica of da Vinci's most famous masterpiece.

BUT IT IS NO FAKE ...

The Louvre has kept this secret for over one hundred years, waiting for the original to come to light, and now they want it back at any cost.

With Marie held hostage and the Louvre curator and his men hot on his trail, Joey is left to run for his life in an unfamiliar city, with the priceless Mona Lisa his only bargaining chip. While formulating a plan to get Marie back with the help from an unexpected quarter, Joey discovers hidden secrets within the painting, secrets which, if made public, could change the world forever.

In this elaborately plotted, fast-paced thriller, Phil Philips takes you on a roller-coaster ride through the streets of Paris and to the Jura mountains of Switzerland, to uncover a secret hidden for thousands of years ...

MORE FICTION FROM PHIL PHILIPS

Last Secret Chamber

A Joey Peruggia Adventure Series Book 2

Where is ancient Egypt's last secret chamber, and what is concealed within?

When an archaeologist is murdered in his Cairo apartment, an ancient artefact is stolen from his safe – one believed to hold the clue to the last secret chamber.

When Joey Peruggia discovers that the dead man was his long-lost uncle, he travels with his girlfriend, Marie, and his friend Boyce, who works for the French intelligence, to Egypt, on a mission to find answers.

But once they arrive, they are lured into a trap and become hostages to a crazed man and his gang of thieves. This is a man who will stop at nothing to discover what lies in the last secret chamber.

All bets are off, and only the cleverest will survive this deadliest of adventures.

In this elaborately plotted, fast-paced thriller, Phil Philips takes you on a roller-coaster ride through Egypt's most prized structures on the Giza plateau, to uncover a secret hidden for thousands of years ...

MORE FICTION FROM PHIL PHILIPS

Last Secret Keystone

A Joey Peruggia Adventure Series Book 3

When a cargo plane carrying an ancient vase crashes into the Atlantic, the DGSE – otherwise known as the French CIA – immediately suspect it's deliberate. The vase is believed to hold a key that gives entrance to a hidden cave on Easter Island: a site connected with ancient Egypt and an otherworldly portal discovered deep beneath the Great Pyramid of Giza.

Joey, Marie, and Boyce are once again caught up in a dangerous adventure, forced on them by a trained assassin who is on his own spiritual quest for answers ... A ruthless man who will stop at nothing to get what he wants.

His objective: to find the last secret keystone, and with it activate the portal once again. Joey and his friends must stop him – at any cost.

In this fast-paced thriller, Book 3 in the Joey Peruggia Adventure Series, Phil Philips takes you on a roller-coaster ride from the giant Moai statues of Easter Island to the Greek island of Santorini and back to Egypt, where the fate of humankind once again rests with the most unlikely of heroes.

Fortune in Blood

A NOVEL OF MURDER, THEFT, BETRAYAL AND MONEY ... LOTS OF IT ...

Joey used to be a carefree surfer kid on Venice Beach. But as the youngest son of a notorious gangster, it seems he can't escape the life. Soon he's forced to prove himself by leading a team in the heist of the century. Will he be able to pull it off?

Vince was always worried about getting to lectures on time ... and spending time with his hot girlfriend. But everything changes when he's embroiled in his detective father's world. Now he's on the run for his life from the mob.

FBI Agent Monica is smart, beautiful, tough and unyielding. Caught in the middle of the mob and the police, her loyalty is being questioned by both sides. But Monica seems to have her own agenda ... In a world where corruption is rife, she will be tested to the limit.

Who can be trusted and who will be left standing? And who will ultimately escape with all the money? A showdown is set in motion and no one will be left unscathed.

In this elaborately plotted, fast-paced thriller, Phil Philips takes you on a roller coaster ride that will keep you guessing until the very last page.

MORE FICTION FROM PHIL PHILIPS

Guardians of Egypt

*Short Story - Prequel to the
Joey Peruggia Adventure Series*

When Julien Bonnet finds the remains of an ancient city under the Red Sea, he unleashes the might of the Guardians of Egypt. They carry the burden of destroying ancient sites – and anyone who discovers them – to keep their secret safe.

Only this time, they messed with the wrong guy. Killing him will not be as simple as it seems

Get a FREE copy when you sign up to my mailing list. You also will be notified on giveaways and upcoming new releases. www.philphilips.com